He stood there.

Her tiger man arched a brow with stern displeasure at her careless opening of the door.

He was dressed in black again: black trousers, black vest, black jacket. Elegant, casual, he might have graced the pages of a high-class magazine.

But he was the furthest thing in the world from civilized. In spite of the suit, in spite of his totally businesslike appearance, he resembled a tiger. Taut and vital, he exuded leashed energy, yet remained cool and self-assured.

"Rafe!" she said, standing there.

"Yes, and you should be glad that it is. You might just have thrown your door open to a mugger."

The smile she gave him nearly caused his heart to stop, his blood to boil—superior, aloof, a sensual curve of her lips.

"Perhaps that would be less dangerous."

"Ms. Pozzessere

HEATHER GRAHAM POZZESSERE

BRIDE OF THE TIGER

MIRA BOOKS
NORTHEAST COLORADO BOOKMOBILE SVS
WRAY , CO 80758
(970) 332-4715
(800) 306-4715

MIRA

ISBN 1-55166-146-2

BRIDE OF THE TIGER

Copyright © 1987 by Heather Graham Pozzessere.

Printed in U.S.A.

BRIDE OF THE TIGER

1

The sculpture was magnificent.

It was in the Roman section of the museum, with a plaque beneath it: Anonymous, A.D. 100, Black Marble.

Tara was entranced by it.

It was a life-size tiger, standing—watching. The ancient artist had caught all the tension, passion and cunning vitality of the creature. The beauty was there, the danger. One paw was raised as it stalked its prey, its grace casual, its quest unmistakable. Though the sculpture was carved in sleek black marble, Tara could almost see the true color in the eyes; they would be a tawny gold, like candle flames, like the endless sun, with a heat that was just as piercing. The tiger was all power, all grace.

Tara realized suddenly that she was alone with the beast, and smiled whimsically. She wanted to be alone to marvel at this creature.

There were lions and boars in the room, salukis and mystical cats, maidens and warriors. But nothing compared with the tiger, a fact that was made clear by its position of prominence, dead center, encircled by velvet ropes.

Still fascinated, Tara began to circle the creature. She glanced at her watch, aware that she couldn't linger much longer, or she would be late for lunch. But she did have a few minutes.

The tiger was lean and sleek, yet each muscle and sinew was well-honed and clearly delineated—again she got that sense of sheer power. It didn't need to move or growl to display that power. Primal, subdued, awesome, it touched her senses beyond all logic.

Her back was to the doorway when she became aware that someone had joined her in the room. Watching the tiger? Or watching her?

She looked up. In the glass case around a majestic granite centurion, she could see the reflection of a man. He appeared to be as tall as the centurion, seemed to tower there, blocking her way. He stood in the doorway, as striking and as haunting as the ancient works of art on display.

He was silent, not moving. As powerful as the tiger.

A chill played along her spine in a peculiar dance. Whimsy took hold of her in the most disturbing fashion. Like the tiger, he was a hunter. Subtle, entrancing, deadly. He would tread silently, watch, then encircle his prey. He would play with it, perhaps. When he grew bored of his game, he would pounce with complete arrogance and confidence and lethal precision.

You're mad! she accused herself. He wasn't a tiger, and this was a public museum. Crowds were everywhere; guards lingered just yards away.

Tara took a breath, mentally ridiculing herself. Still, she moved carefully. She didn't want him at her back. She wanted to circle the tiger again and face him, then laugh at herself, because he would just be an ordinary man.

She came around the tiger, casually.

But her ridiculous feelings of hypnotism and tension did not leave her. He was not just an ordinary man.

She stared at the tiger but looked beyond it, to the tall, compelling stranger in the doorway. Silent, hands on hips, he, too, watched the tiger.

Her heartbeat began to quicken.

His short, well-cut hair was dark, nearly jet. He wore black corduroy jeans, a cavalry-style leather jacket. Both hugged his trim form nicely.

A form like the tiger's. Slim, but with strong, smooth muscles at the shoulders, at the thighs, encased in that midnight corduroy. He radiated a sleek and subtle power. Beautiful, dangerous. Taut, tense and vital, apparently casual, never really so.

And she still felt that, like the tiger, he was on the hunt.

She inhaled sharply as her scrutiny reached his face. It was weathered and bronzed, rugged, though still young. Firm jaw, high smooth cheekbones, full mouth, dark, arched brows and—

Golden eyes. Tawny eyes. Alive with their color, like a candle's glow, like the sun...

She was openly staring at him, Tara realized.

He was returning her gaze, aware of it.

Slowly, his sensual mouth twisted into a small, subtle smile.

Tara felt her face flame; she quickly averted her eyes.

She had to go, she reminded herself; she would be late for lunch. But she couldn't possibly go through the doorway where he was standing. The tiger man. All subtle, graceful power...stalking. Stalking—her?

She told herself that she was being ridiculous. Millions of visitors came to the museum, and they did not come to stalk Tara Hill. The notion was absurd.

It wasn't a notion. It was a feeling.

Walk past him, fool! she ordered herself.

And then her breath caught again, because he moved, just slightly, into the room.

His hands remained on his hips. His gaze was fixed on the work of art to which she was mentally comparing him.

He was closer, she realized. She felt hot and flushed, and totally irritated with herself. But there was just something about him, something that was both base and noble, that lured and enticed. She wanted to read the message in his eyes. She was painfully tempted to touch him and discover whether he, too, was of marble or true flesh and blood. Sleek and agile, alive and breathing ...

He captivated one. He touched something beneath the cool exteriors of civility. He lured; he repelled. He fascinated....

And he terrified.

Absurd, Tara thought once again. But she felt frozen, willed to stillness, by the mere presence of a stranger. Her palms were damp; her throat was dry, and the ripples of heat and fear and excitement still played havoc all the way down her spine.

Run past him! she commanded herself.

Walk normally; don't be an idiot!

She moved the silver fox fur of her collar closer to her face, squared her shoulders, and started to walk.

So did he.

They passed each other. He nodded to her. She lowered her eyes, hurrying, breathing deeply.

His scent was subtle, clean and pleasant, elementally male. It was filled, too, with a sense of primal power.

The tiger was stalking. He would strike at any moment.

He walked right on by her.

When Tara reached the doorway, she couldn't help but turn back.

He was staring at the tiger. Tall and lean and as dark as the beast, in his black cords and leather.

She turned, smiling ruefully at her foolishness, and hurried out of the Roman section to the stairs. He'd had no interest in her whatever—just in the treasures of the museum.

Too long in the country, girl! she chastised herself. Well, that was all changing now. She had run, and she had hidden, but it was time to face the daylight.

She had started off rather well. Only a few days in the city and her apartment felt like home again, she was ready to start work on a fascinating assignment, she had come to the museum, and she was meeting Ashley for lunch.

Her smile broadened as she thought about telling Ashley all about her encounter with the tiger-man. Ashley would love it. Paranoid, Ashley would call her.

And, of course, she had been. To have thought of the man as being as ruggedly beautiful, powerful and dangerous as the tiger.

And to have thought that he might actually be stalking her. As if she were prey.

Ashley would definitely be amused.

Tara ran down the steps of the museum to the street, still grinning as she hailed a taxi.

She didn't see the tiger-man tread lightly down those same steps behind her, following her every movement with his eyes, carefully noting the direction of her cab.

Then advancing to the car that awaited him at the corner.

2

Rafe Tyler had no need to hurry. A shift in the wind had brought the soft sound of her voice to him; he had heard her instruct the cabdriver to take her to the Plaza.

As soon as the taxi pulled away from the curb, he raised his hand to the hovering limousine. He hopped in beside the driver.

"Where to?" the snowy-haired chauffeur inquired.

"Follow her cab," Rafe said. He leaned back to rest his head against the seat and closed his eyes. He was tired from a month of constant travel, but this lead on the girl had been too good to ignore. She was the last avenue of discovery he had left.

"Damn traffic!" the chauffeur grumbled impatiently.

Rafe opened his eyes again, grinning. "Don't let it worry you, Sam. I want a few minutes to pass anyway."

"What if we lose her?"

"We won't. She's obviously got a luncheon appointment."

"How do you know?"

"Sixth sense?" he teased, then admitted, "I overheard her. She's heading for the Plaza, probably the Oak Room. She'll be easy to find." He frowned suddenly, turned to push aside the glass barrier behind him, and leaned halfway over the seat to rummage in a storage cabinet.

Warily, Sam glanced in the rearview mirror to watch his employer's movements. "Rafe? What are you up to there, boy? Now I'm not going into that place with you—"

"Sure you are, Uncle Sam!" Rafe laughed, returning to his seat, a dignified suede jacket in his hand to replace Sam's uniform coat.

"I'm not—"

"Hey, I can't walk in alone! I have to have a lunch appointment myself, right?"

Sam started to grumble under his breath. Already the collar that hadn't bothered him all morning had begun to bother him. "I swear, if I hadn't been working for the Tylers since they first set foot in the States—"

Rafe's smile faded. He interrupted his old employee and friend with a flat reminder. "This is all about Jimmy, Sam. I wouldn't be asking you, otherwise."

They fell silent until the limousine pulled up in front of the Plaza. Sam was doffing his cap and changing jackets even as the doorman opened the back door. A little confused at finding no passengers in the rear of the elegant vehicle, he scratched his chin.

In the meantime Rafe had left the car, smiling pleasantly as he approached the doorman with a generous tip. By the time Sam was out—now clad as nondescriptly as any businessman, Rafe had been assured that the limo could sit just where it was until he and Sam were ready to retrieve it.

Rafe rested a hand against Sam's shoulder to steer him through the lobby. Sam always felt uncomfortable at the Plaza. "Too much opulence!" he muttered, shaking his head at the display windows full of gems.

"Sam! We're just going to have lunch. We're not moving in!" Rafe chastised him.

"Ostentatious!" Sam said under his breath.

"Ah, come on! It has warmth and character!"

"It's better than some," Sam admitted. Then he sniffed. "The waiters always look at me as if they think I don't know which fork to use!"

"They don't care if you use a fork at all—as long as you leave them a decent tip," Rafe assured him dryly, stopping Sam at the entrance to the Oak Room. Before the maître d' approached them, Rafe had already found Tara Hill. She was sitting with a redhead who was as svelte and fashionable as she was. Luckily, the table behind Tara, which angled to her right, was empty. He could study her easily, but she would have to twist to see him. He should even be able to hear her conversation fairly easily.

"Mr. Tyler," the maître d' began.

"Afternoon, John. My uncle is here on holiday. He'd enjoy a view."

"A view?"

Rafe grinned. "The blonde and the redhead. Think you could arrange to get us behind them—the table right over there?"

"Certainly, Mr. Tyler. Certainly. Gentlemen, right this way."

"The man reminds me of a penguin," Sam murmured.

"Sam," Rafe groaned, "anyone in a tux looks like a penguin."

He helped his aging "uncle" into a chair, then drew up his own for a nice view of Tara Hill. Engrossed in conversation with the redhead, she hadn't noticed their arrival.

He was glad to see that her silver fox fur was gone—obviously left in the cloakroom. He could study her more thoroughly without the fluffy garment, which concealed her throat and chin. She wore a simple gown, a teal silk with a scoop neckline, her only ornament a gold chain belt about her waist. He was certain, though, that she would look just as appealing in rags. Her beauty was in her height and grace. She was, he knew from experience in sizing people up, about five foot eight and one hundred and twenty well-arranged pounds. Her legs were long, lightly muscled, very sleek. Her hips and breasts were pleasantly rounded; her waist was very small. Her throat was slender, and her cheekbones were exquisitely high. Her eyes, silver like the fur she had worn, were large, expressive, and framed with rich dark lashes that contrasted arrestingly with the golden beauty of her hair, which she wore in fashionable layers at a length just below her shoulders.

Rafe absently picked up his menu. His assessment of her was totally objective. She was a very beautiful woman, but, more importantly, she was—he hoped—the means to an end. She was his last chance to pick up the trail where it had disappeared into South American bureaucracy. She *should* be beautiful—she was Tara Hill. Until two years ago, there hadn't been an American male alive who didn't recognize her.

"Drink!" Sam said suddenly.

"What?" Rafe queried, frowning.

"Am I supposed to order a drink?" Sam asked.

"Do you want a drink?" Rafe asked. He glanced up to see their young waiter standing patiently.

"Hell, I'd like a whole bottle of Jack Black!"

"Then you should have a drink!" Rafe laughed. He gazed at the waiter, amusement deep in his tawny-gold eyes. "Two Jack Blacks on the rocks, please."

"Thank you, sir," the waiter said. "And may I suggest the veal? It's excellent today." He walked away.

"Haven't they got hamburgers?" Sam asked.

"We'll get you a hamburger," Rafe promised.

Sam fell silent, sitting very straight in his chair. Rafe chuckled again.

"For heaven's sake, Sam! Loosen up! You'll have everyone staring at us. And talk. Act natural."

"What should I talk about?" Sam ran his finger beneath his collar again.

"Anything," Rafe replied. The waiter returned with their drinks. Rafe ordered two hamburgers and was assured that he could get them. Their menus were taken away, and Rafe tried to hear the conversation between Tara Hill and the pretty redhead. For several seconds he could barely make out their words. He concentrated harder, then started slightly, aware that they were talking about him.

"I don't know, Ashley," Tara Hill was saying ruefully. "It was just the oddest sensation. He stared right at the tiger—oh, it's really a wonderful, wonderful piece!—but I still had the feeling that he was looking at me." She shivered slightly, delicately, then laughed. "Too much country living, I suppose. He reminded me so much of that damned tiger."

"Primitive, eh?" Ashley queried.

"I guess. But then, of course, I finally got up the nerve to walk by him, and he wasn't after me at all."

Ashley laughed delightedly, picking up her wineglass. "I love it. Maybe he was after you. Men might well be, you know. Are you forgetting that you've been called one of the ten most beautiful women in the world?"

Tara looked annoyed. "Years ago—and any woman can look great with an entourage of dressers and makeup experts. Ashley, he wasn't staring at me for my looks."

"I thought you said he wasn't staring at you at all?"

"I did, didn't I? I—I don't know."

"Well, I'm glad about one thing."

"What?"

"You noticed him. You never notice men. You talk to them, you're polite, but you gaze right past them."

"I don't—"

"There's hope! And I'm ever so glad that it's come now! This trip will be marvelous. I'm convinced we'll have a wonderful trip! Twelve hours of work, and the rest of our time free! And maybe you'll actually be willing to dance with someone." Ashley sobered. "I just—"

"What?"

"Oh, Tara! What happened affected you so drastically that you've hidden away from the world for two years! I just wish we weren't going to Caracas. It's our main port of call. Are you sure you want to go back?"

Tara smiled a little unhappily. "No. But after what happened, George Galliard might be the only one who'd give me work."

"Don't be ridiculous—"

"Oh, come on, Ashley! Admit it—I was involved in a horrible scandal. Guilty or innocent doesn't mean a damn thing once your name hits the media! And maybe it will be the best thing in the world for me. Once we're aboard the—"

"Rafe!" Sam suddenly cleared his throat loudly. "I say, Rafe, I think I'd like another one of those Jack Blacks on the rocks!"

Rafe stared at Sam, ready to throttle his old friend. "Damn it, Sam!" he exploded, quietly but vehemently. "I just missed something important."

"You told me to talk!"

"But softly, Sam, softly!"

"Damn kids these days. Can't make them happy, one way or the other!"

Rafe ignored him. He was a thirty-seven-year-old "kid" but maybe to Sam's seventy-eight that was young.

"Sam," Rafe sighed, "if you want another drink, just motion to the waiter."

Sam started to rise.

"Subtly, Sam, subtly!" Rafe moaned, tugging Sam by the jacket to bring him back to his seat. He caught sight of their waiter and signaled; the waiter nodded and brought two more drinks.

It was then that Tara noticed the men at the next table. The very uncomfortable, older man—and him. The tiger-man. The man from the museum with the cat-gold eyes and midnight hair. And the lithe, tightly muscled build. Unconsciously, she picked up her wineglass—and drained it.

Rafe caught her eyes on him; he saw her stunned—and slightly panicked—expression. Damn! Groaning inwardly, he gave her a smile, raising his glass slightly.

"Well, the best part of this deal," Ashley was saying blithely between mouthfuls of fruit salad, "is that we get to keep everything we model! Can you imagine? Some of those designs are priceless!" Ashley paused, staring at Tara. "What on earth is it? You look as if you've seen a ghost."

"It's him," Tara said.

"Who him?" Ashley frowned.

"Don't look now. It's him, the man I was telling you about. Who reminded me so much of the tiger."

Ashley turned immediately.

"Ashley! I said don't look now!"

"Well, how will I know what you're talking about if I don't look?" Ashley stared straight at him. Tara had to do the same thing. He appeared quite amused. He returned their gaze with a buccaneer's secret smile, then returned his attention to the older man at his side.

"Whew!" Ashley whistled softly.

"What do you think?" Tara asked.

Ashley laughed. "If I had been alone in the same room with him, Tara, I sure as hell wouldn't have run! Or maybe I would have. Ooh! Dangerous type. Hypnotic. You'd have to crawl through half a million singles bars to find something like him. No, you never would. He just wouldn't be there. He's—he's incredible. Snag him, Tara!"

Tara shook her head in annoyance. "Ashley," she whispered urgently. "I told you—I felt that he was watching me, homing in for a kill! And here he is again. Doesn't that seem odd?"

"He's eating lunch, Tara. The same thing we're doing."

"This is a huge city!"

"And coincidences do occur! I once had the same cabdriver twice in the same day. Now *that's* odd!"

"Ladies, excuse me."

Tara quickly looked up. She hadn't seen their waiter approaching, and now he was setting down a silver tray that held fresh wineglasses, an ice bucket, and a bottle whose label made her certain that it was much more expensive than what they had been drinking.

"From the gentleman at the next table," the waiter informed them.

"Oh, we can't accept it!" Tara protested.

"But we will anyway!" Ashley exclaimed, laughing delightedly.

The wine was poured, and short of creating an embarrassing scene in the middle of the dining room, there was very little that Tara could do about it.

"Please thank the gentleman very much for us," Ashley was saying quite cheerfully.

"Oh, hell!" Tara muttered as the waiter bowed and moved away. "Ashley, do you know what you've done?"

Ashley just laughed, her green eyes glittering like emeralds. "Tara, you've been in hiding too long. He's got his eye on you, but if you're not interested, I am!"

"Be my guest, then," Tara murmured.

"Tara Hill, what do you want to do, shrivel up and die because of one unpleasant episode?"

"Unpleasant!" Tara exclaimed.

"All right, that's an understatement. But you can't give up on men just because of Tine Elliott! Oh, Tara, I was right all along. You're taking this job because you can get to Caracas! You think you're going to find him—"

"I don't want to find him!" Tara cried.

"Tara, he made you too... aloof. Too hard, too cynical. Maybe if you did come across him again—"

Tara interrupted her with a soft groan. "Ashley, I'm not aloof. I just learned a lot about the male of the species from Tine."

"Mmm-hmm. They amuse you these days. You don't take a single introduction seriously. You meet charmers, rich men, handsome men. You smile at them over drinks and then politely slam the door in their faces. You've got to let one through that door."

"Ashley, I don't want to let anyone through—"

She paused suddenly with horror, aware that her tigerman had come to their table, that he was, in fact, standing right behind her.

She looked up slowly, and saw his legs first, the way the black cords wrapped around his muscled thighs and lean hips.

Beneath his jacket, his shirt was a soft kelly silk. It clung nicely to his chest, delineating its sinews and muscular structure. The open jacket enhanced the breadth of his shoulders.

And then there was his face.

Handsome, bronzed features. Too dark, too rugged for New York City on a misty, overcast day. His manner was perfectly civilized; his presence was anything but.

Like a great cat, he belonged in the jungle. . . .

"Excuse me, ladies. May I join you for a moment?"

Tara picked up her newly filled wineglass and drained it, eyeing him warily—and discouragingly, she hoped. The wine went down like velvet, and it did help. She quickly composed a courteous turndown.

"I'm sorry; this is a personal—"

"Please, sit down!" Ashley interrupted, awed.

"Thank you." His eyes, topaz, sunny gold, fell upon Tara again.

He offered his hand first to Ashley.

"Rafe Tyler."

"How do you do, Mr. Tyler," Ashley murmured, adding a slight and very feminine Southern slur to her words. "I'm Ashley Kane, and this is Tara Hill."

His pleasantly assessing gaze fell guilelessly on Tara. Yet for a second, she was convinced that he had seen or known of her before. Before the restaurant, before the museum.

"I hope you'll forgive the self-introduction, but I couldn't see another way." He looked at Ashley. "I saw Miss Hill at the museum. And when she appeared again, just a table away, I was rather hoping that it might be fate."

"Fate can be absolutely wonderful!" Ashley gushed. Tara kicked her under the table. Ashley, it seemed, was in no mood for finesse. "Ouch!" she complained loudly.

"Should you be leaving your companion to . . . flatter us?" Tara asked bluntly.

He just smiled and indicated the table behind them. "My uncle had some business to attend to. He's finished his lunch and gone on to his appointment."

Tara glanced at the other table and saw that the older man was indeed gone. She turned back just in time to see a busboy clearing away her untouched salad, as Ashley assured him that they were quite through with their meal.

The waiter poured more wine.

Tara felt her heart begin to beat too quickly, and she tried to quell her irrational fears, as well as the budding sense of excitement his presence brought—despite all her indignation and the inner knowledge that he was nothing more than a tiger on the prowl.

Yet he didn't seem at all obnoxious, or even really interested in her. While she tried to unravel the web of emotions within her, he chatted easily with Ashley. He traveled frequently on business, it seemed, and they were discussing various countries and cities.

The Tylers were into a number of concerns, he said. Jewelry was their main interest, requiring most of his travel.

Ashley laughed, her eyes still bright while she sipped her wine. "Did you grow up in the family business, Mr. Tyler?"

"Rafe," he corrected her softly.

"Okay, Rafe. The question still stands."

"No," he replied. "I've only been back with it about two years."

He turned abruptly to Tara. "You're not drinking your wine," he said. "Isn't it good?"

"Oh, no, it's lovely," she said, picking up her glass, then wondering with annoyance why she had done so. He smiled; she sipped her wine, wondering again at the sensation that rippled through her at the sun-gold touch of his eyes.

He turned his attention to Ashley once more. They were discussing the merits of ocean cruises. Tara thought that he had an accent, though it was slight. Something British, but not English.

She leaned back, wishing once more, very fervently, that she could tell him to go away. But there was really no reason to do that—he seemed to be most interested in Ashley, and Ashley seemed very pleased to be with him.

She should just leave, and she would, as soon as she finished her wine.

Four glasses on a nearly empty stomach, she reminded herself dolefully. And she really couldn't drink wine. Tine had told her that often enough, hadn't he?

Was Tine really the reason she couldn't trust anyone? One affair in her life, and that one affair had led to hurt, then betrayal—and tragedy. Tine...handsome, charming, masterful Tine. She'd been no match for him when she had met him. Too innocent to mistrust him.

But this man, this tiger-man—not even Tine would have been a match for him. Rafe Tyler. What was he after? What was it that he stalked? For a moment it seemed that her blood ran cold. Was he a reporter?

No, no, she assured herself. Reporters didn't order such expensive wine. They didn't dress with the negligent flair that was a part of Rafe Tyler.

He was just a man, albeit an experienced one, an affluent one. Handsome, charming, and alluringly male. If she wasn't so...wary, she might enjoy him. He was flattering and pleasant. Really, she had no right to be rude.

Another glass of wine, she realized ruefully, and she'd be overly charming herself. Why hadn't she eaten? It was something about him. He was talking to Ashley, yet she was the one who was mesmerized. She hadn't even been able to pick up her fork. She didn't seem capable of rising, excusing herself and leaving. The only physical feat she seemed able to manage was that of bringing the wine-glass to her lips.

She just hadn't been back very long. Back in the world, in the company of others. In her upstate farmhouse, there had been little in life that was difficult. She'd seen her neighbors, chatted with Mr. Morton at the store. No worries, no cares. She had never used her real name, nor had she encountered the slightest problem. There had just been the garden, her sketches, an occasional ride in the forest or swim in the lake. It had all been perfect, until her savings had begun to dwindle, and she had realized that she had reached the now-or-never point. She had had to return to work—and to the real world. She couldn't run forever.

Time and events had given her a certain hardness. She could smile through any line, lower her lashes to any flattery, converse, sip drinks, dine—and never be touched. She had met some nice people, too; that was true. And they had become friends. But after Tine, she had discovered that she just couldn't be affected by a man. There had been good times with Tine, but the end had been so horrible that she couldn't remember any of them. Just the betrayal. His use of her; his total disregard for her.

She smiled slightly, off in her own little world. She would never be innocent again. She wasn't cold; she just couldn't be swayed, flattered—or seduced. It was like a numbness inside her, not something she did purposely.

She gritted her teeth, fighting a wave of dizziness.

That had all changed suddenly, hadn't it? Because Rafe Tyler had a massive affect on her. She'd only just seen him for the first time; she'd barely met him. Yet the disturbing impact he had on her was as frightening as the promise of his power.

No, she thought. She was just so startled by it that she had been shaken from her customary poise. She resolved to behave normally.

"Do you live in the city, Mr. Tyler?" she asked with a forced smile, determined to join in the conversation.

Ashley and Rafe stared at her as Rafe hiked a rakishly amused brow. "She's with us again," he said.

"It's the wine," Ashley told him conspiratorially. "And don't you dare kick me again, Tara Hill," she warned as she caught the silver sizzle in her friend's eyes.

"Can't drink wine, eh?" Rafe inquired lightly.

"Not worth beans," Ashley replied bluntly.

"Ashley, are you sure you wouldn't like to give him a rundown on my life from start to finish?" Tara murmured with a warning frown.

But though Ashley was having a good time, she loved Tara dearly. She was convinced that the only way Tara would ever salvage any happiness was to hop right in.

"She's a transplanted farm girl, right out of the dust bowl," Ashley said seriously. "Just seventeen when the George Galliard rep found her at high school graduation. And from there, of course," she teased lightly, "Tara was transformed into the totally sleek and perfect beauty you see before you now. Of course, she does have this penchant for changing into blue jeans. And she looks great with hay in her hair."

"I'll bet," Rafe murmured quietly.

Tara watched as his disturbing gaze subtly roamed her face, so much like a caress that the entire room suddenly seemed to sway and grow hot. Maybe it was the wine....

She smiled, and even managed to do so pleasantly. "Mr. Tyler, it has been a pleasure to meet you. But if you'll both excuse me..."

She attempted to stand, but to her total embarrassment she slid back into her chair.

Rafe and Ashley chuckled openly. He leaned across the table and the expression on his face offered a gentle empathy that touched her despite all her resolve.

"I have to admit," he told her softly, "I have a hell of a time with wine myself. You never ate anything, did you?"

"I..."

Why was she answering him? She owed him no explanations. He was a stranger who had rudely interrupted their lunch.

He was up then, coming around the table, bending his dark head to whisper against her ear, "Try standing again. I'll steady you. We'll go somewhere else and get some food into you."

She moved her lips to form the word No. Sound didn't come, only the gasp of her breath. Because he was touching her. Hand gently on her shoulders, he was offering his support. She could sense him, feel him, and it was causing that horrible rush and confusion of emotions all over again.

He was strong, secure. He was sexually fascinating in a way that defied all reason and description.

She wanted to fall into his arms; she wanted to disappear, to run, to find some safe place where she might never see him again and therefore never feel the lure of his tiger power....

Too late. She was standing, and his arm was about her waist, long fingers played masterfully over her ribs.

Possessively.

As if the tiger had made the first swipe at its prey.

And the prey... the prey was stunned into submission. The tiger could play a while longer before pouncing for the kill.

She leaned against him too easily. Heedless of the wisdom and intelligence of her mental warnings, she felt as if she had been created just to be held by him.

What in heaven's name was wrong with her! She was worldly; she was wise. He was a tiger-man, full of vigor and shocking vitality, exuding energy. Tall, remote, carelessly charming—when he so chose.

Blatantly masculine. So unrelentingly sexual that any fool would fall for him at the slightest invitation.

Tara stiffened and straightened. She wasn't a fool. She had learned a great deal about life, the hard way. She didn't need any lessons from a man like Rafe Tyler.

And, damn it, the man *was* after her!

3

Moments later she was standing, albeit a little weakly, far away from him. Ashley was beside her as Rafe went to the cloakroom with their stubs.

She was amazed to discover that they had been sitting at the table for nearly three hours—it was time for an early dinner, and it might even be logical for them to move to another restaurant with the coming of the evening.

Tara shook her head uneasily. "I don't think we should be doing this. Oh! We didn't even pay the bill!"

"Rafe had it put on his tab," Ashley said blithely.

"Ashley! How could you let him?"

"Tara, it was lunch. Not a night at the Bonsoir Hotel!"

"Still..." Tara paused, not at all sure why she was arguing so strenuously. "Ashley! We don't know anything about him. He could be a murderer or a rapist. A criminal—"

"How many criminals do you know who keep open tabs at the Oak Room?" Ashley demanded dryly. "And who look and dress like that?"

"Jack the Ripper was supposedly quite distinguished!" Tara snapped back.

"Oh, come on!" Ashley exclaimed, laughing. "You don't really believe he's a criminal."

"No," Tara murmured uneasily, and dropped the subject because Rafe Tyler was coming toward them.

He was back, their coats in his hands. Tara found herself watching the way his fingers moved over her silver fox, and unbidden thoughts came to her mind. Thoughts of his fingers, his hands, moving with that same careless ease over naked flesh. She flushed, mumbling a thank-you as he helped her into her coat.

Ashley was smiling sweetly. "You're not a cutthroat or a wild rake, are you, Mr. Tyler?"

He hiked a brow, casting his gaze toward Tara. "Nor any other type of dangerous knave." He chuckled softly. "I've yet to cut a throat, I assure you."

"Pity!" Ashley laughed. "Tara could use a bit of seduction in her life right now. Work on that one, will you, Mr. Tyler?"

"Ashley!" Tara gasped. She was accustomed to the fact that Ashley said whatever came into her head, but she couldn't believe that her friend was going this far—with no discretion at all!

"Well, it's true!" Ashley blandly tossed her short red curls. "She's just come back to the city from years away."

"Years?" Rafe Tyler lightly mocked Ashley's Deep South accent.

"Just two, Mr. Tyler," Tara said flatly, staring at Ashley with a look that promised murder if she didn't cease and desist. She stared back at Rafe. "I believe I'm a bit of a loner. I like life that way."

"Ah, a woman with a mysterious past!" Now he was teasing *her*.

"Not at all," Tara lied as casually as she could. "I'm really quite dull." She had always meant to be dull, at any rate. It was true; as a child she had dreamed of escaping the poverty that had eventually claimed the lives of her parents and that of her baby brother before he'd learned to walk. But her dream had included a house in the country, a husband who loved her, and a whole passel of children. Dreams had taken her from poverty—they had also slashed her heart.

"I know a great Chinese place on Columbus, very casual and busy and lots of people—if you find safety in numbers, Miss Hill," Rafe said, barely concealing a crooked grin.

"Chinese sounds lovely," Ashley purred.

His eyes were on Tara. She saw the laughter in them and was suddenly, perversely annoyed. He was doing this to subdue any wariness on her part, she thought. Sure, lots of people, a totally innocent proposition! It doesn't matter, she wanted to scream. I know you're after something!

But what was it?

He could have any woman, she realized uneasily. He was just that type of man. Striking and assured, fluid and graceful, every movement hinting at a dynamic excitement that women found irresistible. Nor was she immune, and she had thought herself so savvy and smart....

"Shall we?" he queried. Light sparked, yellow and gold, from the depths of his eyes.

A challenge? A dare? She returned his gaze, a silent answer in steadfast silver.

I know what you are! Lean and hard, as cunning as that tiger, and every bit as charismatic. But I've been that route before....

His hand fell on her arm again. In seconds they were outside. Tara was amazed to see that darkness had fallen.

But the fact that Rafe Tyler didn't hail a cab did not particularly surprise Tara. He led them to a waiting limo. It was everything she might have expected—roomy and luxurious, with a bar, phone and a television. There was also a miniature desk, as if someone carried on business from the rear of the vehicle during traffic jams.

Tara was not even seated beside him. She was on the far right; Ashley sat in the middle, next to Rafe Tyler.

There was little traffic. In a matter of minutes, they were pulling up to a curb again. The restaurant was exactly as he had described it. Neat and clean, but very crowded, with tables almost on top of one another. Tea and noodles were served instantly. Rafe poured tea for Tara, smiling while she sipped at it, saying nothing, understanding that the hot liquid was the thing she needed most.

Curiously, dinner went just as lunch had. Ashley and Rafe talked. She told him about modeling; he listened intently.

And still Tara felt his eyes on her. Felt as if he were weighing her, assessing her, thinking deeply about her. Why? She wanted to scream. But then, in between bursts of panic, she felt wonderful little ripples of excitement cascade along her spine. She wanted to touch him, to feel the texture of his hair, to run her fingers along the muscled flesh beneath his shirt....

Dinner ended, and he offered to drive them both home. Tara became uneasy, realizing he would know where she lived.

Where—but not which apartment.

"Lovely!" Ashley answered.

Tara was struck with the sudden urge to run down the street—run anywhere from this sense of danger. But that would be absurd. And it would be a kind of surrender, too. Yes, I am afraid, she thought. Afraid that I can't withstand him.

They drew up before Ashley's apartment building. Ashley blew Tara a kiss. "See you tomorrow at one! Don't forget—fittings!"

Rafe excused himself to see Ashley to her door.

Alone in the rear of the limo, Tara leaned back, her heart pounding. There was a chauffeur in the front, she knew. A chauffeur who worked for Rafe Tyler. Long accustomed to the man's nocturnal habits?

Nocturnal habits! Her teeth started chattering slightly, and she twisted her fingers in her lap, wondering what she was doing, waiting alone in the back of a luxurious limousine for a man to return. Ashley was the one who had baited him all night. Why the hell hadn't Tara insisted on being brought home first?

Because he hadn't intended to let her go first! And she hadn't even fought, because she had known that she would lose....

No, it wasn't that at all. There'd been no battle. Surely he was a respectable man, albeit a devastating one, assured and adult, and definitely male.

Very male. Very attractive—because of that potent masculinity.

Tara released her hands and nervously stretched her fingers. She envisioned him coming back to the car, sitting beside her, staring into her eyes with that subtle, rueful smile. There would be no need for words. He would reach for her, and she would utter a small sound of protest, but it would be no more than a whimper caught in her throat. His arms would engulf her, and she would be swallowed in heat; his mouth would be firm and persuasive, but brook no resistance, should she find the strength to offer it. His kiss would be like fire. She would feel his fingers moving over her flesh with the same tender expertise with which they had touched the silver fox, but unlike the fox, she would feel that caress, and, knowing that she was a fool, she would still delight in it, gasping when his lips left hers to trail down the bare flesh of her throat.

No! In panic at her own vision, Tara almost gasped the word aloud. Furious with herself for being such a guileless coward—after all she had been through!—she nevertheless began to grope for the door handle. Let him think that she had run. That was exactly what she intended to do.

Blindly, Tara leaned forward. The door handle refused to budge, then quite suddenly gave way. Ready to leap for the pavement, she looked up.

Into his golden eyes.

"Was I gone so long? I'm sorry," he said smoothly.

Tara couldn't think of a thing to say. His foot was already inside; she had no choice but to back away.

Still smiling, he moved in beside her and tapped on the window. He looked back questioningly at Tara.

"Where to, Miss Hill?" he asked softly.

She stuttered out her address, furious at the sound of her voice, more annoyed still with the amusement on his features.

He repeated her address to the driver, and the limousine pulled out into the traffic. Rafe sat back, idly folding his hands before him, watching her with his slight, devilish grin.

The city lights flickered around them, giving occasional glints of substance and bursts of shadow. For a moment she tensed, remembering her fantasy. His arms around her, the potent kiss. The sleek feel of the rugged planes of his face beneath her fingers . . .

He didn't touch her. He didn't lean toward her.

"You've just come back to the city?" he asked casually.

"Yes."

"Long vacation?"

"Yes."

They passed beneath a streetlight. Tara noted that his eyes were really green, with brilliant pinpoints of topaz around the pupil that gave them their compelling quality of yellow gold.

Shadow came between them again. In that shadow he seemed to move slightly. His gaze appeared to change slightly, to become as gentle as the darkness.

He was going to touch her. . . .

She could feel the air grow tense between them. Little shocks seemed to leap through her, seemed to flame and warm her blood, heat her skin. She wanted to cry out, to leap away. . . .

Or into his arms.

"This is it," he said suddenly, and she started violently.

His lip twitched, but he said nothing, and merely opened the door. He stepped to the curb and turned, offering his hand. She took it, swallowing sharply, keeping her eyes lowered as she gained her footing. His hand was so warm. Hot and alive with power.

He released her, and his fingers lightly touched the small of her back as he led her to the door.

The doorman was on duty, but Rafe Tyler walked her to her apartment anyway.

The grand elevator, carpeted and mirrored, suddenly seemed ridiculously small. He filled it. They didn't speak, and as the cubicle took them higher, Tara felt her blood race like lava. Her fingers began to tremble. Her breath came too quickly, and, God help her, surely he could hear the beat of her heart.

She wasn't alone yet. Not yet. His arms could still come around her; his kiss could still sear her. . . .

The door opened. She walked down the hall and stopped nervously in front of her apartment, fumbling for her keys.

He took them from her fingers and deftly opened both locks.

This was it, she thought. He would lead her in and follow, close the door and lean against it. And she didn't know if she would long to scream or slide heedlessly into his embrace.

He stepped back. The caress of his eyes was his only touch.

"Good night, Tara," he said, his tone low and husky.

It was a promise in itself, something that touched her as surely as fingers might, with the same effect.

"Good night." She managed to form the words, trembling as she spoke.

And then his hand did move. He raised it slowly. His knuckles came to her cheek and brushed the soft flesh there.

He smiled and stepped away. She watched him move down the hall.

And then he turned back. His eyes fell on her curiously, disturbingly. It was a slow, total assessment. Her blood chilled, then heated. At first she felt his scrutiny touching her, like a breeze, lightly, then intimately. Velvety, vibrant and warm, knowing all of her, from head to toe.

His eyes met hers. She could tell that he had found all he saw appealing. He looked as if he could, like the great beast he so resembled, forget all convention, step back to her side and sweep her into his arms, into his very being. A savage conquest: desired—taken.

She quivered inwardly, wondering what her reaction would be. Outrage, surely.

But maybe not. The urge was almost painful. The urge to go to him, to curl into his arms...

Except that there was more to his look, something very disturbing. As if he hadn't *wanted* to find her appealing, though he had stalked her. But it was as if now that he had caught her, he wouldn't deny what he felt.

But it was only a physical appeal.

Then his eyes softened, if only for a minute. There was the slightest flame of tenderness within them.

"Tara, get inside."

She stepped back.

He smiled. "And lock your door!"

She nodded, not realizing that she was blindly obeying his command.

She leaned against her door once she was inside, having lost the strength to stand on her own.

Tara listened to the light fall of his footsteps as he moved down the hallway, back to the elevator. She gave herself a shake, moved into her apartment, showered, made herself a cup of tea and turned on the television set to watch the late movie from bed.

Rational, normal things to do...

But they didn't make her feel rational or normal. She was keyed up, wide-awake and very nervous.

She knew that Rafe Tyler had stepped into her life to stay for a while. What she didn't know was what he wanted.

Rafe walked into his study and headed straight for his desk, then sat and parked his legs on the gleaming wooden surface. Lacing his fingers behind his head, he stared up at the ceiling for a moment, then leaned forward and rummaged in his bottom drawer for the bourbon and the shot glass he kept there.

He splashed out a portion of whiskey and leaned back again, this time surveying the oil paintings on the paneled walls. There were five of them, all of ships at sea. Proud ships, rising high against the horizon.

He downed his drink, shuddering slightly as the liquor burned his throat. Then he opened the top drawer and pulled out a manila folder. He laid it flat on the desk and opened it.

Tara Hill, the woman who had occupied his day and night, stared at him once again from an eight-by-ten glossy.

It was a younger Tara Hill who looked up at him. She couldn't have been more than seventeen or eighteen in this picture. Her hair was longer and very straight; she wore little makeup, and her eyes carried a glint of dreams and fantasy and eager fascination that they lacked today.

Rafe turned sheets of paper, passing more and more photos, until he came to the most recent one he had, one that was two years old. She had changed. Her hair was far more sophisticated, feathered and sensual. She was slimmer. And her eyes carried a look of weariness that was more haunting and alluring than even the bright innocence of the earlier picture.

Rafe slapped the folder shut and readjusted his long legs over the corner of the desk as he leaned back, wincing. The photos had never touched him before. But then, *he* had never touched *her* before. She had been an object to be studied, and now she was real. He had assumed that she would be hard-bitten and cool, careless of her impact on the lives of others.

He didn't—couldn't—believe that anymore. Not when he had been touched by the shimmering silver in her eyes, had felt the soft and fluttering pulse of her life beneath skin as smooth and evocative as translucent silk....

He grimaced. He had touched her hand, no more. Gazed at the perfect ethereal beauty of her face. Rested his fingers against the delightful small of her back, and yet even then he had imagined he felt her heat, warm and subtle and promising a blaze of love and passion, an inferno....

Rafe slammed his feet to the floor, uttering an exclamation of self-disgust. Was this what Jimmy had felt? This overriding, uncanny desire? This lure that had to be followed, this hunger that had to be appeased?

He groaned aloud. Jimmy had been younger. Easily led, easily tricked. And by God, Rafe determined, *he* wasn't Jimmy. He'd seen the world in all its facets; he knew the harlots and the whores, the ladies and the thieves. The world had molded him, touched him with its many cultures, given him a wisdom about human nature that defied country and custom.

But tonight he might as well have been as raw and naive as Jimmy. He had ached, yearned to reach for her, touch her, hold her, caress her—and forget everything. And if he had touched her, she would have surrendered to his hold. Or would it have been he who surrendered, to practiced wiles, to a known beauty?

Rafe raised his hands to his temples. What was she, then, a lady or an elegant tramp? And in that moment he knew the truth. He had touched her but done no more because though she might have gone to him for the moment, she would have run in time. And he still had enough of his wits about him to know that he had to treat her carefully, building her trust, until she decided to talk.

Rafe started suddenly, aware that there was a hesitant tapping at his door. He stood, crossed the room and threw it open. Before him stood a slight woman with silver-dusted chestnut hair and enormous blue eyes. She appeared to be no more than a very attractive forty, but Rafe knew her to be a year or two over fifty.

"Myrna!" he exclaimed, startled at her presence. He moved, inviting her in. "I didn't know you were here."

Myrna smiled wanly and moved restlessly into the room, wandering to the window to stare blankly out at the darkness before turning back to Rafe.

"I'm sorry. I shouldn't be disturbing you. I hope you don't mind—I planned on spending the night. I came around eight. You were out."

"I just got back and—"

"Yes, yes, Maggie went up to her room hours ago—I told her to."

Maggie was his housekeeper.

"Myrna, you know you're always welcome," Rafe told his stepmother gently.

Her smile became a little less hesitant. "You mean that, don't you, Rafe?" she said a little wonderingly. "I've—I've been very blessed to have you."

Touched, and slightly embarrassed, Rafe grinned ruefully. "I don't know about that, Myrna." He continued quickly, "But what's wrong? You seem upset."

"Upset" was an understatement, but Rafe was at a loss for a better word. Myrna had been upset for the past two years, and Rafe sure as hell couldn't blame her. She'd lost her husband to heart failure and her son to mysterious circumstances within a month.

"I, uh, I am upset, Rafe," Myrna murmured. Then she smiled and crossed the room, staring up at the oil painting of the *Highland Queen*. She turned back to him suddenly and chuckled girlishly.

"I was awfully afraid that I'd... interrupt you. I take it you were out with some exquisitely beautiful woman?"

Everything in his body tensed, but Rafe was careful not to let emotion show in his face. He leaned against his desk, crossing his arms over his chest, and grinned in return.

"Yep," he answered, and she nodded, pleased.

"Well, I'm glad you're alone now."

Rafe walked around his desk, indicating that she should sit on the soft white leather sofa across the room. "I think you need a drink, Myrna. Bourbon okay? I can call Maggie and have her make us some tea if you'd rather—"

"Oh, heavens no! Maggie played nursemaid to me long enough tonight!" Myrna protested. "I'd love a good shot of bourbon. A manly drink, isn't it?"

Rafe grimaced. "I don't know about that. It does seem to go down smoothly."

He poured them each a shot, then took a seat beside her. She gulped down hers with a toss of the glass, shuddered, then faced him squarely.

"I saw her picture, Rafe. That model who disappeared. She's back with Galliard Fashions."

Rafe drained his glass quickly, dismayed that Myrna already knew that Tara Hill had emerged from obscurity.

He set his glass on the coffee table and faced his stepmother squarely. "I know," he told her honestly.

"Oh, Rafe!" She clutched his hand, and her fingers were shaking. "I know that you did everything you could, that you searched and searched, that you left your profession behind you, that you did everything already. But I have to know! I just have to know what really happened. If Jimmy is—"

"Myrna, Myrna," Rafe said softly, clasping her fingers tightly, wrenched anew by the bright tears he saw hovering in her eyes. "I'm going to find out," he promised.

She nodded, looking down to her lap. "You're not even my blood, and I've asked you to give up everything—"

Rafe shook his head impatiently. "I gave up working because Dad died and someone had to run his empire. I might have been a wanderer, but he always knew I'd come back when I was needed. And Jimmy was my brother,

Myrna. My little brother. I promise you—I'd never be able to rest if I didn't follow every damn possibility."

She was still looking at her hands, and nodded miserably.

Rafe stood. He'd been fifteen years old when his father had married Myrna; her son, Jimmy, had been only seven at the time. But a tie had formed between them instantly, and in the years that followed, the stepbrothers had become closer than those bonded by blood.

"One more shot of bourbon, Myrna," Rafe said. "Then off to bed with you. You could use some sleep." He brought her a second drink and watched while she swallowed it. Then he helped her to rise and led her to the door. He kissed her forehead. "Get to bed."

She lifted her huge blue eyes to him, eyes that still brimmed with tears. "You've been the very best son, Rafe. The very best."

"Hey, you're a damn good stepmom, too."

Her smile warmed; her tears seemed to dry a little. "Good night, Rafe. I'm in control, I promise. And I'll—I'll trust you."

"Thanks, Myrna. This will take a little time, and you can't make yourself crazy, right?"

She nodded, stronger now. With a smile and a little wave, she moved down the darkened hall to the suite she still maintained in the Tyler mansion on Long Island.

Rafe closed his study door, turned out the lights and went through the connecting door to his bedroom.

He didn't turn on the light. Wearily, he stripped and headed for bed, then paused and turned to the mullioned floor-to-ceiling windows that looked out on the gardens. There was a full moon tonight. There was a breeze, too. The moon's glow fell on the water splashing in the main fountain and made fantasy diamonds of it against the velvet of the night.

A perfect setting for a Galliard girl, Rafe found himself thinking. Not just any Galliard girl. Tara Hill.

Dressed in something flowing, something almost translucent—chiffon silk. A gown that was soft yet would mold to her hips and breasts with each fluid movement of her long legs. Its color would be somewhere between blue and silver, like her eyes. Good God, he could almost see her walking the path, almost smell the fragrance of her perfume and her flesh. . . .

He turned away from the window and angrily padded over to the bed, ripping the covers away with a vengeance. Damned bloody moon! It had been proved centuries ago that the moon gave rise to fantasies.

Rafe slammed a fist into his pillow and curled onto his side. Still she remained with him, her scent seeming to linger on his flesh. He closed his eyes tightly but could not dispel the vision of her in his room, walking toward him. He could discern her figure beneath the diaphanous gown, the lush round rise of her breasts, the shadow between, the dark, entrancingly peaked circles where her nipples rose in anticipation of his touch. The sway of her walk, the length of her thighs, the moon-touched silver of her eyes as she looked at him, the feel of her fingers as they rested first against his cheek and then on his chest. He could even hear her whisper to him. . . .

He sat up, grunting between clenched teeth, holding his head between his hands. Had he been awake or asleep? That touch of her fingers had been nothing but a layer of sweat beading onto his naked flesh as he dreamed.

He closed his eyes tightly and vehemently shook his head. He finally banished her presence and brought to mind his stepmother's glistening tears, recalling the agony in her voice. He thought of his brother Jimmy. Young, good-looking, happy-go-lucky. Sensitive and courteous, and such an easy mark when it came to a beautiful woman. One who might have cried, clung to him, used him.

Tara Hill—pretty poison. Or was she?

It didn't matter. He lay down again, very aware that he could not fall in love with a fantasy. But he smiled grimly in the night. He intended to have that fantasy. She would be dealing with Rafe Tyler this time.

Not Jimmy.

And by God, he meant to have the truth. The whole story. It mattered not one whit how he went about procuring it.

He closed his eyes once more, finally exhausted by his determination. But his dreams wouldn't quit. It seemed that he was plagued by whispers moaning in the wind, clarified by the moon.

Whispers hinting again and again that, despite the odds, despite the facts, she might be innocent. As real and innocent and beautiful as the shimmering silver of her eyes....

4

Tara arrived fifteen minutes late for her fitting, and George wasn't about to let her get away with it.

"Tara, back to work means back to work! Either you're with us or you're not. You don't want a job? Fine—I've got dozens of girls who would die for the opportunity. Girls not yet a quarter of a century old, if you get my meaning, *ma petite*!"

Tara winced slightly behind her sunglasses and gritted her teeth. George had been really angry at first; he hadn't even bothered feigning his French accent through the first two sentences. And George liked to "be French." He might have been born in Brooklyn, but he was convinced that American women wanted French fashions. Maybe he had a point. He had managed to make his name synonymous with fashion the world over.

But he didn't fool her. Not anymore. She had known him too long now. They had been friends; they had endured their squabbles. They had undergone an investigation together—he'd been dragged into it, all because of her! But still, he had tried to shield her, had tried to talk her out of running away. And he had taken her back without blinking when she had squared her shoulders and determined to work again.

"I'm sorry," Tara murmured, lowering her head and trying not to show her grin. His toupee was slightly awry—

and he was a man who did not admit to baldness. He was of medium height, with a wiry build, and his manners were perfect—when he wanted them to be.

He was also cruel at times. He liked to remind Tara that he had taken her on as a dirt-poor ragamuffin and changed her into a priestess of high fashion.

Tine had been worse! she reminded herself abruptly, and felt suddenly frozen. In her two years of solitude she thought she had matured. She thought she had faced all the facts and learned to live with them. But just as she had done through all the previous night, she was reliving the past. Yes, Tine had enjoyed his moments of mastery. Reminding her that even with her scholarships, she would never have been able to leave her parents to go to college. That if it hadn't been for him, she wouldn't have been able to give them relief in their last days. That they would have died in pain and dirt and filth, and she would have wound up just like her mother—except healthier. She would have raised a passel of lice-ridden brats, scrounging in the welfare lines.

Tears pricked her eyes behind her glasses; it hurt even now. She wanted to fight, just as she had always fought Tine. She wanted to rage out that her mother had been one of the kindest women on earth, that she had always been poor because she had taken in any stray, any child, and that her father's only crimes had been his lack of education and tireless efforts to make other men rich by his labor and sweat....

"*Mon Dieu!* Take those glasses off and get over to see Madame Clouseau! Schedules, schedules! *Ma chérie*, we leave in ten days!"

His tone had grown gentle, and Tara sighed, aware that George really did care for her; it was just that he had become accustomed to treating his models either like little children or slaves. He had a remarkable ego—and perhaps it was justly deserved, for it was his fashions that had given them all their tenuous claims to fame.

"I'm going, George," she began. "And I really am sorry—"

"Tara!" he exclaimed, looking at her closely for the first time and frowning. "What have you done to yourself? You look like—like absolute hell!"

She grimaced dryly—she didn't look great, but she didn't look all that bad, either! She hadn't slept more than an hour the night before and had a few shadows under her eyes. All because of that damned Rafe Tyler! He had triggered something in her, and all she had done, hour after hour, was toss and relive her life and...

Dream. Dream of something different from anything she had ever known. A man with the grace and power and fluidity of a tiger—who loved her with the gentle, tender manner of a kitten.

"I, uh, I slept badly last night, George, that's all. I've only been back about a week now; my apartment still seems a little alien and—"

"Alien!" George snorted in disgust. "It has been yours for eight years! Tonight you will take the pills I give you—they will ease you into sleep."

Tara sighed wearily. "I don't take sleeping pills, George."

"You will not work, Tara, unless you learn to sleep. Now, I am serious—I cannot have you looking like a refugee! Like an emaciated pauper. Like—"

"All right!" Tara snapped. "I'll sleep, I promise! But no pills!" She continued to mutter her opinion of sleeping pills as she stepped past him to the rear of the showroom, then to the fitting rooms beyond. He chuckled softly behind her. If nothing else, she was at least off the hook for her tardiness, she thought.

Madame Clouseau was there amid a tangle of measuring tape and sporting a mouthful of pins as she worked over Cassandra Law, a stunning young woman with a headful of nearly blue-black hair. Perhaps, Tara mused, George had taken her back as an employee only because she was a blonde. George, as well as having a flair for color in clothing, loved to play the artist with his models' hair. There would be only four of them on the trip, and they were entirely different in their natural coloring. There was Cassandra, with her raven locks and indigo eyes; Ashley, with her brilliant red curls and green eyes; Mary Hurt, a brunette with deep mahogany eyes; and Tara, with light-blond hair and silver-tinted eyes. Colorful, different—just the way George liked things.

Cassandra was standing on a stool, a white satin strapless gown molding itself around her luscious form and ending elegantly in a froth of rhinestoned tulle around her ankles. She grimaced at Tara in pain as Madame stuck her with one of her countless pins.

"It sounded loud out there," Cassandra murmured, looking anxiously at Tara. "You okay?"

Tara nodded. "Fine, thanks. I've learned to weather the storms around here quite well."

"You're late!" Madame Clouseau snapped, pushing a straying tendril of steel-gray hair behind her ear.

"I'm sorry."

"Start with the black velvet evening gown, please," Madame said. "Cassandra, get this off. Now where is Ashley?"

"I'm here, I'm here! And I'm not wearing this!"

Ashley appeared in a burnt-orange concoction that clashed horribly with her hair. She didn't wait for a re-

ply—Ashley was marvelous at ignoring Madame's impe-
rious manner—but smiled at Tara. "You're late! Does that
mean that something erotic happened last night?"

"No, it means I overslept."

"You will wear the dress! George has said so!" Madame exclaimed angrily.

"Damn!" Ashley swore to Tara. "I certainly will not!"
she told Madame. "I shall go see George right away and
handle the situation myself!" She started for the front,
then turned back. "Tara, I want to hear all about it later!"

"I'm dying to hear about it, too!" Cassandra laughed.

"Will you please get to work!" Madame called out,
clapping her hands sharply.

"What a wonderful kindergarten teacher you would
have made!" Tara told her sweetly, then, secretively smiling and giggling to one another, Tara and Cassandra hurried to the back. They passed Mary on the way; she was
mumbling under her breath as she tripped over the hem of
the elegantly seductive peignoir she was wearing.

It was a long day. Tara went through outfit after outfit
and appeared before George—pinned to perfection by
Madame—with a multitude of purses, evening bags, shoes,
coats, hats and stockings. He picked everything apart and
redesigned each complete ensemble until he was satisfied.
He did the same with the others. Ashley and Cassandra
complained, while Tara and Mary remained silently
amused. In between, Ashley described the tiger-man to
Cassandra, and the two of them plagued Tara to death
with questions regarding her few minutes alone with the
man. Cassandra swore that Tara led the most exciting life,
and Tara silently reflected that excitement had brought her
nothing but misery before. Mary seemed to be on her side,
though.

"Don't ever trust a man like that! If he's that devastating to you, he's that devastating to all women. And he probably keeps a scorecard of his conquests!"

Ashley shook her head vehemently. "Not this guy. He would only be interested in the *crème de la crème*!"

"Ah, but he needs his *crème* all the time!"

"It doesn't matter, anyway!" Tara said at last. "I'll never see the man again. Let's drop it, shall we? Please?"

She counted herself grateful that they did. Mary was taking classes at Columbia, determined to be an architect when her days as a model came to an end. She began to talk enthusiastically about a certain professor, and Tara found herself swept into the mood, laughing with the others. She longed to agree to Ashley's suggestion that they all go out to dinner at the end of the day. But she remembered what George had said. She would have to get some sleep.

"I've got to go home," she said with a sigh. "Sorry— I've just got to get some rest."

Ashley instantly looked contrite and worried. "Are you all right, Tara? Want me to come with you? I can make you something to eat. You can shower and go straight to bed."

Tara shook her head. "No, thanks, Ashley. I'm capable of making my own dinner—honest! Go, have a good time!"

They parted on the street. Tara let the others get the first cab, and, to her frustration, it took her almost half an hour to get another. It was nearly seven when she reached her apartment.

She kicked off her shoes by the door, sighed softly and went into the kitchen to put on a kettle for tea. While she waited for the water to boil, she drew a hot bubble bath. When her tea was made, she took it and a paperback thriller into the bathroom, where she relaxed in the tub, while a frozen dinner cooked in the oven.

She couldn't seem to get into the book. It was wonderful—but her mind was a mess. She didn't want to think about the past, but she couldn't seem to help herself. She kept remembering that she was going to Caracas again. And she kept seeing that city, and then Tine, herself—and Jimmy.

Tara sighed, sipped her tea and set it down on the tile floor, gave up on the book—and settled back into the bubble bath, closing her eyes.

Caracas...

It had been all over by then. All over between her and Tine. She had met him at seventeen, fallen in love with him before she was twenty.

By the time they had reached Caracas, she had almost hated him.

She wasn't quite sure when the beginning of the end had come. She had adored Tine at first. He had been like a benevolent magician, come to turn her world around, to offer her money to ease her family's distress, to give her fame and glamour. He had asked nothing of her—not at first. He had been tall and slim and capable of the slowest, sexiest smile in the universe.

Tine had known how to bide his time. She had been raised rigidly and morally. But on her twentieth birthday she had gone to him, and before her twenty-first birthday they were living together.

The trouble had started in small ways. Her family had embarrassed him; she had been fiercely loyal. He wanted to control her contracts. He didn't want her sending money home; he didn't want her creating scholarships for the local high school students who were caught in the same economic prison in which she herself had been confined. He didn't want her to have lunch with her friends—not even to make phone calls!

When he had begun to insist that she marry him, she had backed away, already disillusioned. When she had begun to fight—he'd eased off, and reminded her that he had made her. Very subtly, he'd reminded her that he could also break her. And, of course, he had still been Tine. So good-looking, so male, so capable of overpowering the staunchest convictions that she could muster.

But in Caracas she'd escaped him. And, wandering through the city streets, joining a tour of the old cathedral, she'd realized that she really was coming to hate him, and that she couldn't stay with him a minute longer. He meant to rule her—and she wasn't about to be ruled or imprisoned by anyone.

On that same afternoon, walking past the shops, she had suddenly paused, caught by the reflection in a window of a young man's eyes.

She had turned quickly to meet him face-to-face. He didn't turn away. He had been young and handsome and more. She was accustomed to men's looks, accustomed to sighing with the realization that they were usually interested in just one thing.

It wasn't that he didn't display that same hunger. But it was tempered somehow with laughter and humor. His eyes had held a wistful appreciation, and he'd smiled so nicely that she discovered herself smiling back.

They talked as they walked along, and they wound up having dinner. He told Tara that he was a tourist. She told him her business. He said that he knew her business—any man with life and breath in him knew who she was.

And somehow she had poured out her story to him. And in speaking to him, she'd realized uneasily that she was afraid of Tine.

"If you need help, if you're ever afraid, just call me. I'll be there, understand?"

She knew his offer was honest. He really didn't want anything; he wasn't making any demands. He was actually offering to be her friend.

That night she'd told Tine that she was leaving him. First he'd reminded her harshly that they were both working. Then he'd tried his subtle magic on her.

And she had known that it was truly over, because she felt nothing for him. When she had told him that, he'd called her a liar, but it had been true.

Sitting in the tub now, she clenched her fingers tightly. Tine had been convinced of his sexual mastery. She didn't think she would forget, no matter how long she lived, how he had forced her that night. And how incredulous and furious he had been when he realized at the end that she had meant it—he could not move her, and she hated him.

He had started to laugh. "You should learn to enjoy it again, baby. When we get home, you're going to marry me. If you try to leave me, Tara, I'll kill you. Do you understand?" He had flexed his fingers, then wrapped them around her neck. "Don't doubt it—I'll kill you. I saw you today with that kid. I'm always watching you, Tara. I'll kill him, too." He'd chuckled again. "Maybe I'll just kill him anyway. I may need to."

"You fool!" Tara had retorted. "You'll never keep me this way. I hate you—and I'm not afraid of you!" But she was; she was near tears because he had just proved to her that he could toss her around easily enough—if he had her alone. She was so humiliated she nearly wanted to die, so miserable that she didn't think that she could ever really trust or love anyone again.

"Sweetie, remember—you're mine. I'll do whatever I want, whenever I want. And if you don't want to leave a trail of blood in your wake, you'll leave the boys alone."

He'd walked out on her then—cocky, cruel, assured.

Tara had hesitated in absolute misery—then called Jimmy.

If she'd been able to think clearly, she might have wondered at his rapid questions, about his lack of surprise that Tine knew about him. He'd told her to meet him at the glass factory, and at that point she certainly should have wondered what was going on.

The glass factory was out of town, up in the mountains. But Tara had gone, determined that she would never see Tine again.

The factory was closed. The taxi driver hadn't wanted to take her there, but she had feverishly convinced him in her broken Spanish that she was meeting a friend there. The kindly cabdriver had stayed with her in the darkness until she had seen Jimmy coming out of the trees.

He'd taken her gently in his arms and told her that he had the use of a friend's little house nearby. There was no road leading to it, so they walked through the trees, up the mountain. She told him something of what had happened—not all, since it was so horribly humiliating—and then regretted quite suddenly that she had come to him, because she was afraid for his life.

That was when the first shot had rung out. They were in a small clearing, the moon overhead, the night beautiful and cool. She could still remember the fresh scent of the trees, damp from a recent rain. She'd screamed, and Jimmy had instantly and protectively pulled her to the ground. Wary, ready. Or so it seemed.

Tine had appeared in the clearing, carrying a gun. She could remember his silhouette so clearly. She could re-

member the flash of his teeth when he smiled. She had lain
there in terror as he casually glanced her way, then stared
at Jimmy.

She could remember the sophisticated and beautiful
brunette at his side—a woman who seemed to know him
quite well, to be quite comfortable with this gun-toting
activity of his.

And, despite her terror, she realized what an idiot she
had been. He'd wanted to marry her—her income potential had far surpassed even his original imaginings—but
there had been other women all along.

Then, to her complete amazement, he had told Jimmy
that he wanted the mask back. And he had laughed and
told the other woman that Tara really was an extraordinary prize—she'd lured Jimmy easily when no one and
nothing else in the world would have been able to do so.

"The mask!" Tine had cried, firing a warning shot into
the trees.

Tara had been incredulous when Jimmy fired back—and
then she didn't know what happened at all, because she
had ducked her face into the ground and shuddered as
volley after volley of shots rang out. Leaves rustled, and
Jimmy was gone.

Sirens had suddenly screeched through the quiet of the
forest as the police had climbed their way up the mountain. Tara had dared to look up—just in time to see Tine
clutching a bloody shoulder, leaning against a tree. He had
stared at her and smiled slowly.

"Sweetheart, someday, somewhere, I'll find you again.
Once more, my love, for old times' sake! And then, as I
promised—bye-bye, darling!"

Tine had disappeared. The sirens had come closer and
closer. She had screamed for Jimmy—but Jimmy, too, was
gone.

She had been alone with the brunette—dead from a gunshot wound—when the police had arrived. She'd been arrested instantly, dragged into interrogation. She had sworn her innocence, trying to explain that Tine had been shooting at Jimmy. When George Galliard arrived to stand at her side in the confusion, they had threatened to arrest him, too. After all, he had employed both Tine Elliott and Tara.

George had sworn her innocence too and threatened to sue for libel and legal retribution. Heads would roll if he and Tara weren't released immediately, he'd insisted.

No one ever did discover who Jimmy was. Nor had Tine been found. After three miserable weeks, the charges against Tara had been dismissed. She and George had come home, and she had decided to disappear after the media blitz. The police had told her that Tine had been suspected of being in on the artifacts smuggling racket for a long time. The papers had picked it up, and she had found herself labeled the lover and accomplice of a notorious criminal.

Tara opened her eyes and took a deep breath. The water was getting cold. Her dinner was probably burning. She didn't want to think anymore—she just wanted to sleep.

She hurried into the kitchen, turned off the stove, and poured herself a glass of wine, which she quickly downed. Feeling a bit better—as if she would at least get some release from her own thoughts!—she dressed in a silk floor-length hostess-type nightgown, brushed out her hair and meandered back into the kitchen.

She bent over the oven door, intending to remove her dinner, then frowned, feeling a little dizzy. Too much wine after a sleepless night, she thought. The doorbell rang. She hesitated. If she didn't answer, whoever it was would go away.

But someone was insistent. The bell kept ringing. "All right, all right!" she muttered, pressing her palms to her forehead.

She should never have just opened the door. She didn't usually do anything so foolish—she always checked through the little peephole to see who was there. Perhaps she had been so annoyed and so dizzy that she had thrown the door open to stop the horrible sound of the bell as quickly as possible.

It was a mistake. A horrible mistake.

Because he stood there. Her tiger-man. Arching a brow with stern displeasure at her carelessness.

He was in black again: black trousers; black vest; black jacket. But a white shirt and a red tie. Elegant, casual. He might have graced the pages of an elite magazine. Sophisticated.

And the farthest thing in the world from civilized! In spite of the suit, in spite of his totally businesslike appearance, he still resembled a tiger. Taut and vital, exuding a leashed energy, yet cool and knowledgeable, on the prowl.

"Rafe!" she said, standing there.

"Yes, and you should be glad that it is. You might have just thrown your door open to a mugger."

The smile she gave him nearly caused his heart to stop, his blood to boil. Superior, aloof, a sensual curve of her lips.

"Perhaps that would be less dangerous. You can't come in, you know."

But he was already in, closing and locking the door behind him, frowning as he surveyed her eyes.

"Are you all right?"

"Of course I'm all right. But you can't stay."

"I have to stay. My dinner is coming here."

"Here?"

"Yes, I've ordered us two steaks, medium rare, linguine with clam sauce, and antipasto. It will arrive any minute now."

"Well, I'm so sorry, but you didn't ask me, and you can't stay!"

Did tigers smile, or did they simply grin? He leaned against the door, watching her, as comfortable in her home as a lover of many years' standing might be.

"You wouldn't really have me eat in the hallway, would you? And besides, your own dinner is burning."

"What?" she demanded, and then she smelled it—her frozen dinner, burning in the oven. "Oh," she murmured, and hurried out to remove the charred remains before the whole place smelled of smoke.

Tara grabbed an oven mitt, quickly threw the tray into the sink and flooded it with water.

Rafe was right behind her. "That was what you were going to eat? For a meal?"

"It was a fine meal!" she retorted. "Models are supposed to be slim, remember?"

She wanted to sail regally on by him and show him the door, but the dizziness overwhelmed her, and right before him, in the narrow space of the doorway, she found herself having to stop and grasp the frame to keep herself upright. She looked from the sleek material of his suit to his eyes and shivered, because it was there, that magnetism so unique, so dangerous, so appealing and sexual that her heart fluttered in a way it hadn't for years. No, never—she had never felt this absolute attraction before in her life.

"Slim?" he inquired softly as he took her cheeks between his palms, then threaded his fingers slowly through her hair. "You're perfect. More beautiful without makeup. Soft, like this, fragrant and natural in every way."

"I—" Tara gripped the door desperately for help. "You—you have to go."

The doorbell started to ring again. He smiled and went to answer it.

It was dinner. Two men in white coats brought it in on a table covered with a snowy-white cloth. They set it up in her living room. Tara couldn't seem to speak as she watched the whole thing taking place. The men tipped their caps to Rafe, then said they hoped she enjoyed her dinner.

And then they were gone. Rafe had taken two chairs from her dining-room table. He held one out for her.

"I told you—" she began.

"It's here. And your own meal is a soggy mess in the kitchen sink. Come on—you have to eat."

She paused, watching him warily. "Who are you, what do you want, and why have you been following me?"

He returned her stare. "I am Rafe Tyler," he replied. "And what I want is you. Can that be so difficult to understand? No subterfuge. I'm being as honest as I can. And civilized! I realize that what I want may not be something you . . . desire, so I want to get to know you. Dinner and walks and flowers. I'll worship from afar—for a while!" he said softly. He smiled, and she thought there was an amazing tenderness in his eyes. A tenderness as great as the primal heat and hypnotic energy that drove him.

She couldn't fight him. Wine and exhaustion were making her too drowsy, costing her too much.

"You're rather sure of yourself, aren't you?" she asked him.

"I'm a determined type of person."

"If I sit down and eat, will you leave?"

"If that's what you want, yes."

"I have to sleep," she told him primly.

He arched a brow. "Did you have trouble sleeping last night? Might it have been because of me?"

"Of course not!" she snapped.

He just smiled and seated her politely then sat down across from her. He served her, talking about the wonders of the restaurant from which the food had come. She ate, asking him questions. She learned that he really lived on Long Island but kept an apartment in the city. He told her that he had sailed quite a bit, traveling the world on steamers right after college. She was barely aware that he had poured wine for her—and that she had kept drinking—until her elbow fell off the table and she nearly lost her balance.

"What's the matter?" he demanded, sweeping around to help her.

She stared at him, shaking her head in confusion. She had heard him; she hadn't heard him. She felt delightfully light, and terribly sleepy. Very soft, very feminine. He didn't seem to be so much of a threat anymore. He was a man. An attractive and attentive one, and it was impossible not to like him.

"Tara!"

He seemed annoyed, though, annoyed and a little too macho.

"What have you done to yourself?"

She smiled, loving the feel of the fabric of his jacket against her cheek, fascinated by the gold and silver color of her hair where it fell across his shoulders.

"I told you—I have to sleep."

"What did you take?"

"Don't yell at me!"

"Then tell me!"

"It's all your fault. George told me to go home and sleep so I had a glass of wine. And then you gave me more."

His face was tense, and his arms were tight as he lifted her and carried her down the hallway, past the bath and the den to her bedroom. It seemed all right. Everything seemed to be all right.

More than all right. She felt ridiculously secure, comfortable. So relaxed, so ready to smile.

"You should be in bed," he said as he stopped in the doorway.

"I would have been. You appeared at the door."

Thick lashes hid the tawny gold of his eyes. She thought that he smiled a little secretively.

"I'm going to put you to bed."

"Wasn't that your plan?"

"No. Eventually, I plan to *take* you to bed. There is a massive difference, of which you will one day be completely aware."

"Ah! No ego problems there!"

He smiled, turned down her brocade coverlet and the sheet below, then laid her down with her head on the pillow. He sat at her side, studying her intently.

"They're quite unusual," she murmured, reaching up to touch his face, smoothing a finger over his brows.

"My eyebrows?"

"Your eyes. They actually have brown in them, and green—and a ring of blue at the very edge. Like crystal. And when you combine all the colors, they seem gold. Like a tiger's eyes, reflecting in the darkness."

"They're hazel," he said dryly.

He caught her hand and pressed a kiss against her palm. She inhaled sharply at the river of sensation that swept through her. She was tired and off guard, yet she couldn't seem to care.

When their eyes met, it seemed as if eons passed. Eons in which they strained to know each other, to absorb each other's soul, and thoughts, and heart.

He leaned toward her. And kissed her.

Never had she felt such magic. Lips that knew hers, commanded, yielded and coerced. Warmth and fever, magnetism, engulfing her.

Never had a kiss coursed through every nerve and fiber of her being, awakening a fever, a heat. His lips were forceful, his tongue demanding. Sweeping all the crevices of her mouth, hungry and restraining, hungry and setting free . . .

She felt his hands cupping her face, caressing her shoulders.

Moving intimately. More intimately than they should have been. She trembled as his fingers curved around her breast, his fingers playing over her nipples. He groaned, deep and hoarse, against her, and sudden truth and panic seized her.

She wanted him. Everything within her quivered for him, like a strung bow, taut and ready to let fly. She was fascinated by him. Where he touched her, she felt alive. Where he did not touch her, she longed to be touched. She wanted to see his shoulders bared to her touch. She wanted to explore his chest and muscular legs. She wanted . . .

All of him. It was like a drumbeat, frantic, insistent.

And it was so wrong! She didn't trust him; she barely knew him, and she couldn't believe she was letting things go so far. She was suddenly very frightened, whimpering slightly in her throat.

Perhaps he heard. Or perhaps some alarm had sounded within him, a warning that the time wasn't right.

He pulled away. Not with an apology. Pensively, painfully. She could see the tension in his features, the pulse throbbing in his throat.

He took her hands, planted a light kiss on each one, then let them go and rose stiffly.

"Go to sleep. I'll see you soon."

"Oh . . . no! Really, we can't."

He shook his head, smiling crookedly. "No, Tara. We not only can. We have to."

He turned and left her.

She struggled to think, to find logic. She didn't trust him. She didn't know why, exactly, but she didn't trust him. He wasn't following her because she was a "beautiful" woman. He would attract women without seeking them, all of them beautiful, all of them sensual.

He knew her, she was certain. He had watched her in the museum; he had followed her to the Plaza.

She shouldn't see him again.

She shivered, knowing that she would. He was right. She would have to.

Seeing him could become as necessary as . . . breathing.

"No," she protested aloud.

But no one heard her, and she gave up all attempts to be rational when sleep overcame her.

5

He was there when Tara finished with her fittings the next day, in the showroom, idly talking to George—waiting for her.

Tara saw him as soon as she emerged from the back, and she held herself still, stunned and, to her annoyance, slightly panicky.

Morning had brought reason back to her. Humiliation, too. The night now seemed part of a dream, a very disturbing dream. She could remember him carrying her, could remember the feel of his arms. She could remember his smile and his laughter, and the way his hair had felt beneath her fingers.

She could remember his kiss, his touch on her breast. And she could remember the absolute feel of fire. Sensations that ripped through her. A wanting unlike anything she had ever known.

And she remembered him pulling away. Kissing her fingers, leaving her be when he could have...

Continued. With her so content, yet at the same time so explosive that she would have never thought to stop him. To seek restraint. To realize that they were virtual strangers and to remember that the one previous affair of her life had ended in absolute disaster.

Easy, she had told herself in the morning. It was a matter of will, and her will would control her actions. She didn't trust him—he was a tiger. Fierce, exciting, wonderful, beautiful—and dangerous. She couldn't quite fathom why, but she knew instinctively that she was being stalked. Therefore, she told herself, don't see the man. The next time he appears, keep the door shut. Don't answer the summons. Simply don't see him. The decision was made, so it would be easy.

He wasn't in black today. He wore a loose off-white jacket, tan slacks and a navy silk shirt casually open at the neck. His hands were in his pockets as he leaned casually against the golden oak bar at the rear of the store, nearly parallel to the models' dressing rooms.

He seemed to be listening politely to whatever George was saying.

"Is that him?" Mary whispered suddenly.

Tara discovered herself nodding reluctantly. Ashley had dragged it out of her that he had stopped by the night before, and the group of them had been teasing her all day.

Tara heard a soft whistle. She twisted and saw that Cassandra had come up behind her, too.

"That's spectacular," she murmured.

"Cassandra!" Ashley joined the group. "Get your tongue back into your mouth before you trip on it!"

"He might be worth the risk," Mary said philosophically. "Don't get too involved, of course. But his type is ... rare."

"What type? Two arms, two legs?" Tara asked nervously. And then she laughed. "We must look like a group of high school girls standing here."

"Right you are!" Ashley proclaimed. "And since I do have the privilege of knowing the man ..."

She smiled sweetly at Tara.

"Wait! I've got to get out of here first—" Tara began.

Too late—she made a grab for Ashley's arm, but Ashley was already on her way out, smiling graciously.

Cassandra and even the world-weary Mary followed behind her.

Rafe was charming. Tara still had not budged from the doorway, but she watched him. He met Cassandra and Mary, shaking their hands, making polite inquiries. George must have decided that he was a man of wealth and influence and, therefore, should be entertained and impressed. He himself was charming, solicitously telling his models what a long day they had endured, asking if they wouldn't like a drink—a question usually reserved for clientele at showings—whether they shouldn't all sit, and where Tara was? Obviously George knew that Rafe had come specifically for Tara, because he went on about how much Galliard Fashions had once done for Tara—and what Tara Hill had come to mean for Galliard Fashions.

"Ashley, where is she?"

"In the doorway," Ashley replied blandly, winking mischievously at Tara from her relaxed perch on one of the well-padded Greco-Roman settees—also customarily reserved for their affluent clientele.

The tiger eyes were instantly upon her. Warm and glowing, golden, and burning with a certain devilry. Damn him! He'd known she would never have opened her door to him again, and so he was here.

"Hi." He lifted his glass to her.

She really had no option. She left the security of the doorway and wandered out. It seemed that a silence fell. He watched her; she watched him. And her little audience of friends watched them both.

"Tara?" Only George seemed oblivious to the sparks. "Ah, *ma chérie*! What will you have? Hmm. We have an excellent Bordeaux."

"Fine. Thank you."

George poured her a glass of wine. She avoided Rafe, nearly sitting on Ashley's foot in the process. Ashley emitted a little yowl of protest, but Tara ignored her.

If Ashley didn't move her damned foot, she *would* sit on it! Ashley had gotten her into this predicament to begin with.

Or maybe she hadn't. Maybe he would have found her and followed her no matter what.

"So tell me again, Mr. Tyler, about this lady friend of yours who is so interested in a showing. We won't be taking any more appointments after Friday—for two weeks, that is—but I'd certainly squeeze her in before, if you wish. Or after, of course."

"Oh? Why are you closing the shop?" Rafe sounded totally engrossed in George's words, but he didn't take his eyes off Tara. There was something totally unsettling about the way he swirled the ice in his glass while he surveyed her with his half smile. She felt herself flushing uncomfortably, wondering what he was thinking.

Whether he was mulling over their last moments together, laughing because the sophisticated and aloof image had proved to be nothing more than a pawn to be taken in the easiest of moves.

"We're having a showing in Caracas," Ashley answered for George, but George went on with enthusiasm.

"Yes, South American buyers. It should be very exciting. Oh, I know, there's a great deal of poverty down there, but I'll tell you, there's no woman better dressed, more feminine, more enchanting than a true Colombian lady. And the aristocracy of Venezuela! Some of the Mexican señoras—the Brazilians! And Argentina! None know so keenly the allure of a truly wonderful fashion!"

"Is that so?" Rafe said.

Cassandra laughed. "Actually, we're all looking forward to it. We'll be aboard a wonderful cruise ship for seven glorious days, all in all. And only three sessions aboard the ship! George's—" she hesitated, smiling sweetly at George "—*grande* showing is in Caracas, and we're free as birds the rest of the time."

"Are you really? Fascinating," Rafe murmured.

George cleared his throat. "Well, Mr. Tyler, shall I make an appointment for this lady?"

What lady? Tara wondered. And she hated herself because she was sick with the thought that he might be married. But if she intended to stay away from him, what difference did it make?

"Certainly. This Friday, if at all possible."

"Certainly, certainly. The lady's name?"

Rafe arched his brows. "Mrs. Tyler, of course. Mrs. Myrna Tyler."

"Your wife, sir?"

"My stepmother, Monsieur Galliard."

"Oh, of course, of course, of course!" George said. "You do seem enraptured with Miss Hill. Should Tara model—?"

"No." He turned full face to George. "I would love to have Ashley model for her, if it's possible. Of course, I realize she is busy preparing for her trip—"

"I won't mind at all," Ashley murmured.

Tara kicked her.

"Well, then. Friday—say at three? Would that suit Mrs. Tyler, do you think?"

"Perfectly," Rafe murmured.

George chuckled softly, clearing his throat. "Strange, Mr. Tyler—wasn't it Miss Hill you asked for when you came in?"

"Oh, it was," Rafe said smoothly, and at his look, Tara felt blood rush to her face. He turned back to George. "Ashley and I are . . . old friends. I came to ask Miss Hill to dinner."

Tara jumped to her feet. "Miss Hill can't possibly go to dinner."

"Tara—how rude!" George protested uneasily. At that moment, she hated him. She was a model—not his damned upstairs maid! She made fabulous money, but she worked for it!

She turned on George. "George! You're the one who's insisting that I need sleep these days." He looked so baffled and confused that she ended it with a smile as she swept over to the bar to deposit her glass.

He sounded curiously like Ashley had the day before as he lowered his mouth to her ear to whisper, "Tara! The man is inviting you to dinner—he's not asking to have you for dessert!"

"Oh, yes, he is!" Tara muttered.

She turned quickly to find him watching her again. To see the amused golden light in his eyes.

"Really, Mr. Tyler. I can't. I have an early fitting—"

"No, no you don't, Tara!" Cassandra interrupted breathlessly. She looked at Tara, her eyes wide and innocent, and Tara decided that Rafe Tyler had hypnotized them all. "Tomorrow is Madame's late day, remember? We're not due in until noon. That's right, isn't it, George?"

"What? Ah, yes."

"How wonderful," Rafe said smoothly. Then somehow George had moved, and Rafe was standing beside her, folding his long fingers over hers, smiling. Pleased with himself. Like the tiger that had just consumed the canary.

"I don't—" she began, but as she watched him, the words stuck in her throat. At his touch she felt an overwhelming curiosity, a desire to be with him. She wasn't a teenager; she would never be innocent again.

And she would never let things get out of hand again!

She lifted her chin slightly and smiled. "Dinner. Since you insist, Mr. Tyler."

"Good night, Monsieur Galliard," he told George, smiling with just a trace of irony at the title, which slipped so smoothly off his tongue. Then he turned, and in a friendly, charming fashion said goodbye to the others, and told them that it had been lovely to meet them. He was certain, he said, that no man had ever been so surrounded by beauty.

"Quite poetic," she muttered as soon as they were on the street.

He arched a dark brow to her. His reply came with a subtle grin. "Jealous?"

"No."

"My God, you do know how to dash a man's hopes."

"Ashley might love to go to dinner."

"We did go to dinner."

She sighed softly. "I'm sure that Ashley would love to go to dinner with you—alone."

"Ah. Because you and I have already had dinner together—alone?"

There was something about the way he said it that made her turn about and smack him on the arm. Not hard. Just hard enough.

He laughed. "I thought you were having a rather good time."

"I was having a wretched time."

Laughing, he caught her hands and whirled her before him.

She found herself standing there, staring into his eyes. Her hands were still held in his. People were walking by them; horns blared, automobiles snorted exhaust fumes, and everything seemed to fade slowly away.

"Why were you following me?" she asked him.

"How can you ask that?"

"Why?"

"I think I've been as blatant as I can."

"Oh. Have you?"

"You know what you look like. You're not a fool. You can't tell me you've never had a man see you and feel compelled to follow you before."

"No, Rafe. I haven't. Of course..."

"Of course what?"

She shook her head and lowered her eyes quickly, moving to his side and hurriedly walking once again. She had almost told him about Tine. That no one had ever dared smile at her or come close to her because Tine had been there—her determined guardian.

"Hey!" he said, striding quickly to keep up with her. "We need to turn at the next corner."

"I'm not so sure—"

"Oh, yes you are." He caught her elbow and spun her back around. "French tonight, Miss Hill. Right this way."

"I just said—"

"What? What is it?"

"All right! I feel like your chosen prey! As if you know exactly who I am. As if the past..." She didn't know why, but she hesitated, inhaling sharply.

"You're behaving ridiculously. All right—I know who you are. Tara, you've been in dozens of national advertisements. I was fascinated; I am fascinated. Tara, for God's sake, what is the matter with you? Haven't you ever dated? Gone to movies? To plays? For long walks in the park? Met someone for dinner after a long day?''

''I...'' She started to make a retort, and then it occurred to her. ''No.''

She had never dated. Not really. Not gone out, done all the little things to get to know someone. She had been at home, and then there had been Tine. And she had wound up with him—just as he had intended. But they had never dated. Never gone to movies. Never laughed in the park.

Rafe squeezed her hand. ''It's fun. Give it a try.''

She lowered her head again, horribly confused. She couldn't let herself be taken in by someone, not again. She just couldn't. Any remnants of youth and innocence had died on that last awful night in Caracas.

''La Maison,'' Rafe murmured softly, and she realized that they were at the restaurant. He was opening the door, ushering her in, his hand supportive and light against the small of her back. Inside the foyer, he gave his name to the maître d'. Seconds later they were escorted along a deep-maroon velvet pathway to an intimate table of dark, heavy oak. The lighting was dim; the tables were situated so that each was private, a trellis of dark wood separating each one from the next.

They sat down; Rafe ordered wine. His interest was in the menu. He mentioned various dishes that he had tried. Tara just sat there, watching him and wondering what she was looking for. Might there be a break in his facade?

Tara realized that she didn't want anything to be wrong. There was more to her feelings than just the tremendous physical pull the man had on her senses. She liked him. She liked the way he smiled, the easy way in which he had swayed George, the charm that had brought her friends around him like moths drawn to the light.

He looked up from the menu, caught her tense scrutiny—and smiled. "Am I passing muster?"

Tara flushed, but she refused to be swayed. "If you know who I am, you obviously know something of my past."

"Oh, yes. The mysterious past."

"There was no mystery about it," Tara said bitterly. "The papers had a field day."

"And hence, Tara Hill disappeared."

She shrugged. "I wasn't so much afraid of the papers as..." She hesitated, then shrugged. "I needed to get away from everything for a while. I'd made some rather serious mistakes in judgment."

He set down the menu and leaned back against the booth, smiling as he watched her. He picked up his glass, clinked it against hers where it sat upon the table, and sipped his wine. Tara didn't pick up hers.

"What are you—twenty-five?" he asked her.

"Twenty-six."

"Excuse me." He laughed. "Still, rather young to give up on the world, don't you think?"

"I didn't give up on the world. I simply had a lot of experience shoved into very few years."

"Oh." Still smiling slightly, he looked back at the menu.

"Are you laughing at me?" she inquired sharply. "I don't intend to be patronized."

He didn't answer, because their very French waiter had appeared. Rafe asked her if he should order for her, and she shrugged, not caring what she ate.

Rafe ordered in French. Not the high school or college French so many people liked to practice in French restaurants—the kind that caused waiters to grin scornfully as soon as their backs were turned. It was obvious that he spoke the language fluently.

When the waiter was gone, Rafe stretched a hand across the table. "I'm not patronizing you, and I'm not laughing at you. I believe you had a rough time of it. But you're still very young, and to judge the entire world by one previous experience is a mistake. Is that why you're afraid of me—your relationship with Tine Elliott?"

Tara stiffened. Of course he knew about her; she imagined that he sat down with *The New York Times* and coffee every morning. He'd study the headlines and move on to the stock exchange and the sports pages—she wasn't sure in which order.

So, of course, he knew all about Tine Elliott. About the fact that she had been charged with murder, suspected of smuggling—and had her life recorded in boldface black on white.

It just hurt her somehow. It made her feel as if she had to defend herself.

As if she had to convince him that she wasn't the woman they had portrayed in those pages.

"I didn't do it," she blurted out.

He leaned back, grinning an amused devil's grin once again. "You didn't do what?"

"Any of it." She picked up her wineglass and sipped at it nervously.

He leaned closer to her, catching her eyes intently. "Tell me about it," he told her.

She inhaled, not meeting his eyes. "It was a mess. I wanted to get away from Tine. I'd met a...friend. I was supposed to meet him, and I did. Then suddenly Tine was there with the woman who died. He wanted some mask—shooting started. And that was it. Tine and Jimmy disappeared; the woman was dead—and I spent the night in the police station."

She didn't mean to, but she shivered with the memory of fear. Fear of Tine. Of his threat. He had said that he would find her somehow, someday, somewhere.

And she was going back to Caracas. Back to the very place where Tine had disappeared.

She gazed up at Rafe quickly, then frowned at the tense, penetrating quality of his stare. It was as if she had said something that had touched him personally. She sipped her wine again, her throat dry.

But he leaned back, easy once again, darkly handsome and charming. "You're still frightened," he commented.

She shrugged, determined to talk no further. "It was a long time ago. Never mind—I think George was the only one who ever believed I didn't know a damn thing about any mask. The police didn't even want to believe that Jimmy existed. Do you believe me?" she inquired coolly.

He lifted his hands. "You said you were innocent. You're innocent, then. Go on, tell me more."

She shook her head vehemently, alarmed at the way she was feeling. Warmth flooded her veins, something secure that seemed to ease her shudders. Her thoughts of Tine had filled her with a reverberating fear; Rafe, so close, so sure, made her feel as if she had a buffer against that fear.

She didn't like it. It was the physical thing. It was the fascination, the longing to touch, the fire that scorched her when he looked at her, when he touched her. Like something that would grow until the heat was too much—and had to be appeased. She couldn't trust him; she didn't dare. So she had to keep her distance.

And she was going to have to go to Caracas alone. No buffer zones. She didn't think that she was looking for an answer to the past, but maybe she was.

She determined to change the subject. Picking up her wineglass, she challenged Rafe. "Where did you learn to speak French so fluently?"

"Ah, Miss Hill! You weren't listening to Ashley and me the other day. I was in the navy for a while after college, then I worked aboard a French freighter."

She shook her head. "I thought you went into your family business."

"I only came back to it recently."

"And that is . . . ?"

"Various things. Shipping, jewels, trade." He shrugged, as though it wasn't important.

Their salads arrived, but even as she thanked the waiter and bent her head over hers, she thought that he was being purposely evasive. Why?

Or was she imagining things?

"What other languages do you speak?" she asked.

He seemed to hesitate, then shrugged again. "Spanish. A little Italian. Some German."

"Quite accomplished."

He laughed. "No, just well traveled. I always liked to see distant places."

"The life of an adventurer."

"No, the life of a laborer. I worked my way around the world. It was good experience."

"But you're back on terra firma now."

"Basically. A lot of the wanderlust is out of my system. I still travel, though."

"Business?"

"And pleasure."

"You grew up with a silver spoon in your mouth and went off to labor anyway. Very commendable."

"And you grew up in coal dust and went on to enchant the world."

He always managed to turn the conversation back to her!

But the wine was good, and the veal *cordon-bleu* delicious. The service was impeccable, the atmosphere intimate and private. She slipped off her heels somewhere along the line and relaxed. She studied him again and again, and could find no flaw. Not in his manner, not in his looks. And the more the night waned, the more she wanted everything about him to be just as it seemed. She would find herself staring at his hands and remembering their touch. Watching his mouth and remember how it had commanded hers, fierce and gentle all in one, practiced— unique in her experience.

"Pennsylvania, right?"

"You do read the papers," she responded dryly.

"Tell me about it," he said.

And to her amazement, she did. She tried to make him see it. The weary struggle on the miners' faces, the wives who strove so hard to make better lives for their children. The children who did grow up to a better life—and came back to demand that safety measures be taken as far as they could go, that doctors be sent in early so that fewer men died of the black rot that formed in their lungs.

"It seems amazing for this day and age," Rafe commented.

"Well, it exists," Tara murmured. "My parents..."

"What?"

She shook her head. "They're—they're both dead. But they were wonderful people. The best. My mother..."

"What, Tara? Go on."

"I just—" Now it was her turn to shrug. "Tine Elliott always liked to pretend they didn't exist. They were on and off welfare all their lives. Perpetually broke. But whatever they had, they shared. My mother took in orphans and the elderly—anyone who was down knew they could come to our house. She never had a decent dress, a nice haircut—and I think my father was able to take her out to dinner twice in her life. She was still the greatest lady I ever knew.''

His hand closed over hers. ''I'm sure she was, Tara. Greatness is always in the heart.''

She was suddenly embarrassed by the ferocity of her defense. Idly she moved her food around on her plate and sought desperately for a means to change the conversation. ''You have a stepmother, you said. What about your family?''

''Myrna? She's a sweetheart. My mother died when I was about five. All I remember is a gentle smile and a beautiful scent. Myrna married my dad ten years later. We're very good friends.''

''And your father?''

He paused and sipped his wine. ''Gone now, too.''

''I'm sorry. Recently?''

''Fairly.''

''That's why you're back—taking over the business?''

''Something like that.''

''Do you have any brothers or sisters?''

He seemed to hesitate a long time.

''Just one. A stepbrother. Younger. Have you looked at the dessert menu? How about a coffee liqueur?''

They had marvelous napoleons and brandied coffees. Somehow the conversation turned back to her early years in the small mining town in Pennsylvania, and she discovered herself answering questions she normally avoided.

''You've sent a lot of money back into that town,'' he said without her having told him. ''Is that why you've decided to come back to work now?''

She hesitated a second. The warmth of the brandy filled her veins, and she really couldn't see any harm in telling him things. After all, he knew almost everything about her anyway.

"Yes."

"But you didn't run home two years ago."

"No, I, uh, bought a little house in northern Michigan."

"Why?"

She sipped her coffee again. "I don't know. Yes, I do. I moved to a very small farming town. No one knew me. It was quiet, and nice. I learned how to grow marvelous vegetables."

He smiled. "I guess I'd better get you home."

He paid the bill and led her from the restaurant. Once again, his hand was on the small of her back. She leaned against him, inhaling deeply.

And though warnings screamed within her mind, she thought that she was all right. It was fun to dine with him, fun to lean on his arm.

Fun to imagine that they might get involved. That she would feel his kiss again, his hands upon her—

Slow down!

And then, of course, she was nervous. She wondered if he would take her to her door and insist that she owed him a nightcap. If he would stare at her with those tiger eyes on fire. Then she would be in his arms, and before she was aware of what was happening, their clothing would be gone and...

He stepped into the street and hailed a cab.

On the way to her apartment he talked to the cabby about the traffic.

Once there, he walked her through the lobby and to the elevator. And when they left the elevator behind, he walked her to her door.

Fire brushed her fingers when he took her keys from her.

He didn't step inside. He took her cheeks between his palms and stared into her eyes, searing golden magic in his.

His lips brushed hers, barely touching them.

"You are beautiful," he murmured. "Stunning. I don't believe that even Webster would have the perfect word for you."

She felt that she couldn't breathe. She longed for him to release her, before she could sigh and throw herself against him.

But she was no one's fool, she insisted. "Why were you really following me?" she demanded.

"I told you."

"I think you're lying."

He started to laugh, and for just a second his arms swept fiercely around her, crushing her against him. Letting her feel all the vibrant and electric heat of his body, all the muscled tension.

All the desire.

"If you don't believe that I want you, Miss Hill," he whispered softly, "you are not in the least observant!"

Now, he would come in now....

"You are beautiful," he said simply, and added in a curious tone, "I think I'm falling in love with you. Do I have half a chance?"

"I—"

"Don't answer. Wait. See you tomorrow night."

He released her, stepping back. "Get in. Close and lock your door."

He wasn't going to budge until she did, but she wasn't certain that she could move.

Eventually she did. She smiled and stepped into her apartment, and obediently closed and locked the door, and only then did she hear his light footfall down the hallway.

See you tomorrow night.

She hadn't agreed. He hadn't said when or where.

But she knew it would happen.

6

Rafe stood by his bedroom window, staring out at the fountain, not seeing it, yet seeing it completely. In a different way. In his mind's eye, she stood there. The perfect Galliard girl, soft and flowing, shimmering blond, subtly smiling, the silver light of the moon dazzling in her eyes.

He saw her everywhere he looked. At his dining-room table, in the foyer, before the fire. Seated at the piano, walking through the garden. In his kitchen, in his bedroom.

He had told her that she was beautiful. Any fool could see that; the harshest cynic would not deny it. He had said it; he had meant it.

He had told her that he was falling in love with her.

And that, too, had been the truth.

Fool! he raged against himself, and he turned from the window and padded naked back to his bed, throwing himself on it, twisting to stare up at the ceiling.

She had to be real. The real thing. He could not sweep her from his mind.

Well . . . she was supposed to be on his mind.

Ah, yes! He was supposed to be the great detective. Dispassionate, ruthless in this quest. God knows, such things happened. It had happened in Caracas. The day she had met Jimmy, Jimmy had disappeared. What had she done to him? What had she embroiled him in that he hadn't been prepared to handle?

Rafe remembered Jimmy's last communication—a postcard from Caracas. A postcard of the glass factory. Brief, in Jimmy's scrawl, telling him that "things" were under control, but he had just met the most beautiful woman in the world and would stay to see her clear.

See her clear. Of what?

Had she been smuggling? Part of some larger scheme? That was Jimmy's business. Locating lost and stolen treasures. Had Jimmy latched on to her because he knew something about her? Or had he been watching Tine Elliott—while Tine Elliott watched him?

Rafe sighed and gave up on sleep. He rose and slipped into a robe and walked out through his balcony window. He could see the fountain again from here, catching and reflecting the moonlight. He could see her there.

It was better than imagining her in his bed—beside him.

Fool! She was yours for the asking. Things could have been cemented in one night. An intimate relationship to bring you closer and closer, to win her confidence...

It hadn't mattered. He'd forgotten his stepbrother; he'd forgotten half of what he'd set out to do that night at her apartment. She had smiled so wistfully during dinner, had kept her eyes on him so warily. And she'd sat before him in that lovely flowing gown, devoid of makeup, silver eyes huge and innocent, angel trails of hair spun upon her shoulders. And when she had been in his arms, he had felt the most urgent need to protect her.

And the most urgent need.

He groaned out loud again and murmured incredulously, "It's as if I'd die if I thought I couldn't have her in the end...."

He'd been in the most exquisite pain when he'd left her, he thought dryly, remembering her arms around his neck, her laughter, like a melody that crept under the skin, like a siren's song that played throughout his entire body.

Jimmy! he reminded himself.

Had that same innocence captivated and swayed his brother? Young and idealistic, Jimmy might have touched her—and fallen for anything.

Just like I'm doing . . .

He stiffened, thoroughly aggravated with himself. The police had arrested her. The media had harpooned her. For God's sake, she had been Tine Elliott's protégée for seven years; she had lived with him for nearly four of those years. How could she be innocent?

Rafe leaned against the coolness of the wall. Jimmy had disappeared; Tine Elliott had disappeared. Had they died on the mountaintop? He couldn't believe that Jimmy could be dead.

But he had to be. Otherwise he would have contacted them by now. And if he was dead, that death rested upon her elegant blond head. And here he was, falling in love with her, too. . . .

He pushed himself away from the wall and gripped the wrought iron railing, staring out into the night, his face ravaged. She could be innocent. When she spoke to him, he believed every word she said. He wanted to promise that he was no Tine Elliott. . . .

After two years, she was going back. Maybe it had all been planned. Maybe the rest had all been a charade. Tine Elliott might well have been on to Jimmy. He had used Tara to beguile and entice him. He had found Jimmy and found the mask. He had disappeared—Tara had faced the police and the press—and then he'd gone into hiding.

And now, two years later, maybe she was going back to him.

But maybe she was innocent.

He gritted his teeth harshly. He knew that he wanted her to be innocent.

It didn't matter, he reminded himself. Nothing could change his actions at the moment. He had to stay with her; he had to earn her confidence.

Damn it! He slammed his fist against the railing in sudden fury. He was thirty-seven years old, he'd been around the world and back a dozen times—and he was no high school kid, falling in love.

He could have been with her.

Should have been with her. Finding her, wooing her, seducing her—winning her complete trust. The golden opportunity had been there. And he had been so in awe of her smile, of her laugh, of her silver eyes, that he had felt like any anxious lover, determined not to mar everything beautiful between them. And ego had been there, too. Total scorn for anything less than her totally conscious and eager anticipation of the night.

He sighed again and left the balcony. He showered and dressed and went downstairs at five. The newspaper had come. Thank God; he could read and escape his own thoughts.

And wait . . . for the night to come. He would meet her at the salon again. Dinner and then a show.

Dinner and the show and then . . .

Slowly! Take it slowly, fool! You're supposed to be the hard one; you've been given a warning that Jimmy never had.

He set the paper down suddenly, feeling slightly ill.

What if she *was* innocent? The thought brought a harsh, bitter laugh from him, because if she was, she would never forgive him once she discovered why he had been following her.

To hang her, if he could. To use her, if he couldn't. No, she would never forgive him.

But he couldn't stop. God, he couldn't stop. He had to know if Jimmy was alive and needed help....

Or if he was dead, beyond all help.

"I think he sounds marvelous," Mary said bluntly. "I don't know what you're worried about. You practically attack the man, and he leaves—he takes you to dinner and doesn't expect a thing. Most unusual, in this day and age."

"I didn't 'practically attack'!" Tara protested, changing from a sequined ball dress to her linen sheath. "And he barged in when I didn't intend to let him."

"Yes," Cassandra interjected, "but trust me! Half the oafs out there think that dinner at a French restaurant is a ticket straight into the bedroom—and they actually get hostile when you say no!"

"And you still think that he's after something?" Mary queried.

"Of course he's after something! Her body!" Ashley said cheerfully. "What on earth is so unusual about that?"

"Well, nothing, really," Mary replied. "Except that according to what Tara said, he could have had that already."

"Now, wait a minute—" Tara protested again.

"Well, you said that you were feeling perfectly comfortable. And you'd have to be an idiot not to appreciate the man's . . . his, uh—"

"Body," Ashley said bluntly. "God knows, the man definitely has one!"

"No, no, no, it's not just size and muscles," Cassandra said dreamily, flouncing about on the plain corduroy-covered sofa in the lounge area of their dressing room. "It's—it's—"

"Sex appeal?" Mary queried. "Some men have it and some men don't. And—" she glanced at Tara curiously "—he's a have."

"And he's definitely infatuated with you," Cassandra said. "So just what is your problem?"

Tara shook her head. "I don't know."

"I do," Mary told her. "Tine Elliott was a striking man. You knew it the minute he walked into a room. Are you afraid that you're becoming involved with another Tine?"

Tara shrugged. "I don't know. Maybe. He knows everything about me—"

"Your sordid past," Ashley said cheerfully.

"Ashley!"

"Well?" she asked innocently. "That's just my point. What are you worried about? If he thought you were an easy mark because of all that stuff about you and Tine and the mystery man—"

"Jimmy," Tara said stubbornly.

"Whoever." Ashley waved a hand in the air. "You're missing the point. Obviously he's a very well-behaved gentleman."

"He's more than that," Mary suggested seriously.

"What do you mean?"

Mary smiled and tossed her rich mass of hair over her shoulder. "Children, children, while you gibber and speculate, I take things into hand. I checked up on the man."

There was a stunned silence in the room. Mary, enjoying her moment, walked regally toward the sofa. Ashley was quick to sit up and give her room. Cassandra and Tara glanced at each other and hurried over to her.

Tara planted her hands on her hips and stared down at Mary squarely. "Well?"

"His name is Rafael Tyler—"

"Mary!" Ashley snapped. "We all know that!"

"Aha! But do you know what that means?"

"No, what?" Tara demanded.

"Well…" Leisurely, Mary stretched out, setting her long legs on the coffee table, studying her blood-red nail polish.

"Mary, get to it!" Tara persisted.

Mary drew her legs up and smiled excitedly. "He can't be after your money, Tara. He's incredibly wealthy. He inherited one of the largest fleets of privately owned ships in the world. He also owns at least a dozen fine jewelry stores—somebody in his family learned early that the Caribbean ports could legally supply wonderful gems that could be sold in the States. Oh, and of course, the stores are all over the Caribbean, and South America, too. They're called Tyler and Tyler. Not terribly original, perhaps, but I doubt that he named them. His father was a sailor out of Glasgow who found the American Dream."

Tara lifted her eyebrows. "Sounds all right so far," she murmured. Mary still looked excited.

Tara grimaced. "Go on. You're going to choke on your information if you don't get it all out soon."

Mary laughed. "Okay. The man has never been married. He's considered one of the most eligible bachelors in the world. He sails, races, plays polo and keeps his finger on the pulse of his varied interests. He could court heiresses—or princesses!—and be considered quite suitable."

"So why would he be interested in Tara?" Ashley queried, confused.

"Thanks a lot!" Tara told her.

"Well, you're not a princess. Or an heiress."

"He doesn't need money!" Cassandra exclaimed. "Just love! I think it's marvelous. Just like a fairy tale. He sees her once. Their eyes lock across a crowded room—"

"It was an empty museum," Tara said matter-of-factly.

"Oh, quiet! You're destroying my fantasy!" Mary said, annoyed. She cleared her throat dramatically. "Their eyes meet—and it's love at first sight. Passionate, desperate love. He trails her, he finds her, he sweeps her away to a life of luxury—"

"She already lives in a penthouse overlooking the park," Ashley interjected, laughing. "And she isn't exactly cleaning out chimneys at the moment, either."

"It's still just like a fairy tale," Cassandra persisted.

Tara shook her head, looking at Mary. "That's all? You didn't discover anything... strange about him?"

"Strange? No. He's done a great deal of traveling. Seems his father believed that a young man should follow his calling. He could have had a cushy job from the beginning, but he joined the navy instead, then worked his way through foreign shipyards. Oh! He's been in on a few smuggling busts."

Tara stiffened instantly. "So that's it! He thinks I'm a smuggler."

Cassandra giggled. "You arrest smugglers—you don't take them to French restaurants for dinner."

"Mary, where did you get your information?"

"I've got a friend at the bank where Tyler keeps lots and lots of his money."

"You still don't trust him?" Ashley asked Tara. She fastened her zipper and walked idly to the door. "Why?"

"I don't know," Tara murmured.

"Give him a chance!" Cassandra exclaimed. "Do you know what happens to old models, Tara?"

She smiled. "No, Cassie. What happens to old models?"

"They shrivel up and die—all alone—unless they fall in love and get married."

"Thanks. I'll keep that in mind."

"Well, you'd better decide quickly what you're feeling!" Ashley whispered, hurrying back over to the sofa. "He's out there again—with old George eating right out of his hand!"

"He's what?"

"He's out in the showroom again."

They all jumped up and hurried to the door. Ashley was right. He was talking to George, who was gesticulating in flushed pleasure.

Rafe was in black again. A stunning black tux with velvet lapels, a starched white, pleated-front shirt, black cummerbund and a deep maroon ascot.

Tara moved back into the room and leaned against the wall.

"I wonder where you're going, Cinderella!" Cassandra breathed.

Tara looked over at Mary, who always seemed to be so steady and poised.

"Good God! Don't be an idiot! Grab him!" said Mary, which Tara found no help at all.

"George is coming back here!" Ashley said. She was right again. George, wearing a wonderfully pleased expression, was hurrying toward them.

He came in and shut the door, staring at Tara. "The theater! Tyler has plans for the theater. It's quite possible the photographers will be there. You must wear a Galliard design. The black, Tara, with the sequined flounces. That will be perfect! Sexy and austere all at once!"

Tara wasn't sure whether to be indignant or amused. "What am I going to see, George?"

"See? What? Oh! The Albee play. What did he say the name of it was? Oh, what difference does it make? A Galliard girl on the arm of *the* Rafe Tyler. What matters is what you *wear*!"

She yawned elaborately. "I think I'll have to give him an apology, George. I'm so tired these days. And you were commenting on how awful I looked—"

"Don't be absurd, *ma chérie*!" There was mild irritation in his voice—desperation, too. "Really, Tara, how can you be so ungrateful? You needn't worry about sleep. Your fittings are well along. You can sleep late tomorrow."

"A day off?" Tara queried sweetly.

"What?" George blustered.

"I'm down to where I believe Madame is sticking me with pins for the fun of it," Tara told him.

"Oh, for heaven's sake, then. Fine, fine. You've got the day off. Just get the black on and wear it with élan!"

"I'll do my very best, George," Tara promised.

He nodded, turned around in a daze and left them. They were all silent for a minute; then they burst into laughter.

"What more could you want from a man?" Mary asked, and they all laughed again.

Ashley pinched Tara's cheek. "Well, you get into that black dress, *ma chérie*. And take your time. I'm going to run out and cheerfully greet tiger-man and see if old George won't pull out that marvelous ancient Scotch of his again!"

"Sounds good to me!" Mary agreed.

Cassandra chuckled. "Now, now. We make a ridiculous amount of money. We can afford our own Scotch."

"But it's so much more fun to drink George's!" Ashley retorted, rolling her beautiful eyes. "Especially with Tara's tiger-man. If she blows this thing, I'll be around to console the poor fellow." She grinned at Tara. "Get out there and be beautiful, kid!"

Tara grinned as the others left her. She went to the rack and found George's grand creation. It *was* a stunning dress. And it suited her coloring well.

She paused, hoping there would be no photographers around. She didn't want the mud raked up by the press again; George should have thought of that.

She shook her head. His creations were all George ever thought about. He was internationally known—a sleeveless cotton blouse by George Galliard cost well over a hundred dollars. But it was a two-way street. Galliard clothed the rich and the famous—and the rich and famous had made Galliard because they wore his clothing.

And, she thought, smiling smugly, she had earned a day off. Not a bad agreement. Maybe she had something to thank Rafe for after all.

Minutes later she entered a scene much like the one she had encountered the day before. Rafe, totally resplendent, her three color-coordinated and bewitching friends arrayed around the bar—George amid them, the supreme ruler.

They were chattering when she came out. All of them except Rafe.

He stared at her in a fashion that was bewitching in itself.

Stared at her as if she was a goddess suddenly descended to the earth. Silent, still, a golden message of enchantment in his eyes. He didn't move; he didn't come toward her.

For a moment she couldn't move either. She could only meet his eyes, feel their golden heat. Feel it move into her, enthrall and hypnotize her. Become liquid and mercurial as it swept through her, making her feel dizzy, as if the room were spinning, as if the world had faded away...as if there were only the two of them. Meant to come together, the earth itself screaming that it should be so.

Ashley broke the spell. "George! My God, that's a stunning creation."

"Woman," Rafe corrected her.

And he stepped forward, coming to her. Reaching out a hand. She raised her own slowly; he enfolded it in long, strong fingers.

"My God," he breathed, his eyes locking with hers, then moving slowly over her bare shoulders and the cleavage displayed by the silken bodice and velvet trim. Over the length of her body, hugged and draped by fabric. To the slit along her thigh, the froth at the ankles.

It must have been at that precise moment, she would think later, when magic entered the night. It was the way that he looked at her, the way that *he* looked. So tall, so elegant and so darkly masculine.

Suddenly she wasn't aware of anything around her. She knew only the light in his eyes. The subtle but persuasive scent of his after-shave. The shivery feel of heat and energy that surged around him, engulfing her. She felt his hand on hers; she felt that this was a fantasy, that this was magic. And maybe she did feel a little bit like Cinderella at the ball—she'd danced that first dance with the prince of her dreams, and she was falling in love. There was something so right about him. Not in appearance, not in height or stature or any other tangible way. Just him. His touch. The message in his eyes.

Had he been dressed in rags, she would have felt it. The absolute need to put her hand in his, and with that, the trust she couldn't logically give him.

"Shall we?" he murmured, and she nodded, unsure of her voice.

George said something to her; the others all waved and called goodbye. Ashley came running out with Tara's silver fox fur, and she accepted it gratefully.

Then they were out on the street, where his limousine awaited them. He ushered her in.

"Are you cold?" He adjusted the fur more closely around her shoulders. She shook her head.

He sat back. Day was still with them, fading to twilight. She could see his features so clearly: all the hard and handsome planes; all that was rough and rugged; all that was keenly beautiful. All that created that most intricate animal—man.

And still the magic held her. Held her so firmly that she could not find words to speak.

He reached over and took her hand, brought it to his lips and kissed it with a bewitching reverence. His eyes had not left her.

He touched her cheek. "Do you really want to see a play?"

"I love plays."

"That's not what I asked. Do you really want to see a play right now?"

God help her. She shook her head. She knew what she was saying, what she was doing. She hadn't had a single drink; but she knew exactly what she was saying by not speaking.

He watched her for a moment. Something inside her cried that she should protest, that she should ignore all she felt and gaily say that she was just dying to go to the theater.

He wouldn't have protested. He would have gone ahead. And he would have been a charming companion for the whole evening. He would have taken her to dinner, and then he would have taken her home, and he would have left her at her door with a good-night kiss that would have left her aching for more.

But she didn't speak.

He tapped on the dividing window and murmured something to the chauffeur, then sat back.

They stopped in front of an apartment complex that was nearly as well known as Rockefeller Plaza. Dear Lord—she couldn't think of the name of the place. It wasn't far from hers.

The chauffeur didn't appear. Rafe himself helped her from the car.

The doorman greeted him deferentially. Tara felt her lips lift in a smile as he nodded to her.

The lobby was muted luxury. Marble and oak, ferns and pillars. The elevators were subtly etched in gold.

She still didn't speak as they entered and rose high above the world, high above any normal concerns.

The elevator door opened. Tara would have stood still, staring blankly at the door. But her hand was still in Rafe's, and he was walking, so she followed.

A few steps brought them to a set of double doors. Rafe opened them and released her, standing slightly behind her to turn on a light.

She blinked, seeing the place arise from the darkness.

They were up on the roof, on the corner, and both sides of the back wall were glass, looking out on a panoramic view of the city, of the park. The stars were reachable through those sparkling panes. Even the moon—she could stretch out a hand and touch it, and she reflected that perhaps she already had.

It was contemporary, completely so. Mexican tile flooring in the entry gave way to deep pile beige carpet, white leather sofas, and a redbrick and copper fireplace. To the far left of the windows was a door, so artfully planned by some architect that it blended with the open beauty of the room yet led out to the balcony, where the heavens would seem even closer.

A little breathlessly, Tara stepped into the room, down from the Mexican tile to the sunken carpeting beneath. The fur trailed from her shoulders.

Watching her, Rafe could barely breathe. As usual, she was part real, part fantasy, her hair a golden contrast against the black of her gown, the silver fur just dangling over her shoulder. Her other shoulder bare.

Long, lithe, slim, elegant. He swallowed. What was it that she had? Whatever it was, it went far beyond the obvious. Was it the silver mercury of her eyes, the timbre of her voice? Motionless, poised, she might have been Tara the model, the face and shape that had seduced and enticed from a million pages of print. And that alone could humble a man.

But it was in motion that she had enchanted him. In motion that she had gazed, spoken, whispered, touched. It was the essence of the woman that had been his downfall. Something inside her, something undiscernible.

He followed her, reaching for her coat. "Do you like it?"

"It's spectacular."

"I like the sky."

"Yes."

Rafe set her fur over a chair. He moved to the left, to the kitchen, which was done in white and chrome. His fingers were shaking when he opened the refrigerator.

"Wine?"

It seemed that she hesitated, that she trembled.

"Yes, please. May I—may I go out?"

"Of course. I'll be right with you."

Tara stepped across the room to the camouflaged door; it opened to her touch. The chill hit her as she stepped out. She shivered and wrapped her arms around herself but did not think to return for her coat.

Night had come in full. There were plants on the balcony, fragrant from a recent rain. The sky seemed a blanket of velvet, and she had the feeling that she was wandering in that velvet.

He came up behind her, offering her a fluted stem glass from behind. She clutched it and sipped from it too quickly. Almost like a drowning man reaching for straws...

He touched her then. His body, the length of it behind her. His hand upon her shoulder pulling her close against him. His fingers stroking her neck. His breath falling upon her with warmth.

Tingling, rippling sensations played havoc throughout her. He simply stood there, and she felt liquid. She wanted him.

She closed her eyes. It had been two years. Two years since that horrible last time with Tine. Two years since she had felt that everything inside her had died, that she could never want anyone again, that she could never feel again...

She was afraid. Eager, anxious, nervous—and afraid.

"I've ordered dinner," he murmured, and she nodded.

He pointed over her shoulder to the stars. "Ursa Major. Perseus. Cassandra."

"You know them all?"

"Most. You learn the stars when you sail a lot. On a ship, in the middle of the ocean, it's as if they're all that exists. You feel very small."

"I can't believe you would ever feel small."

"Any man can feel small."

He paused, lightly rubbing his cheek against her hair, inhaling its clean fragrance. The night, the sea, the stars. They should have been a perfect opening, he thought. He could have quizzed her about sailing, asked her about Caracas.

No. He couldn't. Something had touched them. Something unique. He could no more end it than he could cut his own throat. He felt her tension; he felt the need to walk on eggshells, to hold the magic.

She sipped her wine and said nothing. For the longest time they stood there, staring at the stars, silent. And through all that time it grew. The knowledge, the awareness. His hard body against hers. Her soft one leaning against his.

At last she heard a little buzzer. He excused himself. Through the glass panes Tara saw two men arrive with silver serving dishes.

She turned back to study the night and sip her wine. Seconds later, Rafe was back. The men were gone. He led her back in and seated her, filling her wineglass again, dexterously removing lids from chafing dishes and filling her plate—seafood tonight. A thick bisque of shrimp and scallops and *langoustines*. Delicate puffs of rolls. Asparagus salad.

"You serve food superbly," she told him, trying to joke.

"I've worked in food service. I cook superbly, too."

"How commendable—if it's true."

He laughed. "Someday you can judge for yourself."

He sat down, and they lifted their wineglasses to each other.

It was then that she began to tremble. Really tremble, so that her glass tilted precariously.

She didn't know that her face had turned pale, that her hair was sun gold, her lips rose red against it.

Quickly, anxiously, he was on his feet. More quickly still, he was at her side, on one knee, rescuing her glass, taking her hands in his.

Fire, electricity, all the tension of the evening leaped between them. He looked into her eyes.

"You're afraid of me," he murmured.

"I'm just . . . afraid."

"I'll take you home." He started to rise.

"No!" She caught his hand; she still quivered. She lowered her head and idly inspected his fingers. And then she looked at him with such whimsical, wistful appeal that it seemed his heart had stopped.

"Will you be tender? Patient?"

It was that softly voiced question, the haunted emotion that colored it, the melody of her voice, the quiver of it more than anything, that ensnared his heart completely. Not her beauty, not her form, not even the wonder of her scent.

It was all that she laid at his feet in that moment.

He brought her hand to his lips and kissed her palm, then met her eyes again.

"Always," he vowed.

7

Stars were part of a dream, part of fantasy, part of illusion. A velvet-dark sky, rhinestoned with stars.

This wasn't illusion; it was reality.

Tara didn't know what else was in the apartment. Another bedroom, perhaps; a study. She only knew that there was a hallway that passed by the kitchen, that they came to a room where not only the window was of glass but also a pane of the ceiling above them.

She'd been only dimly aware of the hallway, vaguely, from some distant frame of consciousness. She was acutely aware of Rafe's eyes, for during the passage from living room to bedroom, she never lost contact with his golden gaze. It *was* something from a dream: a tall, dark, handsome stranger sweeping her into his arms, carrying her up a short flight of steps from one level to the next.

And then there were the stars.

She saw them instantly, of course, when he laid her on the bed and stretched out beside her.

Larger than life, vivid, eclipsing any other sensation she had ever known.

Something, some logical swell of reason, warned her that he was a stranger—a man she barely knew. But raw emotion cried out against logic and won. She had known this was coming; she had wanted it. From the first time she had seen him, she had felt fascination, excitement, even a touch of fear at the power he had. And she was drawn....

She felt his hand on her cheek, and she swallowed slightly, bringing her eyes from the stars to meet his.

I barely know him! she reminded herself in desperation.

But it did no good, for she felt at that moment that she knew all that she needed to, that she knew him very well. She knew that he was somehow aware of her fear, that he would handle that fear like fine crystal and ease it from her. She knew it all over again, meeting his gaze, feeling his absolute hunger....

And a fascination to match her own.

He leaned over her, slowly. Then touched her lips with his, gently, then searingly. His mouth over hers, his tongue a sensual promise of everything to come. The sudden change was strident, like the sweeping wind of a storm. She caught her breath; she knew no more fear, for the passion as he delved into her mouth with heat and fire was something that demanded to be met, and meet it she did.

The wanting that had begun in fantasy, that had been denied, now spilled out through her. She felt his kiss not with her mouth, but with her body. She responded instantly, fingers digging into the rich dark length of his hair. She was tense, but completely alive, a drumming sounding through her blood, through her limbs, like lava, running, playing....

Wanting.

He moved away from her. In the starlit darkness she watched him swiftly shed his clothing, fluidly, each movement innately graceful.

Like a smoothly muscled cat, so beautiful in form, graceful in any motion, vital, corded, unique.

She stared at him and didn't know that she did so; she recorded in memory all the little things she could catch with the stars as illumination. The breadth of his shoulders, his long torso and longer legs, sinewed, sleek. A thick forest of dark hair on his broad chest, which tapered downward to the point where his sexuality so brazenly, urgently appealed to her senses.

She closed her eyes, shivering, thinking that she should be frightened. That she should have inhibitions, natural reservations, since it had been so long, and the last time had been ...

Her mind blocked out the thought. Blocked out everything but the wonder of him. The tiger, the hunter, the magnificent beast, as captivated as she, a vow that he swore with his eyes, that leaped silently into her heart.

He didn't think he'd ever trembled before a woman, yet he quivered now. Then again, he, who was not whimsical at all, wondered if she was really a mortal woman. No one had eyes like hers, silver like the glow of the stars. Hair that touched his pillow like spun gold. A face like the finest porcelain, heart-shaped, classic, innocent ...

Trusting.

So exquisitely beautiful that it was haunting. As anxious as he was, he could have stood like a spellbound kid, fascinated because she lay on his bed.

He lowered his eyes from hers, stopped at the foot of the bed and unlaced her high-heeled sandals. That contact alone sent his heart thudding.

She made a slight sound. He kissed her again, savoring the kiss, savoring her scent. He knew the perfume, but on her it was unique.

He drew her up to him as he kissed her, finding the zipper of her gown and pulling it down, and with that rasping sound, he felt his excitement increase, rushing and roaring like a tide, sweeping from his loins to his limbs and back again. She was so light. Easy to maneuver, easy to divest of Galliard's magical gown. No, it wasn't the gown. It was the woman.

Beneath the gown was some other magical creation. A strapless teddy thing in sheer, midnight silk. A sound escaped him as he saw her breasts hugged, outlined, erotically draped by it, and he dipped his dark head, taking her nipple, material and all, into his mouth. He heard an answering moan escape her, vaguely, distantly, for the feel of her nipple tautening and swelling within his mouth was almost more than he could bear. Another sound escaped him, and he swept away the material, once again impatiently maneuvering her form, stripping off her clothes with quick resolve.

He burned to hold her, but he held back.

Never, in picture, in substance or in imagination, had there been so perfect a woman. Slender neck; firm, full breasts; slim waist; a provocative flare of hips; and shapely legs that knew no end. No artist's brush needed to touch her to soften flaws, for there were none. She was beautifully, passionately formed, golden and glowing. In wonderful, elegant color, cream and gold, silver and rose. And her eyes . . .

A rain of diamonds, shimmering silver. Beckoning, trusting, innocent, vulnerable. He could see the rise and fall of her breasts, the slightest sign of movement.

Was this what Jimmy had felt? Had his brother, once upon a time, fallen in love with those eyes, with the innocence, with the vulnerability, with the trust?

His hands knotted into fists at his sides. This was it; this was everything that he had planned. Coldly, meticulously. He'd needed to get close to her. This close. Now he needed to know her, to win her trust, to follow her, to find the truth.

His fingers loosened.

It was impossible to be cold. Impossible not to believe.

In her. In magic. In the waves that engulfed them, that radiated between them.

He'd promised tenderness. He'd promised patience. He hadn't said a word tonight about love, but that was hers, too, because he was falling, falling. He despised himself for a fool, but it was the simple truth.

He returned to her and engulfed her in his arms. Took her lips again in fire, plied his tongue within her mouth as he would his body within hers.

And touched her. Oh, yes, he touched her. Her shoulders, her breasts, the elegant line of her back, the thrust of her hips. He felt her kiss, her tongue inside his mouth, her lips, against his. Breaking from his, nibbling his.

He stared at her again. Brought his palm against the line of her cheek.

Her lashes fell. "I shouldn't be here," she said softly, in a tone of awe, not of protest.

"It was inevitable," he murmured. He couldn't endure even those seconds away from her flesh. He kissed the upper swell of her breast, then the lower curve, and finally took the delightful pink crest of her nipple into his mouth.

Her fingers dug into his hair, holding him close. "Since the museum," she said, trembling.

"The museum." His words were throaty against her flesh. He moved against her softness. She could feel him, hard, hot, against her thigh.

"Since the museum," he agreed.

"You were stalking me."

"I was watching you."

"Stalking. Like the tiger."

He paused, and she was horrified that she had spoken, for she thought she might truly die if he left at that point.

He lay at her side once more and caught the wings of her hair in his hands, staring intently into her eyes.

"Stalking...as if I were prey," she whispered, and, again, wondered why she had spoken when her whole body burned for him, when all the terrors of the past had been forgotten, when she had put blind faith in instinct and intuition, knowing that she was hopelessly—if foolishly—falling in love.

A rueful smile curved his lips as he gazed at her, his body so hard against hers, his eyes so intense, muscles taut.

"No, Tara, I am your prey. The hunter is the hunted."

His lips touched her ear, his teeth teased the lobe, and he murmured as if in awe, "My God. I wonder how I've lived without you. Without this...feeling. This wonder."

She wound her arms tightly around him. Something vague reminded her that she hadn't trusted him.

She knew that she could trust his words now. That whatever mysteries there might be about him, this much was true. Here was reality. Here was magic. Between them.

And sensation.

"Ohh..." The gasp escaped her as his kisses, ragged, urgent now, roamed her breasts again, and then beyond.

He touched her, moved her. Gently, demandingly, softly—urgently. She arched to him; she could lie still no longer. She rose, flinging her arms around his neck, feverishly kissing his shoulders, his chest, nipping slightly, testing his reactions to her lips and tongue against his nipples, her hands exploring the length of his back. He groaned softly and let her play, until the groan began to come from somewhere deep in his chest and the heat seemed to spew and sizzle between them. She found herself once again on her back, her fingers entwined with his, her eyes locked with his.

His face taut, beautiful, above her. His body wedged between her thighs. He lowered himself, not entering her, teasing, testing, watching her expression, savoring the little sounds that escaped her, the wonder on her face, making it glow, making it ever more beautiful.

Then she cried out; her fingers eluded his, and she touched him, shivering slightly, a little unsure, brought back to a delirium of passion by his husky whispered words of pleasure, of encouragement.

"Yes, take me. Oh, yes...." He raised himself slightly, watching as they joined together. Holding his weight, holding himself, sinking into her fully, completely, then holding tight once more as her body absorbed him, and watching her face again.

"Yes. Take me. Hold me. Tara..."

She thought that she would burst, that she would scream, and yet her body absorbed him, adoring him. She marveled at the slow, painstaking way he held her and then plunged, withdrew, and stroked....

"Ohh..." She wrapped her arms around him, burying her face against his neck, almost ashamed of the terrible rush of pleasure that consumed her. He stroked her hair; he held her; he whispered.

And lost control.

Deliciously, for by then she was arching to him, reaching. She wanted to hold on forever; she was almost desperate for that intangible thing she craved.

It was the best thing in the world. The best feeling. Being a part of her. He wanted it to go on forever. He held and held, and then release swept through him in great, erratic waves, trembling, pulsing.

From him to her. Like the heat that had brought them together. He arched in his turn, strained, taut, muscles rippling, felt that great fall of unbearable sensation, so great that he nearly collapsed, yet did not. The shudder that came rippling from her, washing him with the flow of her ecstasy, was sweeter still.

Only then did he take her tightly in his arms and roll with her, still a part of her, and determined to be so as nature brought them both back slowly from her splendor.

They were sleek, damp, breathing heavily, and still one. Their hearts pounded. Their breathing eased first, and then the drumbeats of their hearts.

Neither spoke. He had to touch her hair, so golden in the starlight.

And still she didn't speak.

"It was inevitable," he told her very softly.

"I know."

"Are you sorry?"

She moved at last, rising above him. He saw the beauty in the classic lines of her face, the passion in her eyes.

"No, Rafe, never. Never sorry for tonight!"

He smiled and placed an elbow beneath his head, pulling her back to his chest.

"Never—for tonight. Does that mean that I'm supposed to get up and take you home now?"

"I can go by myself—"

"No way," he told her flatly, then spun with a fluid motion, bringing her beneath him, eyeing her with determined passion, and a bit of devilry, too.

"Don't tell me that you have to be anywhere. You have tomorrow off. And you're going nowhere, love. Magic may only come once in a lifetime—I'm not letting mine slip away. I'm going to wake up beside you and know that you're real, and then I'm going to make love with you by daylight."

For a moment he thought that she was going to protest. That she was going to panic and insist on going home.

But she smiled. Slowly. A sensuous smile, a beautiful smile that played upon the senses and sent his pulse reeling once again. Lazily, languidly, gracefully, she stretched out her arms, then wound them around him, arching her body slightly, wickedly taunting him with the thrust of her exquisite breasts.

"We're waiting for morning?" she inquired innocently.

"No. Oh, no!" he told her.

And as his arms tightened around her once again, he lowered his head, his mouth moving hungrily over one of those exquisite mounds that had tortured him with such pleasure.

She responded with a gasp and then a soft siren's moan, sending him spiraling into an endless sea of sensation....

There were no longer stars overhead when they awoke. The sky was a beautiful blue, just touched by soft white clouds.

Tara was staring at that sky, and Rafe watched her silently, not moving.

His first thought on waking was wonder—that she should be there. Blond and luxurious, awakening from sleep in his bed. Innocent again, for though their legs were entwined, the sheet was cast just below her shoulder, and despite the abandon of the night, she appeared as sweetly virginal as Venus rising from some magical seabed.

Innocent...

He closed his eyes fleetingly, wondering if his resolutions of the evening could stand up to daylight. There would always be that infinitesimal difference between night and day. Darkness always brought a gentle velvet cloak to hide scars—and suspicions.

He shook his head slightly, a smile ruefully curving his lips. No. Nothing was gone. He was still in love. If he was a fool he was a fool, and the hell with it.

But then there was Jimmy.

He inhaled. There was only so far a fool could go. He couldn't tell her anything, not yet.

He exhaled. The great, momentous changes inside him couldn't really mean anything. He still had to follow her. To find out if she was a victim, or a catalyst, perhaps.

His heart pounded. Now he had more reason than ever to follow her. To be with her. If she was innocent, if she was returning to the scene of past tragedy, more than ever, so much more than ever, he had to be with her. To guard her against—

Whatever might come.

And then, of course, when he gazed at her again, he saw how she watched the sky above her.

What were her thoughts? Regret, as she mulled over the implications of the night? Strangers and lovers. Was she wondering how to escape? Wishing desperately that she had smiled and said, Oh, dear, no! I wouldn't miss the play for anything!

He touched her cheek. Her eyes, those silver eyes that might have launched a thousand ships, met his instantly. And to his vast relief she offered him a smile, soft and somehow shy, and touched with the same wonder he had known himself.

But there was something more. As if she denied nothing and gave him all—except some thought, some resolution, something that she was holding back.

"You're not sorry?" he murmured.

"No, never sorry," she replied.

He kissed the tip of her nose.

"George is going to be furious," she murmured. "No pictures of his elegant gown in the society pages."

"We'll see that he gets his pictures eventually."

"Oh!" she said suddenly, fumbling to pull her arms from the sheets to gaze at her watch. "It's nearly twelve—"

"You've got the day off," he reminded her.

She laughed easily, relaxing on the pillows. But then she bolted up again, driving him half mad, because the sheet slipped and he was reminded in full, glorious daylight that she had the most beautiful breasts he had ever seen.

"You've got an appointment! At twelve. Remember? You're supposed to be taking your stepmother in for a showing."

"Are you trying to destroy a magnificent day?" he asked her, only half teasing. "Myrna is a grown woman. She's quite accustomed to going into the city."

"Shouldn't you call her?"

"I never intended to accompany her."

"Oh." She paused a minute, studying him, arching a brow slightly. "Curious, isn't it? You wanted Ashley to model for her."

He chuckled softly, rising above her. "What's so curious? I wanted you with me."

"You planned the whole thing?"

"Not exactly. I really had planned on the theater."

"And after?"

"It's always been your choice," he told her softly.

Tara wondered if she believed him or not. His dark lashes had fallen over his eyes with his words, and she shivered slightly. Was she mad...falling in love so quickly, so completely, when it seemed that there were still mysteries here? Things unsaid that she couldn't begin to pin-point? A sense that . . .

He caught her hands and brought her back to the bed. He kissed her vibrantly, passionately, impatiently kicking the covers aside and laying the urgent hardness of his body against hers, brazen, bold, so sensually demanding that she responded in kind. He called to her, aggressive and sure; she sighed quite naturally. Her breath caught as he touched her. Excitement surged through her, and feelings of love and need overwhelmed her again.

He was impossible to deny. He was a force of high, windswept excitement. She loved the excitement, the ab-solute intensity. The male power that called on everything female within her. The feeling of his tongue within her mouth, the warm, living power of his body pulsing against hers, joining them.

She did think—vaguely—before she was so swept up in his rhythm that nothing mattered except the culmination of the passion that raged between them.

Today was his. Today was fantasy. And then she would withdraw, from him and—with much more effort—from herself. From the all-encompassing need he was creating.

She almost sobbed, for so many things combined. The feel of him. The spiraling desire. The soaring emotion that told her there was more, that she loved his touch, his smile, his voice, the way he held her hand, walked with her, talked to her.

Looked at her. With a tiger's eyes. Golden. Possessive, wonderful, alluring, exciting.

Mercury filled her body with heat. After all this time, to know a touch that thrilled . . .

She wanted to lie beside him forever. To share his life. To waken in the morning with his head on a pillow beside her.

She wanted to marry him.

To hear his slightly wicked laugh and have him take her like this, anytime, and know that it was real....

He rose above her, watching her body. Moving. Murmuring.

"Oh, yes...Tara, you're beautiful. Take me in, take me in. Let me see this...us..."

A cry escaped her. Tremors began to wrench her body...his. He shuddered in his final climax, collapsing against her, slick, sated; holding her still; murmuring something that caused a milder tremor to shake her.

She didn't dare look at him. She closed her eyes and pressed her face against the dampness of his chest.

It had to wait, it had to wait, it had to wait. She needed to go away, to avoid seeing him again. She'd been with him now. She knew that it was like nothing on earth, and everything that love was intended to be.

It couldn't be an affair. It couldn't be casual. It couldn't be lost. It had to be real and forever, or it could be nothing.

Then what was it that still worried her?

After all this, why did she feel the niggling suspicions, the remainder of mistrust?

How could she have done this? She, who had been hurt so badly, taken in so blindly. She, who knew that love could grow bitter.

He pulled her atop him, and she almost smiled, forgetting her fears, because the look on his face was simply so male. So triumphant, his golden eyes gleaming like topaz.

"My God, I love you!" he declared intensely, voice low but seeming to shake slightly.

And her smile deepened wistfully. "Do you really?"

"I do."

She lay against him, her heart beating, her thoughts a prayer.

Let it be true.

Please, God, let it be true.

He *was* a wonderful cook, she discovered. He made fabulous omelettes with tiny shrimp and a delicious creole sauce. They ate in bed, loosely clad in robes, beneath the extraordinary blue of the sky.

For a moment she felt as if her heart had stopped, because she realized suddenly that he was, by nature, a passionate and volatile man, and his bed had probably played host to any number of women.

Jealousy streaked through her, painful and cruel. She lowered her eyes to her plate, then realized that he was studying her intently, smiling slightly as he noticed her change of emotion.

He touched her chin, raising it. "What?"

She shrugged, then laughed—because it was so ridiculous, of course. She'd only known that he existed for a few days.

"I was wondering how many women you'd had with you in this bed."

He made no firm denials. He was silent, watching her for a minute. "We both have pasts."

It was her turn for silence.

Once again she took refuge in staring at her food. He wouldn't let her. He caught her chin again, forcing her to meet his eyes.

"Past. As in Tine Elliott. You're not still in love with the man, are you?"

The question was harsh. Too harsh, she thought.

"No," she said sharply, deciding that the one word was enough; he could take it or leave it.

He continued to stare into her eyes, as if seeking something. Tension seemed to leap around them, in the air, part of them. He released her chin, sighing.

"I think you should marry me," he said.

She looked up at him quickly, laughing.

"What's so funny?"

"We're—we're strangers!" she told him.

He smiled as seductively as any cat, grinning with pleasure.

"Strangers?" he said with such insinuation that she blushed.

"We don't know each other," she said loftily, straightening to what she hoped was dignity, her shoulders squared.

Dignity was lost. Her stretching had pulled the terry material of the robe taut against her form, and with no hesitation he tweaked the rise of her nipple, laughing. "I know you very well."

Tara clutched the robe, nearly dislodging her plate. "I'm being serious and rational."

"So am I."

She shook her head, not knowing whether to laugh, too, or to protest vehemently.

He took their plates and set them aside then scooped her into his arms.

"I really need to get home," she murmured a little nervously.

"No."

"But—"

"Not today."

"Not today!"

"All of today, all of tonight, you're mine. I'll get you home in the morning."

"But this is so sudden. So intense."

"You said that we're strangers. I'm trying to let you get to know me." He caught her hand and brought it to his chest. "Feel my heart, my love. That's all you really need to know, isn't it?" The teasing quality left his voice—she felt he was speaking in earnest.

Yet she wondered if he was querying her—or himself.

"Really. I should simply sweep you away and marry you, and keep you forever and forever."

"I have to leave on a business trip."

"That's all right. Your willing bridegroom will follow."

She smiled and wondered just what had been wrong about his words. She thought she almost had it, but then he was moving again, sweeping her into his arms as he rose from the bed.

"What—"

"A shower. We'll have eaten together, walked together, laughed together—and showered together. 'Getting to Know You.' I'd sing it for you, but I can't carry a tune worth a damn."

With her arms about his neck, her eyes imprisoned by the passion in his, she could do nothing but laugh. "Whistle, then," she commanded, and he obeyed, and she laughed all the while that he brought her into the elegantly modern and squeaky-clean bathroom. He set her down to start the water, then he turned, eyes growing dark as amber, and untied the belt of her robe and eased it from her shoulders.

The shower stall was of beige marble, with curving seats cut into each end. As he plucked her from her feet to set her beneath the stream of water Tara noted that his taste was wonderfully attuned to hers. She loved old things, but she also loved the contemporary flair of his apartment.

Then she wasn't thinking about the apartment at all, because his hands were full of soap and moving over her body. Over her breasts, along her hips, between her thighs.

Gasping for breath, laughing, she tried to elude him, tried to elude the evocative sensation. Finding soap, she returned the caress, catching his eyes as she slowly sudsed his chest, his abdomen, his tightly muscled buttocks, in swirling circles.

Steam whirled around her, and she was absolutely fascinated as she heard the sharp rasp of his breath and watched the sexual tension seize his features, sharpening them, darkening his eyes, straining his cheeks.

Then *she* was left to gasp, for he caught her beneath the arms and spun around, setting her on one of the marble seats, kneeling before her. Suddenly, passionately, aggressively. Laving her navel with his tongue, parting her thighs and moving lower.

She cried out at the excruciating sensation, at the intimacy. Never . . . never . . .

She grasped for something to hold. Her fingers raked against the water, then fell into his hair. She whispered incoherently. She begged him to stop, because it was . . . too good. The feelings, oh, the feelings . . . She would explode, burst; she would die.

He did not stop. Until she did burst . . . explode . . . die a little. Drained, drenched, nearly delirious. Clinging to him, amazed.

He smiled his triumphant tiger's smile, and swept her from the tub, dripping wet, back to the bed. She was still limp. He moved over her and entered her, and she wrapped her arms around him, flushed, holding him.

She was amazed that as he fulfilled himself, he could bring her spiraling along with him once again.

* * *

She felt that she still burned with his touch even as she began to doze off, held in his arms, as the afternoon sun rose above them.

She was in love. Infatuated, insane—in love.

And then she remembered suddenly what had bothered her about his teasing declaration that they should marry.

He had said that he would follow her on her trip.

An odd thing, she thought, for her tiger to say. There were things that she did not know about him.

He should merely have said that he would sweep her away. From all of it. From her work, from Galliard. That he would hold her and have her and keep her forever.

That was what he *should* have said.

She shivered, convincing herself more thoroughly that if what they shared was real, he would be here when she returned. That he would wait.

And then the burning sensation swept through her all over again, as she remembered the way she had felt when he had . . .

She closed her eyes tightly.

She had to get away from him so that she could think rationally!

But as if reading her mind, he touched her again, his palm light against her flesh, drawing circles.

She'd promised him today. And tonight.

And perhaps it was something that she owed herself.

Tomorrow—away from him—she would be strong and rational. She would simply decide not to see him again until she returned, and that was how it would be.

But for the moment . . .

She felt his kiss against her spine, and she knew that if she had been standing, she would have been weak-kneed, ready to fall.

Today. Tonight.

A soft, strangled sound escaped her. Whatever came, she couldn't deny herself this living fantasy.

8

"Smile, ladies, smile!"

George, sweeping by them—his own smile completely plastic—voiced the command softly, then turned his charm on the next reporter to snare him. He spoke more glowingly of his "girls" than he did of the creations they wore, yet his inflections were so perfect that any woman hearing him would think that the man was entirely too modest and that it was his stunning genius with material that gave the young women their beauty.

Tara smiled obediently. Flashbulbs snapped, and, blinded, she kept smiling and moving along with the others. The ship was just leaving port; confetti was streaming over the sides, balloons were flying, and there was a tremendous bustle all about. The casinos weren't open yet, but waiters were rushing around with free "Island Coolers," and it seemed that everyone aboard had gathered on the aft of the lido deck to watch the first showing of either the Galliard fashions or the Galliard girls. Or perhaps the press and the critics—all gathered to pounce on Galliard.

They were all dressed in casual cocktail wear. Ashley was in flowing teal, Cassandra in a mist of soft yellow, Mary in black and white stripes, and Tara in an A-line silk of massive orchids against silver that belted at the waist. As George spoke about the gowns, he called each girl forward, describing the material, the casual air of the dress, the comfort, how easy it was to wear. Reporters questioned him; he answered them with ease.

And they just kept smiling away, pirouetting now and then on command when a new question was broached.

"It's amazing what that man can find to say about fabric," Ashley muttered as she passed Tara.

Tara laughed. "He's an expert with words."

She didn't care. It was just after four o'clock, nowhere near dark, yet the sun was filling the sky in a way that kept the day light and bright, the heat at a minimum. The morning in old San Juan had been fun; they had gambled and shopped. And now, aboard the ship, with the tug pulling them out, a sea breeze was arising that caressed the skin with a wonderful feel. She loved ships; the crew was already proving to be extraordinary, and everything should be absolutely perfect.

And it was perfect. It was. She was going to have a glorious time. Except that . . .

Except that her mind was being pulled in two directions, and she was too keyed up and nervous to enjoy a thing.

She was going back to Caracas. Back to the "scene of the crime."

Tara tossed her hair across her face, afraid that her professional smile might be slipping. What was she worried about? Tine had disappeared two years ago. He certainly hadn't spent that time waiting for her to reappear. He had never really loved her. He had been crazy about her potential for income. It was likely that he had disappeared into Brazil or Argentina by now. Perhaps he had even moved on to Europe.

She never had to be alone. Never be a target . . .

But Tine wasn't the only one who had disappeared. Jimmy had disappeared, too. Was that the real reason she had come back? Because she thought that she owed him something? He wouldn't have been involved with Tine if it hadn't been for her.

But that hadn't been the truth, either, because Jimmy, it seemed, had had something that Tine had wanted. The mask.

She shook her head slightly. She didn't want to think about it. But then, of course, it was better than thinking about Rafe, and wondering if she was a fool, if there was really something to fear, if . . .

This trip would have been beautiful if she could have leaned by the rail with his arms about her, felt the sea breeze while returning his kiss, laughed and talked and looked at the stars far out on the ocean.

She had avoided him. Carefully, completely. He'd come after her at work; she'd slipped out the back. He'd come to her door. She'd ignored him. She'd answered the phone only once, to tell him quietly and determinedly that she was frightened of what was growing between them and that if the feelings were real, they would last. He had laughed and promised to be on the trip, and she had been glad to inform him that the cruise had been sold out for months and months and months—ever since the press had broken the news about Galliard's showings aboard ship.

He had been strangely silent. She'd wished she could have seen his face, his eyes. Then he had spoken softly. "Tara."

"Yes?"

"It's important that you know this. The feelings—they are real. I love you."

"I love you, too. I'm just—afraid." She inhaled sharply, held her breath for a second, then rushed on. "And you know why. You told me yourself. You know who I am—you know about my past."

"Tara, take care."

"I will."

"I need to be with you."

"Rafe, even if there were a way for you to get on that ship, I wouldn't want you to come."

"Unfinished business?" he queried softly, and she didn't know if there was an ironic insinuation in the words or not.

"Because I'm afraid."

"Maybe you should be. All right, take care, Tara."

And he'd hung up. He hadn't said that he'd call her as soon as she got back. He'd simply hung up.

Then, in a frenzy, she'd called the cruise line, checking to see if he'd obtained a reservation. No, he was not listed as a passenger. And no, there wasn't a single booking left.

So she was alone. No, not alone—good heavens, not alone! George was with her, and Ashley and Madame and Cassandra and Mary, and five other employees who ran around and bowed down to George.

There was suddenly a smattering of applause. Ashley nudged Tara. "Move! This is it! We're free! Piña coladas on the foredeck. Sun, wind, sand—"

"There's not a grain of sand anywhere near us," Tara interrupted her.

"But there will be!"

Tara laughed and started to follow her friend through the lounge, but just then she heard one of the reporters call out a question to George, and it was a query that stopped her dead in her tracks.

"I see that Tara Hill is back with you, George!"

"Yes, yes, of course," George responded briefly.

"Going back to Caracas. Tell me—was Miss Hill ever cleared of all the charges?"

"Of course," George replied.

Bless him, Tara thought, but she decided that she was tired of praying that the media would forgive her the past. This was one interview she wanted to handle herself.

"Tara!"

Ashley tried to stop her, but Tara swung around and moved to George's side, linking an arm with him.

"You're Sandy Martin—L.A.? Yes, I thought I remembered you!" She gave the man a bewitching smile. "Mr. Martin, all the charges against me were dropped."

"What about the woman who was killed? You still claim that you didn't know her?"

"I had never seen her before that night."

"And what about the man? The man with no known identity—who you claim existed?"

She laughed, as if the reporter was missing something entirely.

"Mr. Martin, obviously *you* think that someone existed—you ran dozens of pictures of the back of his head!"

A ripple of laughter broke through the crowd. She felt a sway of warmth, as if she had brought this particular audience to her side. Martin had turned red—and for once he seemed to be out of words.

"Do excuse me," Tara murmured.

George gave her a wink. She hurried off after the other girls; they hadn't gone far. Linking arms, they hurried through the lounge, smiling at passengers who gave way for their group.

"Bravo," Mary murmured.

"You think I'm off the hook?"

Ashley laughed. "No. You'll never be off the hook. But you did real well back there, kid. Real well."

"Oh, let's forget that nasty man, shall we?" Cassandra pleaded. "There's an absolutely beautiful-looking, tall, dark officer out there in the most becoming uniform. Let's change and get back on deck, shall we?"

"Two hours and the casino opens," Mary said.

"You and your one-armed bandits." Ashley sighed. "We'll meet out in the hall in ten minutes—okay?"

It was agreed all around.

Galliard's party had a majority of the suites on the main deck—just perfect, in Ashley's opinion, since they wouldn't have to run up and down flights and flights of steps all the time. The two pools and two of the main lounges were forward and aft from their cabin; the casino was just below them, as were the two main dining rooms.

She and Tara were in one suite together; Mary and Cassandra were sharing another. They were wonderful cabins, Tara thought, with two real full-sized beds separated by a dresser, a massive closet—necessary for them!—and even what was an extraordinarily large bath for a cruise ship. Across from the beds was a full-length mirror—another must, Ashley declared, quite pleased with it all.

She spun around with pleasure before pouncing on her chosen bed. "I love it, I love it, I love it!" she declared ecstatically. "Why, Tara, anytime we want—anytime day or night!—we can pick up this wonderful little phone and a gracious room steward will come bearing a silver tray of anything we might want! Breakfast in bed, coffee brought right before my nose! I'm in love."

Tara smiled and dug through her luggage for a sunsuit in white knit. They didn't eat until the late sitting, and she was determined just to sit out in the breeze until dinner. Even her sunsuit, she reflected, was George's creation. They weren't to appear in anything but his designs for the duration of the trip.

She shed her heels, dress and stockings and slid into the little suit, then sank onto her own bed and smiled at Ashley.

"Ash?"

"What?"

"You employ a full-time housekeeper. And she's a love. She'd bring you breakfast in bed anytime you wanted."

"Oh, you're missing the whole spirit of the thing!" Ashley sat up suddenly, eyeing her friend speculatively. "I know what your problem is. You're upset—and you should be—because you left that man behind. You're sitting there with your Galliard Girl smile in place, but underneath . . ." Ashley rose dramatically, walking to their little draped porthole to look out. "Underneath you're dying. You're wishing that I was nowhere near this room, that you were seated on a sumptuous king-sized bed and that at any moment the door would burst open and there he would be, dark, mysterious, exciting—"

"Ashley, you're getting carried away," Tara said dryly.

"Tell me it isn't true."

"It isn't true." Tara lied, because it was—and it wasn't. She was absolutely determined to be rational and careful about the whole affair. And yet . . .

Ashley's mere words had set her heart pounding. No, it wasn't her heart. It was her blood. Pulsing, growing warm. It was her breath, catching as she remembered him.

Ashley's lips curled into a taunting smile. "You told us it was the best night you ever had in your entire life. That you'd never imagined people could be so intimate."

Tara flushed. "I should have kept my mouth shut."

Ashley laughed happily. "I'd never have let you! In fact, you did tell me dismally little. And you're a liar. I saw it in your eyes. You'd love to have him sweep right in and—"

"Ashley, I'm not denying a thing about the attraction. But I wanted some distance. That's the truth." She paused suddenly, looking curiously at Ashley. "Did you ever remember what it was that you thought seemed familiar about his stepmother?" Ashley had told her that Mrs. Tyler had been gracious and attractive and charming—and very quiet. And that there had been something familiar about her.

Ashley shook her head.

"I never did put my finger on it. Maybe she just reminded me of Donna Reed or Harriet Nelson or someone like that. I didn't really speak with her, you know. George did a lot of finger snapping. I waltzed in and I waltzed out and he talked. I changed while they sipped champagne and she ordered. She was gone by the time I came out."

Tara laced her fingers behind her head and stared up at the ceiling. "I just wish I knew . . ."

"Knew what?"

"What the catch was!"

"Oh, God!" Ashley exclaimed, tossing her glorious wealth of auburn hair over her shoulder. "When Prince Charming walks in, Tara, you're not supposed to ask him about the state of the kingdom!"

"Ashley, you're forgetting—I've been used once. By the best."

Ashley chuckled softly. "I imagine that you haven't seen anything yet. Tine couldn't nearly compare."

"Thanks a lot! So I *am* being used."

"No, no! That's not what I meant. Oh, get up, will you? If I don't get one of those piña coladas soon, I'm going to expire."

"You won't."

"Right on top of you—and you'll be sorry as hell!"

Laughing, Tara rose, and she and Ashley slipped out into the hall, where they were joined a minute later by the others.

Mary's dreams of the slots and Tara's wish to relax in the sun turned out to be just that—dreams and wishes. They were accosted from all sides by people—charming people, for the most part. Ashley did get her piña colada. It seemed that they spent hours answering the same questions, questions about fashion, about George, about the glamour of their lives, about color, makeup, exercise, and on and on.

Tara discovered that she didn't mind a bit. People already seemed to be different—something she had discovered before about cruise ships. It seemed that when you left dry land you left behind the belief that anyone might be a mugger, that being friendly might make you seem like a pervert. It was nice; it kept her mind occupied, and it made her feel great about the whole thing.

Not one person asked her about her past. No one accused her of murder. No one...

Until her friendly reporter "enemy" suddenly appeared at her side again.

"Seems odd, Miss Hill, that you're following your own footsteps. Same trip and all, two years later. What do you think you'll find in Venezuela?"

He was sandy-haired and freckled, with a boy-next-door type of face. Innocuous, friendly.

Like hell.

She smiled. "I'm expecting to find Caracas right where I left it."

He laughed; he didn't redden this time. His smile tightened.

"Some people think, Miss Hill, that you might be going back to look for your lover."

Tara felt her own smile tighten. She strove to remain expressionless—thanks to George's training, it was possible.

"Sorry. Tine and I were through a long time before any of that happened."

"Were you? Or maybe his smuggling really was successful. So successful that he's hoping to find you and smuggle *you* away with him this time to some nice safe haven in South America. Are you sure you haven't been in contact with the man, Miss Hill?"

"No. I'm afraid I haven't."

He was about to say more—another digging, wounding query, she was certain. But suddenly there was a tap on his shoulder. It was one of the ship's officers.

The reporter's eyes widened at the whispered message. "Excuse me!" he muttered excitedly, and Tara was reprieved.

She stared blankly at Ashley. "Saved—by something."

"Another story," Mary supplied ironically.

"What could possibly best Tara?" Ashley demanded innocently. "Illicit love and murder."

"Ashley!"

"Never mind," Cassandra murmured nervously. "Let's escape while we've got the chance. Dinner is in an hour and a half, and we have to go to the captain's reception or cocktail party or whatever it is."

Tara agreed with Cassandra—it was time to escape.

She showered first. When she emerged, wrapped in her towel, she found Ashley studying a door next to the floor-length mirror.

"What are you doing?" she demanded, amused.

"I wonder where it goes."

Tara shook her head, still smiling. "Ashley, it goes into the next suite. I'm sure it's locked. See—there's the closet, and there's the bathroom. And that little door will go right into the next suite. Which will have a door to the closet and a door to the bathroom and another little—locked—door that goes into the *next* suite."

Ashley grinned secretively and shook her head vehemently. "Tara, it isn't locked."

"Well, it should be," Tara said, rubbing her wet hair with a second towel. "I'll speak to the cabin steward about it. Someone has been lax." She paused and shrugged. "Maybe it's someone in our party. Maybe that's why they left it open."

"No. We're the tail end of our group."

"Then I'll say something about it."

Ashley was still standing by the door.

"What are you doing now?"

"Well—it *is* open."

"You shouldn't have even tried it! That's—that's sneaking into someone else's privacy!"

"How do we know that they haven't snuck into ours?"

"Oh, Ashley!"

"Aren't you the least bit curious?"

"No!"

Tara watched her friend. Ashley's fingers were still on the knob. "Ashley."

"Oh, come on!"

"Ashley—all we would see is a bunch of luggage! Or worse—what if someone is in there? We could get nice jabs right in the nose, and we'd deserve it."

"You're right, of course," Ashley said.

"Go take your shower."

"Oh, I can't stand it!"

And Ashley threw the door open.

GET ALL 3

We'd like to send you three free books to introduce you to "The Best of the Best." Your three books have a combined cover price of $16.50, but they are yours free! We'll even send you a lovely "thank-you" gift—the attractive picture frame shown below. You can't lose!

FREE!

ONLY FOREVER
by Linda Lael Miller
"Sensuality, passion, excitement, and drama ...are Ms. Miller's hallmarks." —*Romantic Times*

FREE!

SWAMP FIRE
by Patricia Potter
"A beguiling love story ..."
—*Romantic Times*

FREE!

DARK STRANGER
by Heather Graham Pozzessere
"An incredible storyteller!"
—*L.A. Daily News*

SPECIAL FREE GIFT!

We'll send you this lovely picture frame, decorated with celestial designs, absolutely FREE, just for giving "The Best of the Best" a try! Don't miss out—mail the reply card today!

BOOKS FREE!

Hurry!
Return this card promptly to **GET 3 FREE BOOKS & A FREE GIFT!**

the **Best** *of the* **Best**

```
Affix
peel-off
MIRA
sticker here
```

YES, send me the three free "The Best of the Best" novels, as explained on the back. I understand that I am under no obligation to purchase anything further as explained on the back and on the opposite page. Also send my free picture frame!

183 CIH AZHX (U-BB3-96)

Name: _____

Address: _____

City: _____

State: _____ Zip: _____

THE BEST OF THE BEST™: HERE'S HOW IT WORKS —

Accepting free books places you under no obligation to buy anything. You may keep the books and gift and return the shipping statement marked "cancel." If you do not cancel, about a month later we will send you 3 additional novels and bill you just $3.99 each, plus 25¢ delivery and applicable sales tax, if any.* That's the complete price, and—compared to cover prices of $5.50 each—quite a bargain! You may cancel at any time, but if you choose to continue, every month we'll send you 3 more books, which you may either purchase at the discount price...or return at our expense and cancel your subscription.

*Terms and prices subject to change without notice. Sales tax applicable in N.Y.

"No one is in there," she whispered. "We won't get our noses smashed in, which is probably good." She started to giggle. "Could you imagine having to model George's fashions with black eyes? He'd have to make shiners the rage of the season!"

"Get out of there!" Tara warned her.

"Whoa!"

Ashley moved on into the cabin. Tara followed her.

"I wonder who this is for!" Ashley exclaimed.

All the suites had offered a welcoming bottle of champagne and platter of fruit. All the suites were nice.

This one was . . .

Well, the champagne was Dom Perignon. Tara had never seen half the exotic fruits before. And there were cheeses and pâtés and caviar.

The carpeting was deeper, and there was a single large bed with a soft crimson comforter that matched the full-length drapes.

"We've just got little curtains!" Ashley murmured. "I wonder who is in here? Oh—look! Luggage. Let's read the tags!"

"No," Tara protested—but she was the one approaching the luggage.

Before she could reach it, though, they heard a key turning in the hallway door. Ashley let out a little squeak; she grabbed Tara's arm and they started to race back to their own cabin.

Ashley grabbed at the connecting door. Panicky, she pushed it the wrong way.

"Damn you, Ashley! Open it!" Tara hissed.

"I'm trying!"

"Someone's coming in."

"I know!"

"We're going to get caught!"

"We'll talk our way out of it."

"Talk our way out of it! Ashley—you're dressed. I'm wearing a towel! I swear I'm going to kill you if whoever is in this cabin doesn't decide to shoot us both!"

"It's going to be all right—"

"Ashley! Don't you ever listen? I don't even have any clothes on!"

Someone—a male someone—cleared his throat behind them.

Guilty as sin, they spun around—just as Rafe Tyler spoke, leaning back comfortably against the wall, watching them with golden amusement.

"I rather like you that way myself. Ashley, what do you think? George Galliard would be horrified, of course, but Tara has such a wonderful way with a towel, she could probably pass one off as his latest in casual wear."

"Oh!" Ashley breathed, and she was so relieved that she started to laugh nervously.

Tara wasn't amused at all. She was horrified, confused—and frightened.

The way that he was looking at her...

"What are you doing here?" she snapped.

"That should be my question. After all, ladies, this is my cabin."

"Oh, yes, of course, we're so sorry—" Ashley began.

"What are you doing on this cruise!" Tara interrupted. "I specifically told you not to come!"

He arched a brow. "You told me? This is a cruise ship— a public cruise ship. Not your private property."

"The door wasn't locked." Ashley began to offer excuses, smiling away. "And it just seemed so intriguing. Come on, Rafe, you understand. A woman's curiosity and all that—"

"I don't want to see you," Tara interrupted again.

He lifted a hand. "This is my cabin," he reminded her.

Ashley looked from one of them to the other. "Listen, I really think I should be going now—"

"Ashley, stay!" Tara commanded.

"Ashley, I would like to speak with Tara alone."

"Don't you dare leave me standing here alone with him in nothing but a towel!"

"Tara, come on!" Ashley pleaded. "Be serious! Let me out of this. I mean, after all, the man has seen you in much less than a towel—oops, I mean—oh, please! Let me out!"

She tugged furiously at the door, which still didn't give. Rafe started toward them. Tara clutched her towel and backed away. Ashley smiled nervously and stepped aside.

Rafe twisted the knob—and the door obediently opened without a sound.

"Thank God!" Ashley breathed a sigh of relief and whisked through.

Tara tried to follow her. The door closed before she could do so.

She backed away from him, staring, trying to remain calm. Trying to remain ... unaffected.

It wasn't easy; she had fallen in love with him. She should have thought she was in seventh heaven, on a ship with him, sailing away into the horizon, alone, laughing, touching ...

But love was a frightening emotion—just as he could be a frightening man. A tiger in the jungle, with golden eyes that seemed to see everything and betray nothing.

"Let me out of here, Rafe," she said flatly.

"Tara—"

"I don't want to discuss it. I told you why I needed to get away, but you're here anyway. You're right—if you managed to book on the cruise, I have no right to want you off. But I don't need to be near you, either. So if you'll excuse me . . .''

"Tara, damn you!" he said irritably. "I'm here because I love you."

"If you meant that, you'd have given me the time I asked for."

"Tara—"

"Let me out of here! Please!" Her voice rose in desperation. She didn't dare give in; if he touched her, she would be lost. She would be with him again, and she would forget that she had been burned badly once, that there were still several good reasons why she shouldn't trust him.

He moved, opening the door for her. She wanted to rush past him, but she stood still, because she would have to touch him, brush by his windbreaker, to reach the sanctuary of her own cabin.

Sanctuary! A fragile door separated them.

She stood still.

"Tara," he said very softly, "I'm here because I'm worried about you—I'm worried about this trip. I'm here for your safety and your well-being. You want time. I'll give you all the time in the world—once this trip is over."

He was here for her safety.

Then he must think that there was something that she should fear. Something from the past. She wanted to believe him—she also wanted desperately to know what secret it was that he held, why he, too, should feel that this trip might be dangerous.

"I'll see to it that the dividing door is locked," she told him stiffly.

"Don't bother. I'll take care of it."

"Thank you, but I'll feel better if I handle the situation myself."

She fled through the doorway at last. She did brush his jacket. And she felt his scent, with which she had become so achingly familiar, touch her, enwrap her...seep into her.

She almost turned around. She almost slipped her arms around his neck to tell him that she loved him, that she was grateful that he was near, that she would gladly pass through that dividing door every night and sleep in the comfort and excitement of his arms.

The door closed behind her. She heard the bolt slide home.

And then she felt like kicking the door. It seemed that it locked easily from his side—but what about from hers?

Hurriedly, feeling ridiculously naked now that she knew Rafe was less than thirty feet away, Tara swept through her gowns until she found the oriental silk she was to wear that evening. Ashley emerged from the shower just as her friend slipped into the dress and looked at her anxiously.

"My God—you look like a thundercloud."

"I specifically asked him not to come!"

"I wonder how he got the cabin."

"God knows. It seems he can get anywhere he wants to go."

"Well, he is frightfully rich."

Tara didn't say anything. She sat in a huff to pull on her nylons, eyeing the door now and then.

Ashley sat down beside her. "Tara, I don't understand you. He's fabulous. You told me so yourself! A man like him comes along once in a lifetime. If you're lucky, that is!"

"Ashley, that's just the point."

"Oh, God!" Ashley moaned. "He's perfect—so ditch him?"

Tara shook her head. "Ashley, come on! He's mysterious. He's not telling me the whole truth."

"All right. He's a modern-day Bluebeard. He has his last six wives locked up in his mansion out on Long Island."

"Ashley!" Tara sighed.

"Tara!"

"Oh, I give up on you!" Tara moaned. "I'm just trying to protect my heart and soul, okay?"

"Well, thank the Lord you haven't got your virginity to add to that!" Ashley laughed. "I'll take odds that somewhere along the line on this trip *I'm* going to be the one sleeping alone on this side of that door."

Tara clenched her teeth and shot Ashley an evil stare. Ashley didn't even notice.

"Tara!"

"What?"

"I'll lay you a bet."

"On what?"

"I'll bet anything that Rafe was the one who somehow managed to get our reporter friend—the old inquisitor—out of your hair."

A shiver rippled through Tara.

She was convinced that Ashley was right.

9

The cocktail party was a fun affair that everyone enjoyed—everyone but Tara.

The captain was a charming, handsome Italian, the purser was a charming, handsome Dutchman, and the various other chief crew members were also pleasant. As Tara noticed before, people in general were simply happy to be aboard. They talked, laughed—they relaxed. She wasn't as besieged now by questions as with dance partners, and under normal circumstances she would have been happy just because it was so nice to see so many people so comfortable and at ease.

Except that Rafe walked in about fifteen minutes after they arrived.

She was determined to ignore him. A difficult feat, for as soon as he walked through the doorway, she experienced the whole gamut of emotions that he always elicited. Longing...no one could ever forget being held in those arms. It wasn't even something in the mind; it was miserably physical. A trembling in her limbs, the feeling that the place had grown warm, that she was flushed...

Which she was, she thought, lowering her eyes from those of her dance partner, one of the distinguished, middle-aged chefs. Rafe's very presence was a call to her senses so blatant that it was embarrassing. If she saw him, imagined his scent, heard his voice—she instantly felt a weak shivering inside her, a heat that came straight from her core.

She ached to lie down with him again.

Don't look at him! she commanded herself. But it didn't matter; she knew he was in the room.

Everyone knew he was in the room. She had seen eyes turn when he entered. He had that quality. A presence, strong, hypnotic, fascinating.

Beautifully powerful, like a tiger...

The chef said something to her; she stumbled, stepped on his foot and apologized profusely, and heard his assurance that she could tread on him any time she chose.

She kept dancing with the chef until the charming Dutch purser broke in. But even as she chatted with him about Curaçao, their first port of call, where his native tongue was spoken, she thought about Rafe and could not resist the temptation to glance at him again.

He was dancing with Ashley, whose head was cast back as she laughed delightedly at something he had said.

Jealousy—that evil demon—slipped into Tara's heart again. Ashley was exotic, beautiful, blazing with vitality, sweet and warm. Surely *she* was the better choice for any man.

Tara lowered her eyes again. She gave the purser a dazzling smile, then felt like a fool, because she realized that she was trying to make Rafe jealous while neither Rafe nor Ashley was attempting any such thing—they were just dancing and enjoying each other.

She stepped on the purser's foot, too, and imagined a little bleakly that if they all got together to discuss the Galliard girls, they might shake their heads sadly and agree that the blonde had been a terrible klutz.

At last the cocktail party came to an end. They moved down a deck for dinner. George discussed the first show with them; Tara sipped her wine idly until she noticed that Rafe was sitting at the captain's table. The delicious dinner became totally unpalatable.

When it was over, Cassandra, Mary and Ashley decided to try their hands in the casino—Tara begged off and hurried back to her cabin, then wished she hadn't, remembering that somewhere along the line, Rafe would go into his own.

Ashley didn't stay in the casino long; she returned to the room. Tara pretended to be asleep, but Ashley didn't fall for it; she perched on the foot of Tara's bed. "Dreaming, huh?"

"Trying to sleep."

"No, you're not. You're thinking about the fact that his cabin is just inches away."

"Not inches, Ashley. Feet."

"But still, he'll be right beyond that door."

"Did you have a nice time dancing, Ashley?"

"Lovely. He's not mad at me."

"Why should he be?"

"Well, I did trespass in his cabin. But then, I wonder if he even noticed I was around, what with you there. Especially dressed in that towel and all. He's not mad at you, either."

"Why should he be? I'm the aggrieved party."

"Because he's here? That's absurd."

"No, it's not. It's sensible."

"Sensible. Nice way to spend your life. Lying here, in the dark. In this skinny, single bunk. Imagining that massive bed—just *feet* away. With him in it. Strong arms to hold you. The beat of his heart. The heat of his chest. The pulse, the vitality, the—"

"Ashley, you've been watching the soaps again."

"Okay, Tara. Lie there. Suffer. I just hope you don't talk in your sleep, because it might get a little too erotic for my innocent ears."

"Ashley, haven't you got any more money to lose?"

She laughed. "It's much more fun to torture you."

Tara rolled over. "I'm going to sleep now, Ashley."

Ashley laughed wickedly once again. "Sweet dreams."

"Thanks."

They were docked in Curaçao when Tara awoke in the morning. Determined to get off the boat and onto the island as soon as possible, she rudely shook Ashley awake and called to have breakfast served in their cabin.

She dressed quickly, while Ashley was still attempting to prop her eyes open with her first cup of coffee. "Come on, Ash," Tara urged her.

"We'll stop for breakfast?"

"We'll stop for breakfast. At a lovely little café with a table beneath an umbrella."

"Did you call Mary and Cassandra?"

Tara did. Mary told her that they were going to sleep in—they had stayed up until two in the casino, then danced until almost four.

"What a way to work!" Ashley declared, laughing, and then she managed to crawl out of bed, apply some make-up, and shimmy into one of George's coolly casual cotton jumpsuits.

Tara was already at the door. "Ashley!"

"I'm coming!"

Tara was halfway down the hallway. Ashley puffed along behind her. "What's your hurry?"

"Nothing. The day is young and beautiful."

"It should be. It's seven-fifteen."

They smiled at the man standing guard at the runway, collected reboarding passes and hurried down. Soon they were in the plaza, and then they were walking along past the storefronts. The buildings were all pastel and charmingly Dutch.

"See, isn't this wonderful?" Tara asked.

"Sure—it's just great. Nothing's open."

Tara made a face and turned a corner, leading them back toward the sea. There was a café at the corner, facing the water. Charmingly colorful umbrellas sat over white wrought iron tables.

"Breakfast, as you wished," Tara told Ashley. She pulled her sun hat low over her eyes, crossed her ankles over one of the extra chairs and leaned back. A young girl came for their order; they asked for coffee and rolls and an assortment of cheeses.

Boats were already moving on the little inlet. Fishermen were hawking their catches. A woman walked along, selling handmade dolls.

Ashley, too, pulled her hat low and sank back. "How did you sleep?" she asked Tara.

"Divinely."

"No dreams?"

"Not a one."

"You're such a liar."

"This coffee is delicious."

"Why did you run off the ship? Chicken?"

"Because I didn't want to run into Rafe."

Ashley chuckled. "He didn't come near you all night."

"I know."

"Poor baby."

"Ashley—stuff a roll in your face, will you, please?"

"Love to, darling."

She started to do just that, then paused, suddenly aware that they were being watched. She turned slightly. There was a lively group of five young sailors behind them.

"We've got company," Ashley said.

Tara gazed past her, then wished she hadn't. One of the sailors winked at her. She didn't want to be rude, but she also didn't want to encourage him. She smiled weakly, then pointedly turned back to Ashley.

"Dutch?"

"I think so."

"Beer for breakfast."

"They're probably on a beer leave."

"Wasn't that for American fighters in World War II?"

"I think it's for any soldier, in war or peace."

"They're just a bunch of kids."

"Drunk kids, I'm afraid."

That was proved true just seconds later, when one of the young men swirled his chair and plopped down beside Ashley. He was darling, Tara thought, blond, blue-eyed— and probably no more than eighteen. It was a shame, she reflected, that it seemed all countries selected their most promising youth to offer up to the possibility of war.

But this young sweetheart had overimbibed. He started talking to Ashley, using language learned straight from the movies. Ashley was polite but firm. It got her nowhere. The other sailors were suddenly around the table, and Tara found herself fighting off hands as if she were surrounded by a pair of giant octopuses.

"Your mother should wash your mouth out with soap!" Ashley threatened one of them.

Fear gripped Tara suddenly, a fear she had never really conquered since Tine. It was a feeling of being overpowered.

She jumped up, suddenly not so sympathetic, and grabbed her bag. She tossed money on the table and took hold of Ashley.

"Let's go!"

But they were followed. Panic started to seize her as they headed back toward the main street with all the pastel shops. She felt a hand on her shoulder and spun around. One of the young blondes was smiling away.

"We make beautiful music, baby."

"No! *Nyet!*"

"Tara—that's Russian, not Dutch!" Ashley exclaimed.

How much English did they understand?

"Please, I know they work you hard on your ship! I know you don't get much liberty. But I'm not interested. I'm not—"

From behind, another hand grasped her shoulder, sweeping her around against something very hard.

She knew the scent; she knew the touch. Rafe.

He said something in Dutch, low, easy, but it was something the sailor understood. He blushed and bowed slightly. "Sorry. Enjoy the island, miss."

He turned and walked away. His friends waved a little uncertainly and followed him.

"Rafe! Bless you!" Ashley declared.

He was still touching Tara, who remained silent.

"They were just a little overzealous with their freedom."

"What did you tell them?"

"Just that you were spoken for."

"You didn't threaten them?" Tara muttered.

His hand moved away from her shoulders. "No, I didn't."

Ashley laughed, completely comfortable once more. "Well, whatever you did, it worked. Thanks! Do you speak Dutch?"

"No, only a few words."

"Why not?" Tara whispered. He ignored her, and she knew that she was being ridiculously rude. Absurdly, she felt close to tears. Could it really be that easy? Could she just smile and admit that she had been a fool and then everything would just be fine? It was easy to wish when he was touching her.

What in God's name held her back?

"Where were you going?" Rafe asked Ashley.

"Window-shopping," Ashley replied. "Want to join us?"

"Well, I have to go *that* way." He pointed.

"That way is fine."

They moved along the street. The shops had opened now. Ashley paused to buy T-shirts for her niece, nephew, sister and brother-in-law, and a little wood carving of a Dutch house for her parents.

Tara didn't know if she wanted any souvenirs or not, and she continued to feel tongue-tied. It didn't matter— Ashley and Rafe kept up a conversation easily.

They were in front of a dazzling window when Ashley suddenly stopped dead still.

"Ooh! Oh, Tara! Look at those emeralds! Have you ever seen such a beautiful necklace!"

Tara gazed into the window. The necklace was all alone, displayed on black velvet. There was one large stone in the center of a delicate gold filigree; it was surrounded by an elegant spray of diamond chips. It was simple; it was elegant. It was one of the most beautiful pieces she had ever seen.

"Do you really think it's good?" Rafe asked her seriously.

"Wonderful," Ashley replied. "Why?"

He smiled and pointed at the sign overhead.

"Oh! This is one of your stores!" Ashley said.

He arched a brow. "You knew?"

"No, no. I mean, not that you had one here. We did know that your family was in jewelry." She blushed. Her words betrayed the fact that one of them had done some research on the Tylers.

"Come on in. Try it on."

He stepped ahead of Ashley and opened the door. Tara wanted to remain in the street. Ashley hesitated just a second, then pulled Tara in with her.

Rafe was in white shorts and a navy polo jacket; somehow, he still seemed to fit the old-world refinement of the shop. There was a young girl behind a glass counter in which other gems were artfully displayed. She saw Rafe, smiled with pleasure and came out to greet him. He took both her hands and pressed a little kiss on her cheek.

Tara hated herself for the familiar jealousy that washed through her. But she found herself wondering about his wide-ranging life. He had been so many places. Would she always wonder about his past? Always feel these little twinges?

Always? There could only be an always if she gave in.

He spoke to the girl for a moment; she answered him cheerfully. He turned back to them.

"Would you excuse me for just a second? I want to look in on our bookkeeper. Frieda will bring you whatever you would like."

He disappeared toward the back. Frieda gave them a sweet, earnest smile and asked if they would like coffee or tea or something stronger.

Tara asked for coffee, just for something to do with herself. Ashley did the same.

But when they were seated in cushioned oak chairs around a small oak table, Frieda returned to them, the emerald necklace in her hands.

"You wished to see this, madame?"

Ashley almost choked on her coffee. Their incomes meant that their lives were definitely comfortable, but the size and perfection of that emerald put the necklace's cost into more digits than either of them could easily handle.

Rafe suddenly reappeared. On the soft carpeting, his footsteps had made no sound. He watched Tara, and he watched Ashley, and he smiled a little secretively. The necklace might well have been made for Ashley—sweet Ashley who had been in his corner through blind faith all along. He realized two things; he wanted Ashley to have the necklace because he was so genuinely fond of her, and he wanted her to have it because it was perfect for her. She appreciated its beauty with evident pleasure.

"Here, let me, Ashley."

He stepped behind her, clasping the emerald with its beautiful filigree and diamonds around her neck. Tara felt a twinge as his fingers brushed her friend's neck.

Frieda brought a mirror. Rafe stood back, surveying the necklace.

"It's perfect. A redhead in emeralds."

"It's stunning," Tara agreed, her heart aching a bit. It was. The necklace fell just above Ashley's breasts in a subtle brilliance. And Rafe had put it there.

"You make beautiful things, Rafe," Ashley murmured.

He laughed. "I don't make them. My jewelers do. But I'm glad you like it. After all, I hire the jewelers. And I'm convinced that you have impeccable taste."

Frieda handed him a memo board with a paper on it. He signed it.

Ashley stared at him suddenly, mischievously. "If emeralds are for redheads, Rafe, what about blondes?"

He looked straight at Tara.

"Diamonds. Nothing less," he said softly.

Again he turned to Frieda, exchanged a few words, then turned back to them. "Shall we go?"

"Wait!" Ashley said desperately. "I've still got the necklace on."

"Oh, yes. Frieda, could you get the lady a box, please."

"Oh, Rafe," Ashley gasped, her jaw dropping as she realized his intention. "I couldn't. Really, I couldn't. It just wouldn't be—I can't. I—"

He smiled with mild amusement while she faltered. "Ashley, if I were a florist, you would think nothing of accepting a rose. Trust me—I have a multitude of stones. Please, keep that one. Just please be sure to tell any admirer that it was created by my company."

He touched her again, taking the necklace, brushing his fingers over her flesh. Once again Tara unhappily realized that it had not been a gesture made for her benefit. Ashley had loved the necklace, it had looked exquisite on her, and he had taken pleasure in giving it to her. Like a florist with a rose.

They left the shop. Ashley continued to protest, glancing guiltily at Tara now and then. But Tara wasn't upset. Not at her friend, anyway. Rafe had a talent for giving a gift. He and Ashley walked ahead, while he told her how to judge an emerald, how to seek out the flaws, how to search for good color.

They came to another café; Rafe suggested a cool drink.

Tara had several, sitting silent while the two of them talked.

At last he glanced at his watch and warned them that it was nearing time for the ship to sail. He paid for their drinks and they returned.

As they walked up the steps, the captain was there—almost as if he had been waiting for them.

He had been.

Rafe excused himself to speak with the man.

"Tara, I didn't know what to do!" Ashley pleaded. "I still don't. I know that a woman of any character shouldn't accept a gift like this, but he has no interest in me. I mean, no interest in that way. You're the one he's sleeping with. I—"

"Ashley, it's probably true. He probably has so many emeralds that he just doesn't know what to do with them. You have dozens of George's thousand-dollar-plus fashions, and you don't think twice about that."

"Yes, but that's my job. Oh, the emerald is beautiful, and I do love it—"

"And you wearing it is the same kind of advertisement. Ashley, he meant it in friendship. You benefit, and so does he. To worry about it is silly."

"I hope so," Ashley said dubiously. "I wish you would stop this foolishness and leap on him."

Tara sighed and leaned against the wall, frowning. "I just wish he didn't have so much money. I mean," she hesitated, "not quite so much. I don't think I realized until today just how much he really does have. That kind of money, it's not just money. It's power, too. That's frightening, Ashley."

Ashley smiled a little sadly. "Tara, love is nice in any form, but you told me yourself that your parents adored each other—yet life was miserable for them. Look at the money you've poured into that town. He would be perfect for you—you can't wipe out poverty by yourself, and you know that being destitute is a rough life. Don't hate him because he has money."

Tara shook her head. "I never said I hated him, Ashley. I—I think I am in love with him. It's just—suddenly frightening to see his power."

"I don't think that has anything to do with money," Ashley said.

"You could be right. Hmm," Tara murmured, gazing over Ashley's shoulder to watch Rafe, who was still with the captain.

"Ashley, do me a favor. Go play with your emerald. I think we're going to have a little showdown."

Ashley smiled happily. "You mean you're actually going to be nice to that poor man?"

"I'm going to ask him a few questions."

"Gotcha. No, on second thought, I haven't gotten any of this! But I'm leaving!"

She hurried away. Tara stretched her back against the paneling and waited patiently. Then she frowned suddenly, noting a man's back as he hurried down a narrow hallway, heading toward the aft lounge. She pushed herself away from the paneling, trying to recall what it was that had been familiar about the man.

"Are you waiting for me?"

She swung around quickly. Rafe was there, his eyes somewhat skeptical.

"Yes. I want to talk to you."

"Do you really. How nice," he said.

Tara set her jaw stubbornly at his caustic tone. "Well?"

"You're the one who wants to talk."

"Will you?"

"With pleasure, Miss Hill. I'm always at your disposal. Want a drink?"

She'd probably indulged in a few too many on the island, she thought. Oh, what the hell. One more couldn't hurt.

"Yes. Thank you."

She wondered herself how she could be so stiff with a man she had come to know so well. She didn't want to be stiff. She wanted to turn around and pretend that there couldn't possibly be anything wrong, that everything about him was exactly what it seemed.

He led her to the forward lounge. It was darker, more intimate, than the one toward the aft. There were little booths here, and decorative little anchors carved in the woodwork separating the niches. Beneath them, the sea was aquamarine, the breeze light. Someone made an announcement in several languages about the ship leaving port shortly.

He ordered them both a beer, then signed the tab. He sat back in the seat, sipping his idly when it arrived, saying nothing at all, but waiting for her to speak.

"I'm curious," Tara began. "Not only did you manage to book passage on a sold-out cruise, but you have a cabin directly next to ours."

"That's no great mystery."

"Well, if it's not, I'm afraid I'm terribly slow. Please illuminate the situation for me."

He smiled slightly. "One of your friends apparently knows something about me, Tara. I'm surprised that you don't know. I own the ship. Or rather, Tyler Enterprises owns the ship. We own several."

"Oh."

At last his hand reached across the table for hers. He was still smiling, but his next words seemed more wistful, more fraught with tension. "Does that make me guilty of something?"

She snatched her hand back. "No. Yes. You could have told me the truth when we talked on the phone."

He shrugged. "Tara, you were determined that I shouldn't come. I was equally determined that I should."

"Why?"

"I'm worried about you."

"Because of Caracas?"

"Obviously."

"I've got another question for you."

"Shoot."

"Yesterday I was being harassed by a reporter who suddenly and rather mysteriously disappeared. Did you have anything to do with that?"

"Yes," he answered flatly.

"I can take care of myself."

"Can you? Seems to me that things went rather badly for you two years ago."

She inhaled sharply. "What did you do, threaten him?"

"No, I didn't threaten him, Tara. What is this thing you've got about threats?"

"Then what did you do?"

"I offered him a better story, Miss Hill. That's all."

"And that was?"

He laughed. "I don't know yet. I just promised him that he could have an important exclusive in the near future if he would quit torturing you. So, do I get hanged for that, too?"

"I'm not trying to hang you."

"Aren't you?"

She shook her head.

"Then am I forgiven?"

She shook her head again. "I don't know. I just don't know."

Tara jumped up suddenly, afraid to be with him. He'd answered honestly; he hadn't hedged or lied. But she could have found out the truth herself, anyway.

But what was wrong with knowing the truth about him? She still wasn't sure. You couldn't hang a man for being affluent. Or for being so affluent that his promise of a story was "better" to a reporter than digging into her past.

It was just that she wanted to trust him so badly. She wanted to believe that this was really it, that their love could go on and on forever.

"Tara." He caught her wrist, and she could have sworn that the depth of emotion in his arresting golden eyes was real. "Tara, I'm here because I care. Because I have to be. Please, believe that."

She nodded distractedly.

"Can you have dinner with me?"

"I, um, not tonight. I promised George I'd stay with the group. He's having pictures taken."

"After?"

"I'll—I'll meet you in the casino, I guess."

She jerked her hand away, a blush suffusing her cheeks. She needed to run away at this moment; she had promised to meet him later because she couldn't have done anything else. The need to be with him was far stronger than any warning signals.

Ashley was anxiously awaiting her in the cabin. "Well?"

"He owns the ship."

"Oh? And?"

"I don't know. I just don't know. We'll see."

Ashley continued to quiz her; Tara remained stubbornly silent as they showered and dressed for dinner. Ashley told Tara that Mary had seemed to have the captain wrapped around her little finger; he was spending all his free time with her.

''Well, that poor man had better watch out!'' Tara said, laughing, but she was still nervous; she felt a stream of energy running through her, and she didn't know when it would slow down.

Sometime during dinner, she did calm down. She had agreed to meet Rafe. She wanted with all her heart to meet him. She dreamed of spending the cruise with him. Being held in his arms while the breeze moved around them.

The photographers arrived, and the models posed with their wineglasses held high. They stood; they sat. They did their very best to look totally elegant in George's creations.

Then they were left alone, talking, laughing—just like the other passengers.

Dinner came to an end when Mary nibbled at her dessert, then yawned softly, stretching. ''Anyone for casino? I've got my numbers all picked out for the roulette wheel.''

''I'll put forty quarters into a slot machine and that will be that!'' Cassandra said agreeably.

Ashley started to rise, and Tara, too. But George halted her.

''Tara, could you stay behind just a minute, please?''

She frowned slightly, then shrugged, sitting again.

George smiled and waved the others away. When they were gone, he took Tara's hands and stared worriedly into her eyes. ''Are you okay, Tara?''

''I'm fine.''

''How are things with Tyler? I didn't mean to feed you to any wolves, you know. It's just, well, naturally, he can do a great deal for my prestige. But secondly, well, it's time that you—that you saw other men again. I didn't make you unhappy, did I?''

She shook her head. ''No, you didn't make me unhappy. I like Rafe very much.''

He nodded.

"Did you know that he owned the ship?" Tara asked.

"Guilty as charged."

"You didn't tell me."

"If he'd wanted you to know, he would have said something. I guess he *has* told you, now."

She nodded.

"Oh, Tara." He shook his head. "I just hope that I've been doing right by you. I thought that you needed to work again. Maybe even face the past. But the closer we get to Caracas, the more nervous I get."

"You can't really believe that Tine has been waiting there for two years on the possibility that I might come back?"

He shrugged. "From what you said, Tine really wanted that mask."

"I never had the damn mask. Who knows, he may have it already. And most likely he's living somewhere deep in South America and he'll never make an appearance again. Why risk arrest?"

George nodded sagely, agreeing with her logic. "To think that I made a nest for that smuggling snake all those years! Ah, well, you'll be with all of us. You won't be out of our sight for a minute! You'll be fine."

"I think so. Thanks, George."

He gave her a little wave. She smiled vaguely and hurried up to the casino.

Rafe wasn't there. She saw Mary at the roulette table and asked her if she had seen him.

Mary gave her one of her all-knowing stares, plunked down a pile of chips and nodded. "He was here looking for you a few minutes ago. I told him that you had been delayed. I'm afraid I don't know where he went."

"Oh. Thanks," Tara murmured, trying not to show her disappointment.

She walked around the ship, going from lounge to lounge, but she didn't see him. She shied away from a friendly, slightly inebriated group who wanted her to join them. She was so keenly disappointed that she felt like crying.

She went back to her cabin, scrubbed her face, touched up her nails and finally decided to go to bed.

She lay awake for about two hours. Ashley came in, tiptoeing once she saw that Tara was in bed. In a few minutes she stretched out in her own bed, and Tara thought that she had fallen asleep.

But then she spoke.

"He's in his cabin, Tara. And I'll bet that the connecting door is still open. I'll lay odds that he'd be about the happiest man in the universe if you dropped in to, ah, say hi or something. In fact, I'm turning around now. I'm falling asleep. I'd never notice if you slipped through that door."

Tara hesitated, remaining still.

"I'm going to sleep now!" Ashley repeated.

Tara felt her heart thump painfully. She hesitated, then threw off the covers and tiptoed across the room.

The connecting door was open.

She twisted the knob, hesitating again, then pulled the door open. There was no logic, no rhyme, no reason. She wanted, needed, to be with him.

The cabin was dark. For a moment she wondered if he was there, or if he wasn't, perhaps, still in a lounge somewhere, in the casino, out walking the decks, watching the stars.

Gingerly, she made her way to the bed, and the moonlight betrayed his form. A shadow. He sat up, and in the darkness, she blushed.

He was waiting for her. She could almost see his smile, see the glitter of his eyes.

She curled up on the bed. His arms came around her.

"I looked for you," she whispered.

"I looked for *you*."

He took her hand, turning the palm up. He played over it with the tip of his tongue.

"I—I couldn't find you."

"You've found me now."

His hand slipped beneath the hem of her sheer gown; he moved, swift, sleek, vital, like a tiger, and the gown was gone, swept over her head, tossed to the floor. His hands cupped her buttocks, bringing her beneath him, and his eyes glittered with a tender magic in the pale moonlight.

"You've found me now," he repeated.

And with a little sigh she wound her arms around his neck, eager to meet his kiss and the excitement of his body melding with her own.

10

Tuesday morning brought them to Martinique.

There were clear skies, a brilliant sun and a soft sea breeze. Rafe and Tara took off alone in a rented car, since he knew the island well. They climbed mountain trails in the little Toyota, stopped by roadside merchants, watched the sea and the harbor from the heights, and stopped at the small museum to see the relics of a time when the volcano had spilled out its wrath. They visited an old cathedral, walked along wet tropical paths and came back into town, where they wandered through the shops. The company had a jewelry store here, too, on a fashionable street. The manager and his assistant, aware that Rafe was coming, had planned a meal complete with French wine and a few of the island specialties. Tara admired a number of the pieces, but when Rafe told her softly that she was welcome to anything she liked, she shook her head with a rueful smile.

"Ashley's morals seem to have remained undamaged by her necklace," he reminded her. "I believe you told her it was all right, or else she wouldn't have taken it."

"It was all right for Ashley."

"Ah. Because she and I aren't involved."

"Exactly."

"Women."

"It makes perfect sense," Tara assured him. He didn't press her. Outside the store, Tara found herself smiling, wondering if she hadn't won the battle a little too easily.

"You didn't insist," she said teasingly.

"Was I supposed to? Would you have changed your mind?"

"No."

He smiled and walked ahead. She caught up with him, laughing. It was amazing what the night had done—amazing how much of any situation was nothing more than a state of mind. Today, with the sun above them, with the wonderful, colorful people all around them, everything seemed right with the world. She knew him. She knew the emotion in his eyes, the timbre of his voice, and she felt that she must have been half mad to want anything other than to be with him.

Rafe took her arm. "Actually, Miss Hill, I did not insist because I have a very particular gem in mind for you."

"Do you really?"

"Emeralds for a redhead, a diamond for a blonde."

Tara had paused to smell a bunch of fresh flowers that were still a bit damp from the morning showers, radiantly fresh. She felt a little tremor sweep through her.

The shopkeeper said something in French; Rafe laughed and paid for the flowers.

"What did he say?" Tara asked.

"That nature seldom created anything more uniquely exquisite than a flower, but you put the most glorious rose to shame."

"Oh." Tara blushed and turned to the man. *"Merci,"* she said softly.

He bowed deeply, offering her a wide smile.

Rafe glanced at his watch. "We've still got time to stop for a quick drink. I have the perfect place in mind."

It *was* perfect. It had a classic little balcony that sat high above the valley, looking over the town and the ships. It was open, and there were flowers everywhere. The umbrellas were candy-striped in a peach that was as soft as the fragrant air.

They sat there for a moment, sipping drinks the same shade of peach as the stripes in the umbrella. Then Rafe reached into his pocket and produced one of the little velvet-covered boxes with the Tyler insignia embossed in gold on top.

"This is the gem," he said simply. He didn't open the box; he pushed it across the table to her.

Curiosity won out over good sense. She opened the box and was not surprised to see that it was a solitaire. A beautiful stone, not huge and ostentatious, but certainly not small. Perhaps a carat, perhaps a little less. Size meant nothing with this diamond, though. It was splendid in the perfection of its cut, in the rainbow spectrum of bursting color created by the sun's slightest caress.

Thoughtful, Tara closed the box, lowered her lashes, then pushed it gently back toward him. "Rafe—"

"Tara, I know you're not sure. I know you feel that time is very important, that we don't know each other well enough. I wish you would wear it anyway."

She shook her head, confused. "Wear it anyway? Rafe, it—it's magnificent. But it's an *engagement* ring."

She loved it when his lips curled just slightly at the corners. It reflected his ability to laugh at himself, at the world.

"Yes, it *is* an engagement ring. But if you're not ready to make a commitment, I understand. I still wish that you'd wear it. For now."

"Rafe, I'm sorry. I'm confused. You're offering me an engagement ring...but you're *not* really offering it to me?"

He laughed. "I knew you wouldn't accept it."

Belying his words, he took her hand. He flipped open the box with his thumb, took out the ring and slid it upon her finger. The fit was just the slightest bit snug.

Still confused, she searched out his eyes. His fingers wrapped around hers as he met her eyes, seemingly about to speak, and studied the ring on her finger again.

"Tara, I've been around the world a half dozen times; I know a hundred ports. I'm in love with you. I'm old enough, experienced enough, to know that I have never felt anything like this before in my life. I doubt if I ever will again."

His expression was a little rueful when he looked at her again. "Really. Any man would know that you're beautiful. Any man would want to touch you. Beauty has its own fascination. I don't know where it changed. When it was exactly that I started to long just to hear your voice. When I thought about you from the time I awoke to the time I went to sleep, and then again in my dreams. I couldn't breathe without imagining your scent. I couldn't look anywhere without imagining you there. It wasn't just the wanting anymore. It was the knowing—albeit not without more than a bit of an internal battle—that I would never get you out of my soul. I love you. The ring is offered in all sincerity—I want you to marry me. I'd marry you today, this very hour—this second. But I understand you, too, Tara. I think that you love me. I know that you're frightened, and I don't blame you. But I'm frightened, too. For you. I don't know if it can help or not, but my ring will mark you as a woman who isn't alone, and that may protect you, telling others that they can't harm you with impunity.''

Tara stared at him, speechless, as his words fell over her like the softest, most enchanting velvet mist. He loved her; she believed it. No man could speak so tensely, so softly, so deeply from the heart—and be lying.

It was just so hard to believe in fantasy. In magic.

And they were coming closer and closer to Caracas.

He ran his thumb down her hand, then closed his fingers over it, encompassing. "Tara, say something. You're making me feel like a fool."

"I don't believe anyone could ever make you feel like a fool."

"You're doing a good job, Miss Hill."

She smiled, her throat constricting.

"Do you love me, Tara? Or are the things you whisper just lies in the dark?"

"I love you," she murmured.

"Excuse me. I didn't quite get that."

"I love you."

"Then?"

"I just wish...I don't know. I wish you weren't quite so rich. Or powerful. Or something."

He smiled. "You're not exactly poverty-stricken."

She laughed. "Oh, but I am! My bank accounts were so low that I *had* to come back to work."

"That's because you give away more than you earn. I'd love to be your tax man."

"You don't understand—"

"Oh, but I do. I wasn't born wealthy."

"You weren't?"

He grinned. "My father was actually a fireman in Glasgow. He had a penchant for the sea. He joined the navy, and he loved it. He found some backers and bought his first ship. He started in the Mediterranean. The first ship was successful, so he was able to fund another, and so on. Then he discovered that there was money to be made in gems and artifacts. By the time he died, well, he had gone from rags to riches. But I still remember the early days. He never forgot them, either. He left half a dozen trust funds to be used for scholarships and other incentive programs back in Glasgow.''

''Did he really? I'd love to have known him!''

''He was an all right guy,'' Rafe murmured.

''That's your accent!'' she said suddenly.

''I don't have an accent.''

''Only a slight one.''

''You're avoiding the issue.''

''I know. I don't have an answer.''

''Tara . . .'' He took her hand again, as if he was going to speak. Then he shook his head. ''We've got to get back. The ship is going to sail.''

''Oh, yes! And we have a showing this afternoon!''

Tara jumped to her feet, making a move to take off the ring.

It wouldn't budge. It was just that shade too snug.

''Divine justice!'' Rafe laughed, taking her arm. ''You see, you're supposed to accept.''

''Oh, Rafe, I really can't—''

''It seems you have to, for the moment.''

''But—''

He pulled her close. She felt as if she sensed everything around her acutely: the birds flying against the sky; soft clouds against the mountains; the buildings below them; the hawkers in the streets; the ships out in the sea; the ground beneath her feet.

His arms around her. She was in love. As she'd never been in love before. Knowing bliss just because they were together, because she could rest her face against his chest. She was dizzy with the feeling of it. The ring was stuck on her finger, where it belonged.

"Let's go," he whispered.

Arm in arm, laughing over everything they saw, laughing just for the pleasure of it, they returned to the ship. He left her at her cabin door, since she had to go to work. The Galliard girls were skipping dinner that night; the fashion show was set to begin at ten.

Of course, Ashley instantly saw the ring, and of course, being Ashley, she broke into a spate of endless congratulations, gasping in an occasional breath of air. Tara was convinced that at least ten minutes passed before she could get a word in edgewise.

"Ashley, I don't think I'm keeping it."

"What do you mean, you don't think you're keeping it? It's an engagement ring! A man asks you to marry him. You say yes, or you say no. You don't say maybe, let me try the ring for a while!"

"I didn't, Ashley. He put the ring on my finger, and it's stuck."

"Serves you right! What kind of a fool would turn him down?"

"I didn't turn him down."

"Then you're engaged."

"No, I'm not."

"Yes, you are."

"Oh, God! I'm going to try Vaseline."

She did, but to her amazement, she still couldn't get the ring off.

"You *are* engaged!"

"My finger is swollen because I've been tearing at it so long," Tara sighed.

"You're engaged."

''We're both going to be unemployed if we don't go and dress!''

Ashley agreed. Moments later, they were climbing into their first outfits of the evening. They were in a crew lounge just off the main ballroom. Cassandra was going on about the romance of it all.

Strangely, Mary was silent.

Madame told Tara that she was an idiot if she didn't marry the man. ''Beauty is a fleeting thing, young woman.''

Tara laughed. ''Madame, these are the eighties! Marriage is not a woman's only option.''

''Being alone is no great picnic either!'' Madame retorted. She sighed wistfully. ''I was in love, once. I wanted my career, though. That was years ago. Men weren't terribly liberated then.''

''What happened?'' Cassandra asked.

''Well, I had a glorious career.''

''And hasn't it been satisfying?''

''Not as satisfying as a handful of grandchildren would be right now. But then, you young things, you know how to do it all. More power to you. You only go around once, you know. When you see something out there, grab it! Take it all, everything you can see!''

''What about love?'' Cassandra asked.

''But she is in love with him!'' Ashley stated.

''Talk about having your cake and eating it, too!'' Madame said, laughing. ''Young lady, you've had some bad breaks. Looks like the good ones are coming your way now. He's a nice man, all right. All the way around. You marry him. Be happy. You haven't been really happy since I've known you.''

''She was once—'' Cassandra said, then broke off awkwardly.

Mary continued for her. "No, she wasn't," she said bitterly. "Not with Tine. She was always fighting him. Right from the very beginning. She was just so young that she had to learn how."

"We get to Caracas tomorrow," Ashley murmured.

"Would you all stop it!" Tara begged. "You're making it sound like a death knell. Madame, I think something is wrong with one of the hooks in the back. Could you check, please?"

She hopped up on a chair. The gold lamé she was wearing was nearly backless, and it didn't feel at all secure.

"Oh, dear! Someone caught this on something. The button is missing. I'll have to use pins."

"Breathe carefully!" Ashley laughed.

"Oh, hush!" Madame told her.

But it was the truth. Everyone knew that Madame was lethal with pins. Tara stood still while the back of her dress was fixed.

There was a knock at the door. Cassandra went off to answer it, then came back in with Rafe. He was greeted with a burst of congratulations.

He was in black. Tara would always love him in black. He wore a vested tux, white shirt, black tie. Smooth, elegant. The black accentuated his hair and eyes and the sleekness of his build. The white shirt made his features look all the more bronzed, all the more striking. All men, she thought, looked good in nicely tailored suits.

But no one looked as good as Rafe.

He listened to the chatter from Cassandra and Ashley, then glanced curiously at Tara. He thanked them and came over to her, then placed his hands around her waist, lifted her from the chair, and kissed her lightly.

She gasped, "Ohh . . . my God!"

He drew away. "The kiss was that good?"

"No—I've got pins sticking in my back."

He shook his head. "Tara, you'll certainly never over-inflate my ego."

The others laughed. He leaned toward her and whispered in her ear. "Are we engaged?"

"I—"

"We'll talk about it later, huh? I just came by to tell you that I'd be in the audience. George caught me in the hallway. He wants to buy us all some champagne in celebration."

"George knows?"

"Tara, everyone knows."

"Oh," she said a little weakly.

"Love me?" he queried, and she felt all the gold and amber tenderness in the eyes that demanded an answer.

"Yes. But—"

"Then it seems that we *are* engaged. Since the ring is stuck and George is buying champagne, and since I love you and you love me . . ."

She paused, but could not control the radiant smile that illuminated her features.

The magic was real.

He kissed her quickly. "I'll be waiting for you, gnashing my teeth each time I hear some guy sigh when you waltz by him!"

He smiled and left.

Ashley plopped into a chair. "That you could even think about turning him down is a sin! He looks just like Gable tonight! I can just see him at the foot of a stairway! If he were going to carry *me* off, I'd probably expire at the thought before I even got to enjoy it!"

"Ashley, I've seen you turn your nose up at a dozen adoring hunks!"

"Never the right hunk!" Ashley complained.

Tara smiled, still wrapped up in her happiness. Just before they left she noticed that Mary was still silent, and she made a mental note to talk to her later to see if anything was wrong.

Rafe stood at the back of the ballroom to watch the show.

The place was packed—this was an experience few people were ever likely to witness again, unless they were with the press, or wealthy enough to visit Galliard's showroom.

And Galliard's shows were all good, Rafe knew. Galliard was not of the belief that a model should be wooden. His models moved fluidly; they smiled. He always addressed them by name, and in a tone of voice that would lead anyone to assume they were people to him, not objects. This added something special.

Along with the lights, the music, the flowing magic of the gowns... and the women themselves.

Not that Rafe really noticed the others. Once he had gazed at her and noted merely that she was beautiful. It had been with an objective, even cold, eye.

Had that ever really been so?

Each time she appeared now, his heart quickened. He couldn't seem to breathe; his collar tightened. Whenever he saw her smile, he melted inside. Her hair trailed behind her in skeins of silk and gold, and he remembered how it felt to his fingers, when it brushed against his chest. Each time she turned his way, he recalled the way her eyes had glinted silver in the moonlight, silver with innocence, silver with trust, with passion, laughter.

He had to tell her. He had to get the words out now, before it was too late. If he lost her...

He swallowed, amazed at the pain that wrenched him. He had been so certain of himself, of his experience, of his immunity. He had told himself that she was just another beautiful woman. But she wasn't. She was unique. She had held away from him; she had come to him. Slowly she had smiled, taken his hand, and still, to his once hardened amazement, he couldn't quite believe that she was now more important to him than air, than water.

He had to make her understand.

But not tonight, he cried inwardly. The ring was on her finger. They would be with others, but then they would be alone, and he just couldn't take the chance of giving up this night.

Rafe blinked suddenly; the lights had come up, the show was over. He stood there, feeling the heat that rushed through him.

No, he couldn't tell her tonight. Tomorrow they would reach Caracas, and once they were there, he would find a way to tell her that Jimmy had been—was—his stepbrother.

He moved through the crowd, ready to wait in the hallway for the girls to appear.

He was still standing there when Sandy Martin, the ruffled, tawny-haired reporter from L.A. came upon him.

"Mr. Tyler!"

Rafe didn't like the man—he was a sensationalist. Rafe quirked a brow, waiting for him to go on.

"You promised me an exclusive," the reporter complained. "The whole ship knows that you and Tara Hill are engaged."

"Sorry, Martin. I wasn't really thinking about the press when I asked the lady."

"Lady," Martin said softly. It sounded a little bit like a sneer. Rafe's fists tightened at his side, and he clenched his teeth, reminding himself to be civil.

"Excuse me, Martin. What was that?"

Martin backed away a little. "I didn't say anything, Mr. Tyler. Nothing at all. But tell me, are you aware that she was accused of murder two years ago in Caracas?"

"I am aware of everything about her, Mr. Martin. And I believe in her innocence of any wrongdoing."

Sandy Martin snickered. "Did you ever know Tine Elliott?"

"No, I did not. What's your point?"

"Oh, nothing. He was as smooth as silk. Some people speculated that she'd bide her time and go back to him. It was supposed to have been a real hot and heavy romance. Which is easy to understand. I mean, Tara Hill has a lot more than beauty. She's like a walking, uh—well, you know what I mean."

"No. I don't know what you mean."

"Nothing bad." He laughed a little awkwardly. "She just kind of makes a man think of the best time he ever had in his life, you know?"

If he clenched his teeth any tighter, they would crack. He reached deep within himself for every ounce of self-control.

"Martin, I can't exactly ask you to leave my ship. I promised you an exclusive—you'll get it. But until then, do us both a favor, huh? Keep out of my way. If I ever hear you so much as whisper her name in your leering little fashion, I don't think I can be held responsible for my re-action. Now, if you'll excuse me—there are a dozen other places where you could be on this ship."

Sandy Martin didn't hesitate. He paled enough so that his freckles stood out on his face, backed away a step or two and started stuttering. "I didn't, uh, I didn't mean anything. Just that you're a lucky man. You know what I mean. Never mind." He turned around and fled just as the doors opened and Tara came out.

Smiling. Her silver eyes were only for him. Rafe caught her against his chest for a second, breathing in the scent of her hair, feeling her warmth, her heartbeat.

I'd throttle him if he touched her! he thought savagely.

"What's wrong?" she asked, suddenly worried, and it touched him deeply that she could read all the subtle nuances of his body.

"Nothing. When I hold you, nothing in the world."

They went downstairs, where Galliard's party took up half of the smallest, most intimate lounge. A few of the ship's officers occupied the remainder of the room.

The captain and Mary were together, Rafe noted, and he grinned, thinking that the man certainly seemed to have a bad case of infatuation.

George bought the first bottles of champagne, then declared that it was Rafe's ship and Rafe's engagement, and Rafe laughed and ordered the next round.

They danced beneath spiraling lights, oblivious of everyone else.

When the wee hours came, Rafe suggested that Tara retire with Ashley, then slip through to him.

She didn't bother with any pretense; they said goodnight to Ashley in the hallway.

And then they were alone, she in his arms.

"It's amazing," he told her. "George creates the most bewitching clothing. This gown is fabulous on you—and I can't wait to get it off you."

She laughed, a breathy, wonderful sound that mingled with the rest of her to arouse him to a fever pitch. Something on the gown ripped.

"I'll buy it," he groaned against her hair.

"You can't. I own it."

"Good."

She fumbled with his tie, brushing his throat with the engagement ring. He carefully stepped out of his trousers, yelping slightly as she caught him again across the belly with the ring.

"Damn! Maybe I shouldn't have insisted on that thing!"

"It doesn't come off."

"From now on, it had better not."

"Stop moaning, then."

"You wounded me."

"I'll kiss it and make it better."

"Wound me, then, wound me."

And, laughing, she began to kiss him, and he began to kiss her, and their laughter subsided into the sound of their heartbeats and the ragged whispers they exchanged.

The cabin phone let out a screech. Rafe sprang from the bed to catch it before it woke Tara, who was still sleeping with the most beautiful, soft smile on her lips.

"Yes," he said.

"Call from the States, sir. Mrs. Tyler. Shall I put it through?"

He closed his eyes. Myrna. "Yes, of course, please," he said softly.

"Rafe, can you hear me?" She was shouting.

He kept his voice low. "Yes, clearly."

"Oh, God, I'm so sorry to bother you. I wouldn't except that, oh, Rafe, I just read the papers!"

She was trying to sound calm. He knew that she had been crying.

"I'm sorry. What are you talking about?"

"It's front page news up here. 'Millionaire Playboy to Wed Galliard Girl.'"

"Oh." Damn! The press did move swiftly!

"Rafe, I don't mean to question you. But you haven't—you haven't forgotten Jimmy? I don't mean to question your judgment, but she's our only hope! You won't risk finding him, Rafe? I mean, I've never known you to be taken in or fooled, but she was there. She was with him...." Her voice trailed away. Pathetically.

"I haven't forgotten, Myrna. Please, trust me."

"I do," Myrna said.

He wasn't sure that the words had conviction. He sighed softly. "Please don't worry."

"You'll let me know as soon as you learn anything?"

"I promise."

"I'm sorry, Rafe—"

"Don't be. Please. Trust me."

"I will. I'll talk to you soon."

"Soon. Take care."

"You take care, too. I couldn't bear it if you, ah, if you were hurt in any way."

"I won't be. Goodbye, and don't worry."

He hung up, then pressed his temples with his fingers. He glanced over at the bed. Her hair spilled over his pillow; she was still wearing that smile that could have melted rock.

He closed his eyes. He loved her; he believed in her.

But he couldn't tell her anything. He couldn't afford to have her turn against him.

And no matter what he felt, he couldn't jeopardize his chances. Myrna's chances. Jimmy's chances. What if it were all a lie? What if she had smiled at Jimmy the same way she smiled at him?

No...

He walked over to the porthole and moved the draperies.

They were in Caracas. He saw the mountain, purple and green, shrouded in mist, rising in front of the ship as they approached land.

Caracas...

He closed his eyes tightly. They were here; he could feel it, feel the tension rising like the mist. He and Tara had been coming closer and closer to the past.

They were here.

She stirred, shading her eyes against the morning light, then smiled tentatively, only half awake. "Are we here?"

Her lashes shaded her cheeks; her hair was sun against the sheets. The exquisite lines of her body curved as she stretched.

He came back to the bed, lay down beside her and took her in his arms. "We're not quite there—we're here," he murmured. And he kissed her forehead, then her cheeks, and then her lips.

The day could wait. It seemed urgent that he make the dawn last.

11

It should have taken most of the day to make the move from the ship to the hotel. Between everyone's personal belongings and the Galliard creations and accessories, there was quite a bit to be transported.

But there were no delays, no customs problems, no traffic. And at the hotel, there was absolutely no wait at the reception desk. The manager himself greeted them. Everything had worked out incredibly smoothly.

Ashley and Tara were together again, on the fourth floor.

The room was very similar to the one she had stayed in last time in Caracas—with Tine.

Ashley laughed when the bellhop left. "What do you want to bet that this room has a connecting door?"

Tara smiled. "It does. He called in before we left the ship."

Ashley arched a superbly shaped brow, then grinned. "Why didn't you just move in with him?"

Tara shrugged. "Well, I'm working."

Ashley frowned suddenly, stood and walked over to the window. "Where is he now?"

"Well, I expected this to take all day. His firm buys a lot of its gold here. And he has a store here, too. He had some business to attend to. I don't expect him back until late afternoon."

"We don't have to do anything tomorrow until the big showing for the South American aristocracy. We could stay here, of course, but why on earth would we want to? Tara, are you really all right?"

"Yes, I'm fine."

"I mean, being here hasn't made you queasy or anything?"

"Ashley, I've always loved Venezuela. The people are great. I can't blame the place for what happened."

"Are you afraid?"

"Of what?"

"Of Tine being here somewhere."

Tara shook her head. "I'm sure I'm not worth waiting two years for when he could get arrested here. No, I'm not afraid. Besides, I'm not going to run off anyplace by myself."

"Think we're safe enough in public?"

"Sure."

"I was just dying to go back to the glass factory. Last time I bought the most beautiful swans! I wanted to see what else they have that might complement—oh! I forgot! It was at the glass factory—"

"The glass factory wasn't guilty, either!" Tara exclaimed, laughing. "That's just where I met Jimmy. And it's all in the past, Ashley. If you want to buy some glass, we'll get a taxi and go right now."

"Maybe we shouldn't. What if Rafe comes back?"

"What if he does? I'll leave him a note."

"But—"

"Ashley." Tara interrupted a little harshly. "I'm in love with him. I want to spend my life with him. But I had a 'keeper' once. If I thought that I had to ask permission to go places, I wouldn't be with Rafe. I'll never live like that again! If I'd been the least bit wiser, I would have understood that Tine had no trust in me and no sense of security in himself—besides the fact that he was a criminal! Let's go. I'll leave Rafe a message at the desk.''

Ashley, a little stunned by the passion in Tara's voice, saluted sharply. "Yes, Ma'am! I'll call for a taxi."

She did. Seconds later, they were outside the elegant lobby, being helped into a taxi by a doorman.

"What a beautiful day!" Ashley murmured. She attempted some of her choppy Spanish on the taxi driver, who good-naturedly corrected her.

He was answering her, showing her something out the window, when she frowned and shook Tara's arm.

"We're being followed."

"Oh, come on, Ashley."

"I'm serious. That taxi left the hotel right when we did—and it's still behind us."

Tara felt as if her heart skipped a beat. She couldn't help it; she was suddenly frightened.

There definitely was a cab behind them. And Ashley could well be right—it might have been following them since they had left the hotel. She squinted; she couldn't see into the cab very well. Even though they were on a crowded street—Caracas was a big, modern city—and moving slowly, the windows of both cabs were tinted.

They came to a traffic light. Tara could see that there was one person in the rear of the cab. A man, who appeared to be elderly.

She looked at Ashley and shrugged. "Ash, one of the big tourist attractions here is the glass factory. I think every tour takes you there."

Ashley thought about it. "I suppose you're right. Maybe I should tell our driver to lose him."

"Not on your life!" Tara protested. Their driver was already moving incredibly fast for her. And they were leaving the city behind them, speeding toward the mountain.

Ashley sighed and leaned back. "Well, don't blame me if that cab catches us."

"Ashley, if we told our driver to lose that cab, it would probably catch up with us anyway. Like you said, the old guy is probably headed for the glass factory, too!"

Ten minutes later, they had climbed high along the mountain trail; through the trees, Tara could see the buildings of the glass factory.

Fear crept over her. Nothing had changed. The sand, the dirt, the stone paths, and the trees were just the same.

Even the sky was the same, just beginning to cloud, beautifully blue above the vegetation that hugged the mountain. Eventually night would come, and it would be completely dark, except for the light of the stars.

Tine had disappeared into the trees. Jimmy, too, had simply disappeared. No one had ever found either of them.

"We're here." Ashley prodded her. Tara made herself smile, because Ashley looked so worried.

Ashley paid the cabdriver, who assured her they would have no difficulty getting back. They crawled from the cab, and Tara was certain that he was right—there was an abundance of tour buses and taxis parked on the grounds.

The cab they had noticed on their way was pulling in behind them. It seemed to slow, then continue—parking behind one of the tour buses.

"What do you make of that? The cab that was following us slowed down, then speeded up," Tara said.

Ashley frowned. "Maybe we should just go back."

"No. It's broad daylight. Nothing can happen."

"Maybe we should get inside. Either the store or the workshop."

Tara shook her head. "I want to see who was in that cab."

"How will you be able to tell? There are a dozen people getting off the buses."

Tara shook her head. "Let's just pretend we're waiting for someone."

"Okay."

They stood there and waited. People came and went. Most of the visitors seemed to be from cruise ships; they were laughing, wearing ridiculous straw hats and gaily showing one another their purchases.

"How long should we wait?" Ashley asked.

Tara shook her head and shrugged with disgust. "This is stupid. Let's just go."

"All right. We'll go in quickly."

"No, we won't! I'm not going to be neurotic. Let's go watch them working, get a soda, and then we'll shop and leave."

"Tara, if you're uncomfortable—"

"I'm not!"

"Okay," Ashley said. "Let's go, then."

They went down a few steps to follow the path to the workshop. Tara loved to watch the glassblowers—it always seemed so amazing to her that the men could take such a mass of nothing, heat it, and then blow and mold it into a thing of beauty. They watched a young mustached man with wonderful showmanship craft an exquisite owl. They applauded with the others and moved around the outside of the protective railing to watch an older man, stout and grim, form an elegant fluted glass.

Tara stared across the room. The railing followed the outline of the building; the artisans could be viewed from either side.

She frowned, noticing an older man on the other side. He was tall and stately and white-haired, and she could have sworn that she had seen him somewhere else.

"Ashley—look casually across. Do you think that man could be the man in the cab? Does he look familiar to you?"

Ashley wasn't exactly casual. She stared. The gentleman moved back into the crowd.

"He saw us looking at him, and he moved," Tara said.

"Ooh, Tara! He did look familiar!"

"I saw him. And I saw his back on the ship the other day! He came in on our ship—that's it! Curaçao! When I was waiting for Rafe. I saw him walking away, down one of the hallways!"

"But Tara, I wasn't there, and I saw him before and—oh!"

"What?"

"The restaurant! That's the man who had lunch with Rafe the day that we met him!"

"His uncle—or so he said."

"Tara! Why would he lie?"

"Why would his uncle be on the ship—why wouldn't Rafe even bother to have him join us once?"

Ashley had no answer for that one. Tara pursed her lips grimly and started walking.

"What are you doing?" Ashley asked anxiously.

"I'm going to ask him!"

"Wait, Tara—"

"Just hurry! Or I'll lose him!"

"Coming, coming," Ashley muttered.

There suddenly seemed to be people everywhere. Tara determinedly moved through them, murmuring a dozen excuse-mes. She came out of the building, into the sunlight again, and saw him hurrying past the soda machines.

She was so busy watching him that she didn't notice the tall, broad Latino she suddenly crashed into full force. He was young. He caught her arms, then gave her a sexy smile. "Hello."

"Hello. Excuse me." Quickly she jerked her arms free and dashed after her prey, Ashley still on her heels.

He was starting to move toward the buses. She followed. "Wait! Sir! Wait!"

She was almost on top of him. Unable to ignore her anymore, he stopped, an unhappy expression on his face.

"Sir! You're related to Rafe Tyler!"

"Uh—"

"Please. You were with him in the Plaza. Having lunch. And you were on the boat. And you were just following us!"

He grimaced sheepishly. "Not doing a very discreet job of it, eh?" he said with a sigh.

Tara frowned. "I don't understand. Why weren't you with us on the ship? You are his uncle, aren't you?"

"In a way."

Ashley, panting, reached them. "Hi," she said, out of breath.

"Hi," the man said.

"I'm Ashley."

"I'm Sam."

"Sam! Good, that's a start!" Tara snapped. "Now, Sam, what is going on here?"

Sam didn't have a chance to answer. From behind Tara came an unknown voice, accented, deep.

"My love! There you are! I've been waiting. How good it is to see you!"

Confused, Tara began to turn. She barely saw the Latin man with whom she had just collided, and then she was gasping, because he swooped her into his arms, holding her in such a crush that she could barely breathe, much less speak.

"Tara!" she heard Ashley scream. She dimly saw that Ashley tried to come after her but that another young man stepped in her way and crudely knocked Ashley down.

The old man, Sam, was white. She was terrified to see him start running and then fall from a well-aimed and determined blow like the one that had sent Ashley to her knees.

Tara opened her mouth and screamed. Her captor's arms tightened more securely about her.

"Someone wants to see you, baby! And it's worth a lot of money!"

She screamed again. She could hear a murmur of voices. She struggled, managing to tear a nice gouge out of her assailant's face.

But all to little avail. Tourists were beginning to murmur, as if they were beginning to realize that this wasn't a lovers' tryst at all.

But could anyone help? She was being swiftly carried toward a waiting compact car, the engine running, a driver ready to hit the gas the minute she was tossed into the back seat.

Panic seized her. She was afraid that she would lose consciousness.

She should have never come back. It seemed that Tine had waited for her after all.

No! She wasn't a fatalist—and she wasn't going to be anyone's victim. Not while she could still scream, still breathe, still move. She started struggling again, and screaming, wriggling so wildly that her captor had to slow down. She could see that Ashley was up again, shrieking that someone needed to help them.

Just then another car drove into the gravel parking lot. She could hear the sudden screech of the tires.

"Let her go! Now!"

Rafe's voice...

The man holding her hugged her tighter against him. She was aware of his cologne, aware of the rough fabric of his shirt against her cheek.

And then she felt another set of arms, wrenching at her, attacking the man.

The accomplice who had tripped Ashley was suddenly at Rafe's back. Rafe turned, slammed a fist into the man's gut, and turned back to Tara. This time when Rafe wrenched at her, her assailant let her go.

Rafe and Tara fell to the ground together.

Both men leaped into the metallic blue car. The tires screeched, dust and rock blew into their faces, and the car careered away down the path.

Rafe's arms tightened around Tara. She could hear the frantic beating of his heart, the rasping of his breath. He tilted her dirt-smudged face upward. "Are you all right?"

She nodded.

He helped her to her feet. Ashley, dusty, too, from her fall, came racing over.

Sam followed more slowly, watching Rafe unhappily.

"I've got to call the police. Ashley, stay with her. No, never mind. We'll all go together."

He caught Tara's hand and dragged her along to the shop, where he explained in Spanish what he wanted. A concerned salesgirl hurriedly handed him the phone. He talked to the police for a moment, describing the car, then hung up.

He gazed at Tara, and she wanted more than anything on earth to believe all the ravaged emotion in the golden gleam of his eyes. But she still hadn't spoken; she was definitely shaken, still trembling.

And still concerned.

Rafe had certainly made a timely appearance. And he hadn't registered the least surprise at seeing Sam.

"The police are coming. Can you talk to them all right?" he asked her.

She had barely answered when they heard the sirens.

One of the officers who came spoke English. He seemed to know Rafe—and he also seemed to be somewhat suspicious of her.

She hadn't met him two years ago—but it was more than possible that he had heard of her.

He questioned her. She told him exactly what had happened. When he seemed a little skeptical, Ashley interrupted vigorously, telling him that everything was exactly the way Tara had told it. Sam spoke up, agreeing with them both and demanding indignantly that the officer treat the victim more tenderly.

"Is someone trying to trail that car?" Rafe asked tensely.

"*Sí.* They will search for the car. We will do our best. Now, Miss Hill, you are certain you have heard nothing from this man, Tine Elliott, in the two years since he disappeared."

She knew that she was trembling. With outrage, with remembrance—with fear. "I'm positive!"

The officer nodded. "We'll take you back to the hotel. Please, don't wander around in the future."

"She won't," Rafe said grimly.

They returned to the hotel in the police car. It was a silent party. Tara was grateful to Rafe for his appearance, but despite her fear, anger was coming to a boil within her. Perhaps it was even the fear that was fueling the anger. She didn't know.

In the lobby, she suddenly balked, staring at Rafe. "Maybe you don't care about your uncle's health, but I do!" She spun around to face Sam. "Are you all right? I don't know why he's ignoring your existence, but I appreciate very much what you tried to do, and I'm concerned that you could have been hurt."

Sam flushed—his face crimson against the white of his hair. "I'm fine. Just a little dusty. A shower will take care of everything."

Sam wasn't going to give her a chance for any more questions. He waved quickly and disappeared into an elevator with an already closing door.

"Someone should find George and tell him what happened," Ashley murmured, and whether she was in earnest or merely wanted to escape the two of them, Tara didn't know. But the redhead gave them a weak smile and disappeared into the lounge.

"Are you sure you're okay?" Rafe asked Tara, looking her over thoroughly. "Maybe I should have taken you to the hospital—"

"I'm fine. I haven't got a scratch on me!" Tara snapped.

"Oh." He gazed at her again, more intently and seemed to stiffen. "Shall we talk upstairs?"

"Definitely."

They went up in the elevator, standing apart, exchanging not a word. Rafe opened his door.

Tara stepped in first. Rafe followed, pulling his dusty polo shirt over his head and tossing it in the corner.

"Should I order drinks?" he asked.

"Yes, I think you probably should," Tara said coolly. She wasn't feeling cool at all. She didn't know if she was still terrified—Tine was here! Alive! After her!—or merely devastated.

She didn't think that she could take it if everything she thought she knew about Rafe was a lie.

He walked to the phone and requested room service, gazing at her questioningly. She didn't speak, so he just ordered a bottle of rum and some Cokes.

He set the phone down and stood there, watching her with his jaw set, but a little warily, too, she thought. He knew what was coming.

"All right. What?" he asked.

"You don't need to ask that."

"Apparently I do."

"Okay. Sam was on the ship. Sam was following me today. Sam was with you in the restaurant. If this man is your uncle, why was he hiding on the ship?"

"He wasn't hiding."

"You gave me an engagement ring. Most men would introduce a handy relative to the woman they claimed they intended to marry."

He didn't blink. He just stood there in his jeans, feet slightly apart, muscled chest bare, flesh a little dusty. She almost lowered her eyes from his. He had that tiger look again. A look of cunning, of sleek power.

"Is he or isn't he a relative?"

Rafe cocked his head slightly. "He is—and he isn't. He worked for my father, and he works for me. But he met me the day I was born, so he's definitely family."

There was a knock at the door. Room service had arrived. Rafe let the man in, signed the bill, then fixed two drinks.

Strong drinks, Tara noticed. Well, he wasn't going to make her veer from her purpose.

He intended to, though. He handed her a glass that held far more rum than Coke and demanded a little harshly, "I don't think that Sam is really the important question at the moment. Someone just attempted to abduct you."

"I'm very aware of that."

"Are you? Good. There's safety in awareness."

"Rafe, what's going on!"

Tara realized then that neither of them had sat down. Nor were they touching. They were very carefully circling each other. For a moment, she thought that she was going to burst into tears. She didn't want suspicions. She wanted to run into his arms and believe that he could protect her against the Tines of the world forever.

And—oh, God!—she wanted to believe that he wasn't another Tine himself!

"Tara, I made Sam come in and eat lunch with me because I knew that you were in there—I overheard you tell your taxi driver to take you to the Oak Room. And I asked him to come on the trip for the same reason that I asked him to follow you today—to keep an eye on you."

She swallowed, feeling a smothering sensation come over her. He couldn't be like Tine, watching her, following her, spying on her.

"And you arrived so opportunely today because Sam called you to tell you that I'd left the hotel?" she asked him incredulously.

"Yes."

"Where were you, really?"

He hesitated. "At the police station. I wanted to see if anything new had been discovered. If they thought that there was any possibility that Tine was still in the country.

All right! Yes, damn it! Sam was watching you, with orders to tell me if you left the hotel."

"Why?"

"Why?" It seemed as if his temper suddenly snapped. "You little idiot, that's obvious!"

"Don't call me an idiot!"

"You went off, alone!"

She shook her head. "I went to the glass factory, to a place that's always full of tourists—"

"And you almost met your ex-lover again. I didn't interrupt something you were looking forward to, did I?"

She remained deathly still; the only sound in the room was her sharp and horrified gasp.

She didn't say anything to him; she merely set her drink down on the bedside table and turned around sharply, heading for the door to her room.

"Tara!" He caught her arm, bringing her back around, closing his arms around her. "I'm sorry, I'm sorry—"

"No! Let me go!"

"I can't, Tara! I'm sorry. I just get frightened now and then myself. My God. I love you so much—"

Something inside her snapped, too. It was the shattering truth of the day. She was in Caracas and Tine was in Caracas, and he was going to get her if he could. She was overwhelmed by a memory of the past that she couldn't bear. A memory of being held and forced, helpless beneath a greater strength.

She panicked. She gasped out inarticulate words and beat against his chest.

And Rafe didn't understand. He knew only that he loved her, that deep inside he was very afraid. He was afraid that she could be taken, that he wouldn't be there to help her.

Fear that he was a fool. That she didn't really want his help. That he had given his heart and soul to some beautiful temptress, the same one who had caused Jimmy's downfall....

"Tara, stop it, I love you!"

Savagely, he swept her into his arms, carrying them both down hard on the bed. He was half tenderness, half fury. He wanted to touch her; he wanted to assure her. He wanted to erase the past.

"Tara!"

She stopped hitting him. Her eyes were blank. She was as pale as a sheet.

He knew an even greater terror as he watched her.

He moved to the side of the bed, kneeling beside it. He stroked her face, his heart thundering madly. A doctor, he needed a doctor.

"Tara, it's all right. Tara! Come back to me! I won't touch you. My God, what's wrong?"

He drew a shaking finger down her cheek. "I love you. Talk to me. Talk to me. Tara, what's wrong?"

Tears came into her eyes and overflowed when she saw him there. "Oh, Rafe!"

"I'm here!"

Her arms curled around his neck. He held her there, smoothing back her hair while she cried. And somehow, in whispered words, in broken words, the whole story of that last awful day came out, and what she didn't say, he could piece together. He stiffened as she spoke, knowing that if he ever met Tine Elliott, he would want to kill the man, to tear him into fragments of spindrift to throw to the wind.

She was quiet after a while. He stretched out beside her and held her, her head against his chest, still moving his fingers through her hair with a trembling tenderness.

"I love you, Tara. I would never, never hurt you."

"I know. I'm sorry."

"My God, I'd like to kill him." He felt the little skip and beat of her heart.

"He wouldn't be worth it," she whispered. And then she buried her face against his chest in such aching trust that he could hardly bear it. "He is out there, though. I know he's out there."

Then where is Jimmy? He almost shouted the words, but he didn't. They'd gone too far today; she couldn't take any more shocks.

And no matter how he loved and trusted her, there was always that last little doubt that he couldn't ignore. If it were just him, he would. He would be a fool; he'd gladly give his life; he'd gamble on his love.

But it wasn't just him. Jimmy was still somewhere. Either dead or alive.

Her tears were damp on his chest. Mechanically, he continued to soothe her, his thoughts meeting a blank wall. He brought her tear-streaked face to his and kissed her, and that kiss led to another, and suddenly it kindled a fire. Dirt and dishevelment didn't mean a thing as they made love.

The room grew dark. Rafe mixed another drink; they were able to laugh at each other's appearance, and then move into the shower together.

Rafe emerged before she did. He stood by the window and looked out as darkness began to descend in earnest on the city.

He should make her go home. He should dress, drive her to the airport, make reservations for two, and go home with her.

But he couldn't do that. There was Jimmy to think about.

And there was Tine Elliott. Rafe had too many scores to settle with the man.

The only thing that he could do was stick with Tara. Stick tighter than glue.

And be ready.

12

Tara awoke the next morning because the phone was ringing. She really didn't want to open her eyes, and she didn't have to at first—Rafe picked up the phone.

But when she heard him say a sleepy good-morning to George Galliard, she knew that she was going to have to take the call. Rafe handed the receiver to her expressionlessly, and she took it.

"Good morning, George."

He called her *"ma petite"* and went on and on, telling her that he hadn't called last night because he had been sure that she had been resting. Tara thought that he knew she hadn't actually been resting, but perhaps he was being polite.

He went on and on—she didn't really get a chance to say anything for what seemed like a full five minutes. He was terribly worried. Perhaps she should board the next plane back to the States. Was she all right? How did she feel? If she couldn't manage the show, they could manage.

"Ah, Tara, Tara, Tara! I thought it would be good to bring you back here. I thought that nothing would happen, that you would go back to living normally—relaxed, you know. And instead, this!"

"George, I wasn't hurt at all," Tara said. "I'm fine. I can do the show with absolutely no difficulty."

"But your safety, *ma chérie*!"

"George—what can happen to me in an entire roomful of people?"

"Perhaps it was not Tine at all. Perhaps it was a random happening."

"Perhaps it was," Tara agreed. She didn't believe it—not for a second. She wished that she could. Tine Elliott was out there. God alone knew why; he hadn't really loved her. Ever. He was probably incapable of really loving anyone.

"Still, maybe you should get on the next plane."

That was definitely another thing she had thought about herself. Rafe had suggested it last night, quietly, when room service had delivered their dinner.

And it had been a great temptation. But it would have been wrong. What she needed to do was plan a way to trap Tine. If he wanted her—for whatever reason—he could find her. Maybe he had just been lying in wait down here, but she would never doubt that with his resources he could obtain false papers, a false identity—and come after her, wherever she went.

"I'm fine, George. The police have been alerted. I don't want to go."

"Bravo! We should end this thing, don't you think?"

"Yes."

"Then I shall see you soon. I'm sure that you are as safe as you can possibly be, with Rafe Tyler at your side."

She didn't glance Rafe's way. "Yes," she told George softly.

George repeated that he would see her soon and rang off. Rafe silently took the receiver back from Tara and set it on its cradle.

He gazed at her with arched brows, and she drew the covers up around her chest, hugging herself a little nervously.

"He thinks I should leave."

His eyes moved from hers, and he spoke very quietly. "So do I. And then again, I don't. I don't like the idea of your being frightened for the rest of your life because Tine Elliott might reappear."

"It's not just Tine," Tara murmured. She lowered her eyes to her hands, nervously clutching the sheets. "I don't think anyone ever believed me about Jimmy Saunders. No, I shouldn't say that. George believed me, and the girls believed me. But—well, I wasn't really that close to any of them. Not the way I've become now. I could only have lunch, shop and do that type of thing when Tine was off on business—smuggling, as it turned out. The fact that I met Jimmy, that he had become such a friend so quickly, was something I hadn't told anyone about, and so of course it looked like I was making things up."

She looked up; Rafe had moved. His feet were on the floor; his naked back was to her.

He seemed so stiff, as if all the muscles in his back and shoulders had tensed.

"Rafe?"

"I'm going to hop in the shower," he told her.

He stood, heedless of his naked state, entirely graceful and natural, and started for the shower. He disappeared into the bathroom, then paused a minute and turned back to her.

There seemed to be a careful mask over his features. He smiled. "Are you going to join me?"

Something in her expression must have given away her concern at his appearance. He came back to her and kissed her nose, then her lips.

"Going to join me?" he asked more huskily.

"Rafe?"

"I love you," he told her suddenly. He said the words with a vehemence and passion that was startling, then caught her chin in his palm, tilting her face to his and repeated his words more softly.

"I love you, too," she whispered. They stared at each other. The phone started to ring. Rafe swore softly and answered it.

"Mary. Good morning. Yes, she's absolutely fine. Yes, she's coming down to work. Here, I'm sure you'll feel better talking to her yourself."

With a grimace, he handed the phone to Tara. "I'll start without you," he told Tara in a mockingly aggrieved tone, clamping a hand over the receiver as he gave it to her. She laughed softly and told him she'd be there in just a second, covering the receiver herself to hide her own whisper.

Tara watched him walk into the bathroom, her heart thudding harder with emotion. He was beautiful, she thought. A bit savage, a bit primitive, and completely sophisticated all in one. A very elite tiger, a totally unique and independent cat. She bit her lip softly, so glad that he existed, so glad that he had chosen to love her.

Especially now. Any other man would have turned from her with all of this hanging over her head, with an ex-lover who was a smuggler, possibly a murderer...

And seeking some form of revenge, or something, from her.

But Rafe loved her. And it was so easy to love him back. The attraction was as natural as breathing; the ecstasy that had been such a physical tie had become something so much more.

She remembered that Mary was on the phone, and she jerked her hand off the receiver. "Mary!"

"You okay?" Mary asked, although Tara was certain that Mary had already been informed that she was fine.

"Yes, completely. Thanks for asking, though. Thanks for caring."

"Well, I suppose a person always wants to hear it from the horse's mouth."

"I look like a horse, huh?"

"Sure. A Thoroughbred. Where's Rafe right now?"

"In the shower. Why?"

"Good. I didn't want your expression to change any. I have to talk to you, Tara."

"About what?"

"I don't want to talk over the phone. You are coming down for the show, right?"

"Yes."

"Don't run off as soon as it's over. I have something to tell you."

"About Rafe?"

"Yes."

"Mary..."

She fought it; she fought the horrible sensation sweeping over her. She had been so in love. She was still in love, terribly in love, ridiculously in love. The fear didn't change that. But it did make her skin damp and clammy, caused goose bumps to appear on her flesh.

There just couldn't be anything wrong about Rafe, about the depths of her feelings, the need, the desire.

"Mary." She forced herself to inhale smoothly. "Mary, should I be afraid of Rafe?"

"Afraid of him? Of him harming you physically? Oh, no! Sorry, Tara, I forgot how sensitive you must be. No, no. That's not what I meant at all. I just think there's something you ought to know if you don't already."

"Mary—"

''I don't want to talk on these phones. I'll see you downstairs.''

The phone clicked and buzzed. Mary meant it—she wasn't going to talk on the phone.

''Great!'' Tara muttered. ''Get me all upset and hang up on me! Just what I need!''

Her heart suddenly took off too quickly as she gazed toward the bathroom, and she wondered painfully what Mary was talking about. Her breath came too quickly; her palms were damp.

''No,'' she murmured.

The shower was running, but suddenly he was looking around the door frame; his seductive eyes were on her.

''Are you coming in?''

Her mouth felt dry. Of course! she wanted to cry.

She shook her head and fought for speech. ''I'm just going to grab your robe and slip next door. All my things are over there.''

His expression didn't change; she couldn't tell what he was thinking. Was he worried, anxious, suspicious, disappointed—or did he simply accept that she was supposed to be downstairs soon, cool and collected and ready to work?

''Don't leave that room without me!'' he warned her darkly.

She smiled. ''No, I won't.''

His head disappeared back into the bathroom. She tossed the covers off and bolted out of bed, shivering miserably. She drew in a deep breath, grabbed his robe and slipped into the next room, anxious to ask Ashley if she knew what Mary was talking about.

Ashley wasn't there. There was still steam coming out of the bathroom; she had probably showered and gone down to join Cassandra and Mary for breakfast.

Tara sighed. If Mary had something to tell her, she wouldn't have told it to anyone else anyway. Mary was completely capable of keeping a secret.

Tara hurried into her own shower. She was still shivering; still anxious, still a little bit in shock.

And feeling miserably ill. As she stood beneath the hot spray of the shower she reminded herself that Mary had been appalled when Tara had asked if she should be frightened of Rafe. So it couldn't be anything too bad, could it?

She prayed not. She thought that she'd rather be thrown over a cliff by Tine than discover that she had been a fool, that she had been used when she had given in to instinct and fallen head over heels in love.

Twenty minutes later, she was dressed and ready. She almost left the room alone, but then she remembered the events of the day before and slipped back into Rafe's room. He was standing in front of the mirror, grimacing as he adjusted his tie.

Instinct prevailed again. Tara moved over to him and took the tie in her hands, her eyes on her task, her fingers trembling only slightly. She felt the warmth of his breath and slowly looked up into his eyes.

"What's the matter?" he asked her.

She smiled. "Nothing. And everything, of course."

"Why did you leave?"

She shrugged, concentrating on his tie once again. "Because you're a little bit too tempting in the shower, and this is George's big day before the grandes dames of South America. And I need some coffee desperately."

She knew he didn't believe her. But he didn't challenge her. When he moved to open the door for her, his jacket was slightly drawn back, and she stopped, gasping, aware that he was wearing a shoulder holster—and carrying a gun.

The blood must have drained completely from her face.

"Tara," he said impatiently, "this is protection. For you. God knows what that man intends. I only know what *I* intend, and that is that he isn't going to have a chance to pull anything. Let's go."

She didn't have a chance to reply; he took her elbow and led her out into the hallway. He was subtle, but she realized uneasily that he was prepared to have something jump out at them from every nook and cranny.

Nothing did. They met the others down in the dining room. Everyone else had eaten; they were all on their second cups of coffee. Tara knew she couldn't eat a thing. She kept staring at Mary imploringly, but Mary carefully kept looking away. George and Rafe talked, everyone asked after Tara, Madame showing special concern. Tara wanted to scream. It felt as if the tension was mounting with no break. What had she expected?

Not for things to happen this fast! Not for the attempt against her to be made in the first few hours that she had been here.

George rose, calling over to the assistants that they had better get started; they were scheduled to begin in an hour. He told the girls that the dressing room was stage left in the grand ballroom, and then he softly asked Rafe, "You'll be around?"

"Right outside the doorway," Rafe assured him. "And we'll have police in the audience."

George nodded and signed the breakfast check, and the party began to move.

The tables in the grand ballroom were beautifully set in peach and cream, with single fluted candles and white and peach roses. A small orchestra was warming up. There was a podium for George, and a special table for the press. George had the girls walk the runway to accustom themselves to it, and reminded Madame of the order of the program. Madame listened, then muttered that she was no fool, George should realize by now that she knew exactly what she was doing—and his models weren't dummies, either!

Rafe stood, arms crossed, beside George while the models tested the runway. As soon as they were ready to start for the dressing room, he returned to Tara's side, and fell into step with her. Before she entered the dressing room, he squeezed her elbow and told her that he would be right outside.

She stared into his eyes, those fascinating amber orbs, which were studying her so intently.

So caringly, so passionately. She sensed that he would gladly die before he let anything happen to her, and felt herself melting inside, because she loved him so much.

What in God's name did Mary know?

He kissed her lips lightly. "I'll be here. Go dazzle South America."

She smiled and slipped into the dressing room. She looked instantly toward Mary, but Mary shook her head, indicating that the others were all around them, Madame and one of her seamstresses, Cassandra and Ashley. And of course Ashley, bless her, kept close to Tara like a second skin, still concerned about the events at the glass factory.

Tara mechanically put on her first outfit. Madame moved around her, brushed her hair, touched up her makeup. They all talked, and Tara made conversation, too, without the least idea of what she was saying. She didn't know if she was more distressed about the knowledge that Tine was out there somewhere...or that Mary knew something about Rafe that made her acutely uneasy. Tara wasn't sure she could go through the whole show without knowing. She was afraid she would stop somewhere on the runway and simply start to scream.

But she didn't, of course. She was well trained. She moved on time; she smiled; she spun. She opened jackets, pivoted, smiled some more. Silks and gauzes flowed behind her. She even saw the audience, or parts of it. There might be a tremendous amount of poverty in South America, but not at this elite showing. The audience glittered with gold, silver, diamonds. She didn't think she had ever seen such an array of beautiful, elegant and sophisticated women, dark-haired, demure, aristocratic. Beautiful young women, beautiful mature women.

Each model had ten changes. Every time Tara walked around the end of the runway back to the dressing room she saw Rafe in the shadows and knew that he waited.

The show seemed interminable. She began to pray that it would end. And, of course, like all things, it did. George finished his last speech in his French-tinged English, added a few words in faulty Spanish, and then there was a tremendous burst of applause.

Tara knew that her employer was in his element. People were rushing up to him, complimenting his genius. He was ecstatic.

She gave him little thought, though. They were all back in the dressing room, the Galliard creations all being carefully replaced in their garment bags.

Mary caught Tara as she pulled her cool cotton sarong back over her head. "Dress slowly! I'll talk to you as soon as the others are gone."

Tara nodded. That feat wasn't as easy as it should have been—Ashley, concerned, kept urging her to hurry.

"Darn! I ripped my stockings!" Tara lied guiltily. "Ashley, please go on out and wait with Rafe, would you? Keep him entertained for me for a minute?"

"Okay. Mary are you going to be in here?"

"Yes, I'll wait for her. I won't leave her alone for a minute, I promise."

Ashley went out. Madame was still fussing around. Mary pretended to have a bunch of snarls in her hair, but then at last Madame left, reminding Mary to lock the door. Though the gowns belonged to the girls, they were still to be kept under lock and key. Not just anyone could own a Galliard.

The door closed. Tara turned to her friend. "Mary, I'm about to go insane! Damn it, tell me!"

Mary did, quickly. "Maybe I shouldn't tell you this. Maybe I should just have left things alone. I can't help it, though. I feel you have a right to know."

Tara frowned. "Mary, you've suspected something for a while, haven't you? What is it?"

Mary sighed. "Remember the captain on the ship?"

"Of course. He was charming. Oh, you thought so, too."

Mary nodded unhappily. "He is a charming, charming man. And horrible at deceit of any kind."

"Please, Mary, go on."

"I tried to tell you yesterday, but you were with Rafe, and then you and Ashley were already gone when I called your room. And then, well, no one could have gotten to you last night."

"Mary, please!"

"The captain let something slip when we were together. I had been casually talking about Rafe, saying what a wonderful, approachable human being he was for all his wealth and power. He agreed with me—he admires him

very much. I started saying how happy I was for you—
you'd had such a raw deal before. And then he told me
that the whole thing two years ago had been a tragedy for
Rafe, as well as you. I tried not to pounce on him, and I
must have been fairly casual, because I got him to tell me
the whole story."

"What story?" Tara nearly screamed.

"Tara—remember Jimmy Saunders? The man the police wouldn't believe even existed?"

"Of course," Tara said dully. "I could never forget
him."

"Well, he *did* exist. In fact, he was born James Saunders, but his legal name was—or is—*James Tyler*. Tara,
he's Rafe's stepbrother. Apparently, from what I could
discover from my captain, Jimmy used his natural father's name at certain times for business reasons, to keep his
association with the Tyler company unknown—I don't
know exactly why. But he *is* Rafe's stepbrother. His family."

The world began to spin, black and misty. Tara knew she
had to sit down before she fell.

Mary was prepared. She shoved a chair beneath Tara,
who sank into it numbly, praying that she might stay that
way.

"He's looking for his brother," she said tonelessly. "He
found me, followed me, seduced me—assuming I could
lead him to his brother."

"He never told you, then," Mary said unhappily.

Tara shook her head. She buried her face in her open
palms. "Oh, God."

"Tara, I'm sorry—"

"Don't be. Thank God you knew. Oh, Mary."

"Tara, it may not mean anything. He might have looked
for you because of Jimmy, then fallen in love with you for

yourself. Tara, he can't take his eyes off you when you're together. And beyond a doubt, if Tine is out there, it's a damn good thing that you have Rafe's protection."

"Yes," Tara breathed. It truly had been a good thing.

"What are you going to do?"

Tara took a sustaining breath. She straightened her shoulders. The numbness left her, and a horrible pain took its place, but she gritted her teeth against it. "I'm going to have a chat with Mr. Tyler," she said.

"Tara—"

"That son of a bitch."

"Tara, give him a chance—"

She shook her head. Tears clouded her eyes. "No. It took me too long to see the light with Tine. This is much worse."

"Of course," Mary murmured. "Tine was only lethal to your health. The problem here is that you love Rafe Tyler."

Tara shook her head vehemently. "Then I'll just have to stop loving him."

"Talk to him. Give him a chance. Oh, Tara! Maybe I should have kept my mouth shut."

"No. Thank you, Mary."

She stood up. "Help me get out of things gracefully if anyone insists that we all lunch together or something. I have to talk to him. Right now."

"And then?"

"And then I never intend to speak to him again."

"Tara, you're forgetting! It's dangerous for you here. And I don't think it's that simple. I don't think you can just go home. You know that Tine is alive. And he knows that you're alive, and he'll be able to trace you eventually, even if you leave right now. You can't believe anymore that he's just gone under cover, hoping to survive and escape arrest.''

''I don't know what I'm going to do right now,'' Tara murmured miserably, adding in a whisper, ''except confront Rafe. Help me.''

Mary lowered her head and nodded miserably. ''Tara, listen to him, though, if he defends himself.''

Tara didn't argue with Mary; she was too wounded. She still didn't want to believe the obvious; she didn't want to feel the pain. She had to end it.

She tossed her hair over her shoulder. ''Come on.''

Outside the dressing room, George was indeed trying to talk everyone into staying together for lunch. He was still concerned about Tara.

She struggled to stay calm, a difficult task, for as soon as Rafe touched her she wanted to scream, to burst into tears, to beat her fists against him.

She smiled. ''George, I'll have to pass on lunch. I'm exhausted.''

Rafe looked at her curiously but didn't dispute her decision.

''You'll be with her?'' George asked.

''I'll be with her.''

Tara smiled. She kept smiling as they moved away. She kept her head high, her hand lightly on Rafe's arm.

They entered the elevator and went up to his room. He opened the door, then closed it, standing behind her.

''What's the matter?''

She turned around and smiled at him, then sat on the foot of the bed and patted the spot beside her. ''Come here.''

He raised one dark brow high. He came to her.

She gazed at him, and stroked his cheek. ''I'm still amazed,'' she murmured softly.

He caught her hand and kissed her fingers.

She shivered. With love, with hate that he could have used her so well.

"Amazed at what?"

She lifted her shoulders, still half smiling. "That you saw me in that museum. That you were so taken—with me!—that you followed me. That you fell in love with me. That you're with me now, when I have a cunning criminal after me."

He didn't reply.

She twisted slightly, aching. He leaned back, bringing her with him, half atop him on the bed. Ragged, jagged edges of agony scraped at her heart, stopped her breath.

"Love is amazing," he told her softly, his fingers moving into her hair in a soft caress.

"Yes, when it happens so quickly."

One last time. One last time, she had to stroke his face. Give him a wistful and alluring smile. Ease her fingers over the tautly muscled breadth of his chest. Hear the sharp intake of his breath. Know that he wanted her.

That had been real, at least. The passion. The physical thing that had sprung up between them.

In that he hadn't lied. He had wanted her. Still wanted her.

Just as she wanted him...

"Tara..."

His body tensed and tightened beneath her, his flesh heating. The touch of his fingers betrayed the urgency he felt. His lashes were low over the glimmering fire in his eyes, and by God, she wanted her revenge, something to still the anguish that twisted and burned inside her.

"You were just captivated by me, weren't you, Rafe?" she whispered softly.

"Yes. God, yes."

"And it really is . . . love."

"Yes. You know how I love you."

She pushed against his chest, wrenching his hands from her body, slamming them away from her.

"You filthy liar. You're looking for your brother."

Amazement lit his eyes; then they turned hard, as hard as flint.

But she knew. She knew from that one second that it was true, and it was all she could do to keep from crying out.

"Tara, you don't understand—"

"I understand perfectly well. And I never want to see your face again, as long as I live."

She tried to move. He caught her, shifting his weight with startling agility. She was pinned down, a powerful thigh thrust between hers, an arm around her waist.

"Damn you—"

"Well, Tara. That was charming. Tease the man to death, then deliver your blow. But it's not that simple."

"Stop it!" she cried out. She was trapped. The fear was rising again. The panic. This was force, and she was overwhelmed. "Rafe! You know how I feel about—"

"Any feminine ploy in the book, huh? It won't work, Tara, because you know I'd never hurt you. I'd never force you."

She closed her eyes in absolute misery—but not fear. It was true! True, and horrible. She wasn't afraid. Not of his strength, nor of the power that held her there. It was different. She hated him; she had to hate him. But she didn't. She wanted to cry. She wanted to reach up and touch his cheek and feel all his wonderful fire. It was still there, the tension, the wonderful, explosive tension between them. The absolute dizzying need to touch him when he was near, and then, after that touch, to explore the simmering fire . . .

"Rafe, it's all a lie! I want to go; I don't ever want to see you again. I don't want you touching me."

What a lie. But he had to believe her. Because if he didn't, she would burst into tears of fear and uncertainty and misery. She would throw her arms around his neck. She would want him to comfort her, to soothe her, to make love to her. . . .

How she wished there had been no past.

But there had been. And that was the only reason for the present.

"Rafe, let me out of here," she managed to whisper coolly.

"Not until you've listened to me!"

"I don't want to hear anything you have to say."

"You're going to hear it! And with your eyes open. Look at me, Tara!"

She did. She felt the warmth of his hand just below her breast. The power of his thigh cast over hers. The tension in his face, the vibrance of his eyes.

"Tara! Yes! I looked for you because of Jimmy. He's my brother—"

"Stepbrother, I understand," she interrupted blandly.

"Brother—we were raised together. God, what difference does it make? I loved him. I had to find him, for myself, for his mother. Is that such a horrible thing?"

"You seduced me—used me—to find him. You lied. God alone knows what you're really thinking or feeling."

"I'm trying to tell you! I do love you, Tara. I think it happened the first night we were together. Before we were together, even. Tara, forgive me! Maybe I was wrong, horribly wrong, to begin with, but that changed, and I couldn't just tell you then, because—because there was someone else involved. His mother was desperate. I was at my wit's end. If you'd turned away from me, I'd have lost her last chance. I'd have let Myrna down. In love or not," he said very softly, "I owed it to Myrna, to my brother, to take no chances. Can't you see? Please, Tara! Damn it, how can you believe that I don't love you now?"

She kept staring at him. She *didn't* know how. Then she grew desperate, because she was going to burst into tears at any moment.

"I've listened to you. Now let me go."

He didn't respond. She shoved at him in a fury, with an incredible burst of strength.

Still, if he hadn't chosen to release her, she wouldn't have been free.

"Tara—"

"Leave me alone. Just leave me alone." She rose, turning on him, commanding, begging.

"You've got to believe me!" He stood, then walked toward her. He couldn't come any closer. He just couldn't.

A strangled sob escaped her. She rushed to the connecting door, ran through it and slammed it shut.

"Tara!"

His voice thundered after her, and she burst into tears as she slid the bolt into place.

13

"Tara!"

His voice, rough, urgent, came to her through the door.

"My God, Tara, I'm not going to try to touch you or see you, but please, listen to me! I had no choice. If I'd tried to meet you with the truth, you wouldn't have given me the time of day. Myrna—Jimmy's mother—tried to reach you right after it all happened. But you had disappeared yourself. Galliard wouldn't let anyone know where you were. Tara, I do love you. I've wanted to tell you, to explain. Can't you see, it wasn't just me involved! I believed in you, but no one knew anything about Tine Elliott. At first I couldn't be certain."

He lost control for a moment. Tara felt the door shudder as he slammed a fist against it. "Tara!"

She felt numb again. So miserable that she was numb. A dead thing, with no strength, no will.

"Don't do this! Tara, Tine is still out there somewhere. You need me now. You—"

His words broke off with a sharp expletive. Distantly she heard the phone ringing in his room.

She knew when he left the door to answer it. She knew before he spoke when he returned.

"Open the door and come with me. That was the police. They think they have the man who attacked you yesterday."

She clenched her teeth. She couldn't go. She didn't think she could even stay standing.

She didn't recognize her own voice when she spoke. It was cold and hoarse. "I'm sure you'll recognize him. And I'm sure anything that can be dragged out of the man can best be obtained by your dubious means."

"Tara! This has to be done."

"Go do it, then."

She imagined that she could hear him breathing. She could even imagine the tension in his handsome features, the pulse ticking in his throat.

She did hear it when he inhaled sharply in decision. "I'll leave Sam and a house detective outside your door. Don't open it to anyone."

She didn't reply. She leaned her head wearily against the door.

"Tara!"

"I have no intention of opening my door."

"When I get back, Tara, you're damn well going to open it!" he promised her.

She heard him walk away. She closed her eyes, furious with herself, because silent tears streamed down her cheeks.

She didn't know how much time passed before she went over to one of the beds and lay down, ridiculously tired. Facts kept passing through her mind, events, sights. Foolish. They only hurt worse.

She didn't know if she'd dozed or if she had just lain there partially asleep. She became slowly aware of a tapping at her door, slow and hesitant at first, then growing louder and more urgent.

Keyed up and suddenly aware that she had every right to be frightened, she leaped from the bed and stared at the door. Silly—Rafe had said that Sam and a house detective would be there. If he had said so, it would be the truth.

But she walked to the door carefully. "Sam?"

"No, no, Señorita Hill. It is the maid. *Por favor*, I must come in."

Tara frowned. It was definitely a woman's voice. And most probably the maid. But she had to be sure.

She bit her lower lip, then hurried to the door connecting her room to Rafe's. She unbolted the door on her side and tried to open it, only to pause, baffled, to realize that it was now locked from the other side. She couldn't slip into his room to peek out into the hallway to see who stood at her door.

Where was Sam?

She went back to the door. "I don't need any maid service right now," she said.

There was a pause outside, then a whisper reached her, a whisper that she recognized.

"Tara, please! It's me. Jimmy Saunders."

"Jimmy!" she exclaimed. Could she be wrong? No, no, she recognized his voice! The moment he had begun to speak, she had known that it was him.

"Tara, I can't stay out here in the hallway!"

She fumbled with the lock, then threw open the door. For a moment, terror struck her. She might have made a mistake. He was in a hotel uniform, and his hair looked darker than before; he was standing next to a beautiful Venezuelan woman, with a room service table between them.

And he was sporting a rich, full handlebar mustache.

"Jimmy?"

She backed away. But he started laughing good-naturedly even as he stepped into the room with the nervous-looking woman.

"It's me! It's me!" He ripped off the mustache—crying out a little at the sudden pain, then grimacing and stretching out his arms. With a glad little gasp she hugged him. He returned the hug and softly closed the door behind him.

"What are you doing? Where have you been?" Tara demanded. Then she lightly batted him on the shoulder. "Now that I can see that you're alive and well, I could strangle you! No one believed me! Why didn't you contact the authorities? Why didn't you—what the hell was going on that night?"

"Shh!" he warned her. Then he smiled and pulled the pretty woman forward. "This is Tanya. After the fracas was over, I apparently managed to pull myself to her doorstep. Tara, I nearly died. I never would have intentionally deserted you. But I didn't know who I was—and Tanya was frightened. She knew that something had gone wrong with the authorities and that I had been involved. She nursed me herself." He gave the woman a warm smile with so much tenderness in it that Tara felt a new wave of anguish sweep through her.

"Tanya, Tara. Tara, Tanya. I would have died without her," he said very softly.

Tanya, who didn't seem to understand what had been said, did understand the love in his voice. She blushed and offered Tara a shy smile.

Tara smiled wistfully at them both, then gave herself a little shake. "Jimmy, what are you doing here now? Like this? Why didn't you just call me? Why—"

"Sit down. And keep your voice down. The walls around here may well have ears," he told her.

She looked skeptical, but sat obediently. Jimmy paced before her while he spoke. "I started a new life here, Tara." He laughed. "I learned to blow glass! But that's beside the point. About three weeks ago, I saw in the newspapers that Galliard was doing another showing in Caracas. There was a picture of you on the front page. When I saw it, I suddenly remembered everything.''

''So why didn't you call someone, Jimmy? Why—?''

He smiled patiently. ''I'm going to go back further in time,'' he explained ruefully. ''My family is into gems. Shipping and gems. That led us into antiquities. You know, financing expeditions for various museums, that type of thing. Anyway, I had gone to Mexico as a guest of the government to work at a Mayan site. We dug up some fabulous things!''

''The mask!'' Tara interrupted.

''Precisely. Anyway, a number of things were stolen one night. They disappeared quite cleanly. We assumed they would take a nice circuitous trip through South America before appearing in some private collection somewhere in the world. But we did have a bit of a clue—the authorities had been investigating Tine Elliott. I had followed him here, and snooping around, I found his little cache up in the mountains. I took the mask as proof of what he'd been up to. I planned to go to the authorities, but then I met you, and from what I had learned of the man, I was afraid for you. I waited, and then you called me, and, well, you know the rest. Except that I came here like this today because I don't want Tine Elliott to know that I've found you again, or that you've found me. I know he's back, Tara. He wants two things: you and the mask.''

''I don't believe this,'' she murmured. ''Why wait for two years to try to—''

''Tara, that mask is made of gold, diamonds, rubies, emeralds and sapphires. Millions of dollars' worth, even on the black market.''

She shook her head. ''But he *had* money!''

"Not enough, apparently," Jimmy said. "Tara, he has to be caught this time—before he hurts anyone else. That's why I had to lie low. For your safety, and for Tanya's."

She stared at him, still incredulous. She was so glad to see him alive that she wanted to kiss and hug him again—except that she didn't want Tanya to get the wrong impression.

She started suddenly. He didn't know! He didn't know about Rafe! And despite her bitterness, she acknowledged Rafe's right to know as quickly as possible that his brother was alive.

She smiled at Jimmy. "We may have a clue. Your brother is at the police station right now, trying to identify a man who attacked me yesterday. He must be associated with Tine."

"What? Rafe is here?"

The gladness on his face and the pleasure in his voice touched her heart. He also sounded relieved—as if he had infinite faith that big brother could handle anything—and a little amazed.

"Yes," Tara murmured. "He's here. Or, rather, he's at the police station."

"You know each other?" Jimmy demanded.

Tara's mouth twisted in a wry smile. "You didn't read enough newspapers. We were supposedly engaged."

"Supposedly?"

"Long story. Anyway, that's over. Now that you've appeared!"

Jimmy was frowning. "You were attacked? I can't believe that Rafe would leave you alone after something like that."

"I'm not alone. Sam is out in the hallway. And a detective."

Jimmy shook his head. He and Tanya glanced at each other; then he shook his head at Tara again. "No one is out there."

"But I'm sure they are! Sam—"

Jimmy laughed with little humor. "Tara! I grew up with old Sam. Trust me. I'd know if he was out there!"

"Maybe—"

"Let's not worry about the maybes," Jimmy said worriedly. "Let's get to the police station as quickly as possible. Tanya—" He paused, and switched to Spanish to talk to the beautiful Venezuelan. She nodded; Jimmy explained the exchange to Tara.

"She's going to call the police. They'll send a car for us, I'm sure."

"The phone is right over here—" Tara broke off. As soon as she had said the word "phone," the thing starting ringing as if on cue.

"Maybe that's Rafe right now," she murmured.

Smiling a little too eagerly, she pounced on the receiver, speaking into it breathlessly. "Hello?"

"Hello, Tara. Have you missed me?"

It wasn't Rafe. Her heart seemed to skip a beat, then slam against her chest.

"Don't hang up, Tara. Speak to me, love. I promise you'll be very sorry if you don't."

Seconds ticked by in which she couldn't talk. She could just hear him breathing on the other end, and she knew that he was laughing.

"What do you want, Tine?"

She stressed his name, looking anxiously toward Jimmy, raising a hand when he would have rushed over.

"A couple of things, sweetie. I want the mask. And I want you. For the time being, at least. I watched you yesterday. Nice. Old George put on a real good show."

She sat down on the bed, afraid that she would fall. He had been able to watch her, all that time.

"They're going to arrest you, Tine. And put you in jail for years and years. You could even be charged with murder, Tine. Your blond friend was killed, remember?"

"She wasn't murdered; she just got in the way of a bullet. Her destiny, it would seem," he said pleasantly. "But nobody's going to get me, Tara. Know why? Because you're going to leave there. Right now. You're going to go down to the lobby, and you'll see a man who you're going to greet like a long-lost friend."

"You're crazy! I'm going to hang up and call the police immediately."

"No, you're not. You're going to bring Saunders and his pretty little girlfriend and come downstairs."

She couldn't restrain her gasp. How could he possibly know that Jimmy was here?

She heard him chuckle. Anger swept through her, along with the fear. "You're still out of your mind, Tine. Why the hell would I do a thing like that?"

"Why indeed?" he mocked her. "I'll tell you why. I just couldn't seem to reach you, Tara. Tyler was there, every damned place you were. But he's gone now. What did you do, have a blowout with him, too, sweets? All the better. I still have this little yen, you know? I always was the possessive sort."

"The criminal sort, you mean. You should be shot, Tine. But that's not my concern. I'll never come to you."

"I think you will. You see, Tara, you were nicely, safely guarded. Forewarned, after those fools messed up yesterday. I had to rethink my plans."

"What are you talking about?"

"An old friend of mine. A certain lovely little redhead. She's sitting here with me right now. So pretty, so young.

And if you don't do exactly what I say, I'm afraid that I'll have to kill her. Ashley will die, and it will be all your fault, darling.''

Tara sank all the way to the floor, the blood draining from her face. Jimmy came rushing toward her, ready to grasp the phone. Life came back to her even as desperate tears rushed to her eyes. She shook her head vehemently, holding the receiver tightly.

"Got you on that one, didn't I, love?" Tine inquired lightly.

"I don't believe that you have Ashley!" she cried.

"Oh, but I do. It was easy. She stepped into the hallway all alone. She was at the door, Tara, just about to open it. And we simply put this little cloth over her face and she was as docile as a lamb. The annoyance was getting rid of the old man. And the detective. Quietly, of course. You want to talk to her?"

Tara didn't answer, because Ashley was already on the phone, her voice definitely scared, but her words full of bravado.

"Tara, don't you dare do a thing he says! Go to the police right away! He—"

Tara closed her eyes, because Ashley broke off with a small scream, and Tine got back on the phone.

"Don't call the police, Tara. If I see so much as a hint of the police, I'll shoot her. Maybe I'll take out both her kneecaps first. I can't tell you how bad that hurts, baby. Nothing, no tricks. You and Saunders and his little tramp do exactly as I say. Go downstairs now. Come to me, baby. I've been waiting for you."

Jimmy tried to snatch the phone again. Tara covered the mouthpiece, shaking her head, tears in her eyes.

"He has Ashley. He says he'll kill her if we don't come right now. I know that he has her; I heard her. I heard her...scream."

Despite her protests, Jimmy wrenched the phone from her. "Elliott, you idiot. My brother is here, you know. He'll tear up half the country to find her!"

Tara didn't hear Tine's answer, but she could tell when the phone went dead in Jimmy's hand, because he stared at it for a minute and then hung up.

"What?" she whispered.

"He, uh, he, he expects to get in contact with Rafe. I imagine he wants to make a trade. Us for the mask."

"But Rafe doesn't have the mask."

"But I do. I had it when I stumbled into Tanya's doorway, and it's still there. Hidden."

Tanya said something to Jimmy. Tara came to her feet. "How did he see everything? What has he done with Sam? And Ashley!"

"We'd better go," Jimmy said.

"There has to be something we can do. Something that won't jeopardize Ashley's life."

"I think there is. Where's your purse? I can leave a note in it for Rafe. Unobtrusive, in case Tine sends someone in here to check after we're gone, but it's a place I'm willing to bet Rafe will think to look."

"Couldn't we call—"

"I wouldn't trust that phone. Hurry, get me a paper and a pen."

"But what are you going to say?"

"I've got a pretty good idea of where we're going. You forget—I stole the mask from him."

Tara gave Jimmy her handbag, paper and a pen. He scribbled a note and placed it inside the purse. Tanya remained quietly at his side. She must be frightened, Tara thought. But the other woman remained silent and poised. Tara decided that she was going to do the same. She couldn't do anything less. Of all people, Ashley didn't deserve to be in this mess.

"All right, let's go," Jimmy said.

He didn't bother replacing his mustache, and the three of them went down in the elevator together in silence. When they reached the lobby, Tara prayed wildly that a score of policemen would jump out from behind the counter and produce a handcuffed Tine.

It didn't happen. Some tourists walked by, chattering in French. A group of Americans went past, boisterously discussing the delicious meal they'd had for lunch.

Then a tall man with broad shoulders and a Latin accent suddenly threw his arms out toward Tara.

"There you are! Come, give your old amigo a hug!"

Tara gritted her teeth as the man embraced her. He reached past her, smiling as he shook hands with Jimmy and Tanya.

"Now. Out front," he ordered under his breath.

They stepped outside. A black limousine swept into the circular drive. The man who had met them tipped the doorman and hugged Tara's shoulders again—then shoved her into the back. She stumbled, because he was pushing Jimmy and Tanya in almost on top of her.

Instinctively, she grabbed for something to hold. A hand came out, steadying her, becoming a vise around her wrist as she sat down, horrified, next to Tine.

For a moment she could only stare at him. He hadn't changed a bit. He was still trim, sandy-haired, with blue eyes, as handsome as only the all-American boy next door could be, the high school football team quarterback, tanned, broad-shouldered, appealing.

Except that now she knew. Knew that his smile hid a wealth of cruelty. That the glitter in those blue eyes was the glitter of avarice.

He smiled at her, a smile that grew broader and harder as she tried to wrench her hand away.

"I've missed you, Tara."

She didn't respond; she only returned his gaze coldly while icy trickles of fear skated down her spine.

"Leave her alone, Elliott," Jimmy said.

Tine chuckled. "Just what will you do, big man?"

"I have the mask—she doesn't."

"That's right. But Tara and I have a few old scores to settle."

"Where's Ashley?" she demanded.

"You'll see her soon. Just sit tight, sweetheart. We've got a little drive ahead of us." His fingers curled around hers. Suddenly he stretched her arm out, catching sight of Rafe's magnificent diamond—the ring she still couldn't remove.

All traces of his smile disappeared. "You were going to marry him?"

"I *am* going to marry him," Tara lied smoothly.

"Take it off."

"It doesn't come off."

He smiled again. "I'll see that it comes off," he promised her. "One way or another."

Tara lowered her lashes, fighting the temptation to scream with fear and rake her nails across his face. She had to be calm; there was Ashley to remember.

She stared at Jimmy and Tanya, who sat silently, hand in hand.

The limo's windows were darkly tinted. She had no idea of where they were going, except that they were beginning to climb high into the mountains, and it seemed that the afternoon sun was waning. It would soon be dark.

"Relax, sweetheart," Tine said softly, slipping an arm around her shoulders. "You really haven't got anything to worry about—not for a while yet."

But she did. He was right next to her. Very fit, a strong man, agile and powerful. She had learned that once the hard way. It seemed that every nerve in her body cried out. She couldn't bear being next to him.

She had no choice.

She closed her eyes, clenched her teeth tightly and prayed for the ride to end—no matter what that end brought.

"Another ten minutes or so and we'll be home," Tine said, as if he were addressing a group of old friends. "Home, Tara. Nice, cozy home. Luxurious, intimate."

She still refused to react, and he laughed, a grating sound that was entirely horrible.

Rafe returned to the hotel in disgust—not one of the men in the lineup had even remotely resembled the man who had tried to abduct Tara the day before.

The only good thing about the trip had been that he had been able to spend some time with Lieutenant Costello, the one man who had given him a serious hearing when he had attempted to find Jimmy two years before. Of course, by the time that Rafe had realized Jimmy was missing, it had been long after the night on the mountain. The lieutenant had been stunned to hear that the man had actually existed; he'd admitted that they'd suspected Tara Hill of inventing him in a wild bid to exonerate herself. Costello was a good man; Rafe definitely felt more comfortable knowing that the police now believed wholeheartedly that Tine Elliott was alive and well and in their country. Costello assured him that it might take time, but they would find him.

He knew something was wrong as soon as he reached the hallway. He didn't think the detective would have left—and he knew damn well that Sam would never have voluntarily deserted his post.

He hurried into his room. It was empty; nothing seemed amiss. He rushed to the connecting door, ready to break it down if she didn't answer him.

He didn't have to break the door down. It was locked only on his side. And he hadn't locked it.

He burst through. Tara was gone, and there was no sign of Ashley. The room was neat and clean—no sign of a scuffle, at least.

Trying to remain rational and calm, he started toward the phone to call the police, but he never reached it. The phone was ringing in his own room, and he raced back to answer it.

His hello was anxiously hopeful.

"Rafael Tyler?"

"Who is this?"

"Just listen carefully. I have a number of people you care about here. Your brother. And—"

"My brother!" Jimmy. Jimmy was alive. Rafe had always believe that, but ...

Where the hell had he been? Why hadn't he called, written, let those who loved him know that he was all right? Why in God's name—

A chuckle interrupted his thoughts.

"Yes, I have him. Your brother. Excuse me—stepbrother. Yes, *I have him*. It was the strangest thing! I've been pulling my hair out for the last two years looking for that boy myself. Seems I did hit him last time. Good hit, right in the head. Erased his memory. He's been wandering around down here with a native girl all this time—and then Tara shows up and triggers something in the boy's memory. It all worked out real well. So now I have him—and his Venezuelan girlfriend. I also have a redheaded model and, oh, a lady who we both know and love. The illustrious Tara Hill. Nice rock you gave her, Tyler. And I have a paranoid detective, and an old man."

"Elliott!" Rafe breathed between his teeth.

"How perceptive, Mr. Tyler."

"If you touch her, Elliott, you're a dead man," Rafe said quietly.

"Well, that rather remains to be seen, doesn't it? I want the mask, Tyler."

"I don't have the damn mask, and you know it."

"True. But you're going to get it for me. You and your brother."

"You can have it. But I not only want Tara back here—entirely safe and sound—but the others, too. I want them released, and then the mask is yours."

"Now, now, you know it's not that simple. First things first. I'll meet you at the glass factory—way out in the open. At midnight. I'll have your little brother with me. He'll tell you where the mask is and how to get it. And he'll be careful, because he knows I'll shoot his girlfriend if he lies. And you'll behave, too, I'm certain, because there's an entire memory lane that I could travel down with Tara—before I shoot her. Now, if you're even five minutes late, I'll start proving my point by shooting the old-timer. Got it all? Oh, no police. If I see anyone with you, anyone remotely near you on that mountain, I'll begin by breaking his kneecaps."

"I'll be there at midnight. Alone."

"See that you are. You know, I'm smiling at your girl-friend right now, Tyler. Ah, memories! She's something, isn't she? Just like a centerfold, huh?"

Rafe almost snapped the phone wire; it took all his willpower not to reply.

"How nice, a silent pair. Don't mess up, Tyler, huh?"

The phone went dead. Rafe started to click it to call the police, then wondered if Tine Elliott had enough power behind him to have the wires tapped.

He sat down, shaking. He tried to fight back the rising sensation of panic. He reminded himself that his brother was alive, though he'd never believed in his heart that Jimmy could be dead. And it made sense: injury, amnesia. Jimmy would have never let them go crazy with fear if he had been able to do anything about it. He had been hurt, but he was alive. Rafe should be grateful for that, at least.

But he couldn't be grateful. He felt too much panic. Tine Elliott had Tara. Tara. All that he could see in his mind's eye were pictures of her. The beautiful soft silver fox fur clutched to her throat. Her eyes on his when they had met over the marble tiger. Tara...that night in her apartment. Half asleep, her guard down, the attraction calling to them both.

Tara...the softness of her lips. The beauty of her passion. Her love pouring around and over him, and becoming more a part of him than his flesh or his blood or even his mind. He couldn't stand the fear, the horror, knowing what Tine Elliott had done to her, knowing that Tine Elliott had her again.

You can't panic! You can't sit here like a helpless idiot! he screamed silently.

Something inside him came to the fore, something sharp that reminded him that he'd never been helpless in any situation before—he'd always looked to action. But then, he'd never been in love before, not like this. This time another person was the essence of his soul, and the danger was all directed toward her.

Think! Act! By God, of all the times in his life, this was when he most needed to be effective!

Rafe forced himself to breathe deeply. He clenched and unclenched his fists. He looked at his watch. Eight o'clock, and it was almost completely dark outside.

Four hours. Four hours in which Tine Elliott could be doing anything to anyone.

Not to anyone. Tara.

He inhaled, exhaled, and gripped his fingers to stop them from trembling. How many people did Elliott have working for him? Probably not more than five or six—it would be too dangerous for him to have any larger a group.

Rafe knew he was probably being watched. But he hadn't been told not to leave his room. He'd have to risk it.

But he didn't have a damn thing to go on.

He walked back into Tara and Ashley's room, blindly groping for some kind of clue. The beds weren't perfectly made, he thought. And it seemed that the makeup and perfume bottles on the dresser were a little out of order, considering the kind of organization both girls were accustomed to, being quick-change artists.

Someone had been here. Either to take them...or check the room out after they had gone.

He sat down on the bed. If anyone had left him anything, it was surely gone.

He stood up, pacing the room, reminding himself that he had never been a defeatist. He paced and prowled, looking at the carpeting, stripping the beds, searching through the drawers. There was nothing.

But then he paused, opening the top drawer again. Tara's leather handbag was there. He pulled it out and dumped the contents on the table.

He almost raked the entire mess on the floor with disgust, then paused. Among the lipstick, compact, wallet, address book, pencils, pens, stamps and other paraphernalia was an old shopping list. He studied it, tossed it aside, and noticed another slip. It looked like the floor plan for a runway.

Except that it wasn't. It was some kind of a map. And it had been written by Jimmy and meant for him. At the bottom the words "Tanya's walk" were written.

His blood seemed to race and make him dizzy for a minute. He sat down on the bed and studied the map more closely. He began to make out the mountain by the glass factory. The forests, the main road, the dirt paths. Shacks and houses.

His fingers started to tremble again. Jimmy had been here. Tine Elliott had bided his time well. Jimmy had come to Tara; Elliott had snared them both together. But Jimmy was alive, and apparently he remembered something, someplace.

Rafe rushed out of the room. He had no illusions. Tine meant to get his hands on him, too, and probably dispose of the lot of them together. That way there would be no one except for an overburdened police department left to hound him.

No, he had no illusions. That was why he had to reach Elliott before Elliott could reach him. And he couldn't charge in like a fool; he had to have help. With luck, Elliott would count on his feelings, on his sense of panic. Elliott would be pretty damn sure that Rafe would do exactly what he had promised, that he wouldn't go to the police, that he would be where he'd said at midnight.

Midnight would be too late.

14

They stopped once along the way. Tine got out of the car, but when Tara and Jimmy would have burst into conversation, they halted, because the man who had met them in the lobby took Tine's place—smiling and pointing a pistol at Jimmy's face.

Tine returned, pleasantly informing her that he'd made an important call. She knew that he wanted her to cry and plead and question him, so she didn't. He had contacted Rafe, she knew. She didn't need to ask, and she was sure that he wouldn't tell her anything until he felt like it, so she was determined not give him the pleasure of her anguish.

But with him next to her, Tara's only help was a complete retreat into herself. She had to think about something else. Of course, that was nearly as painful, because she thought about Rafe. The funny thing was that she'd felt that she had been betrayed by him just as she had been by Tine.

And now she knew. There were no comparisons between the two men. Rafe had lied to her—by omission. But he would never have hurt her. And he had lied only because he'd loved his brother.

And she'd never known fear with Rafe. Not the kind of horrible fear that was engulfing her now. He'd tried to talk to her.

She lowered her head, wishing bitterly that she'd given
Rafe a chance. She'd been afraid to believe him. Afraid
because she loved him so much. And right now she wanted
nothing more in the world than to be back with him. To
give him the chance to tell her that though their love might
have begun in deception, the magic between them had been
stronger than anything else, and if they let it, it could be
with them forever.

But oh, God, did he really love her?

What did it matter now? She was certain that whatever
else he had in mind, Tine did not intend to let her go.

By the time they came to a halt, Tara was numb—it was
her only defense. She didn't know where they were, only
that they had left the sophistication of the city behind, and
the poor ramshackle cliff dwellings that crowded the
mountains were far behind, too. They had climbed deep
into the upper countryside, where there were few roads and
few houses, and where the bracken and trees were the only
life to be found. Rocks and treacherous ledges abounded
here, and the darkness had fallen swiftly tonight, like evil
wings.

"Here we are, love," Tine said. "Home. Please, come
in."

He didn't help her out of the back; he jerked her out.
Jimmy started to protest.

"Should have left that mask alone, kid," Tine said, then
added, "along with the lovely Miss Hill. Let's keep moving, huh?"

Tara was glad to move, except that she didn't know
where to go. She could barely make out the dusky path
before her. As soon as they had gotten out of the car, it had
been driven away. She realized with a sinking sensation
that it appeared that there was nothing up here, nothing at
all.

No one would find them.

"You remember the way, Saunders, don't you?" Tine asked pleasantly. "Back to the great scene of your crime."

"Where are Ashley and the others?" Tara demanded.

"Straight ahead, love. We'll have a nice little reunion with them, and then we'll have a nice little reunion alone. Sound cozy?"

She didn't answer. He prodded the small of her back, and she started walking along a narrow pathway through the trees.

She spun around to face him. "You can let Ashley go now. What good is she going to do you? And Tanya. Why on earth—"

"Tara, shut up. Go."

She turned around and started walking again. Jimmy was behind Tine. Tanya silently followed him.

The man with the pistol was behind Tanya.

Tara wouldn't have known that they had arrived if the hut hadn't been pointed out to her. It was made of wood and tin and seemed to blend right into the cliff that harbored it. As they approached, the door burst outward. There she saw the man who had nearly abducted her. He spoke to Tine in Spanish; Tine answered him.

"Go on, love. You want to see Ashley, huh?"

Tara went in, stepping past her assailant with distaste. She entered some kind of a crude living room with an ugly-looking fifties couch and a few chairs and a table.

She didn't see Ashley or Sam, or the unknown detective. She looked at Tine, and he indicated that she should go down a hallway.

She did; there was another man standing in a doorway. Tara ignored the massive weapon slung over his shoulder and raced past him.

Ashley was there. Ashley and Sam and a young, strapping Venezuelan man. The detective, she assumed. Sam and the detective were sitting on a cot; Ashley was pacing.

"Ashley!"

The door slammed and was bolted behind the newcomers; Tara was barely aware of it. She was dizzy with relief that Ashley seemed to be unharmed.

Tara rushed to her. The two of them clasped their arms about each other. Tara felt Ashley quiver, and felt her self-loathing grow stronger, having dragged others into this. "Oh, Ashley!" she said, then turned. "Oh, Sam..."

But Sam, straight and proud, was standing with a wonderful grin on his face despite the circumstances. He had seen Jimmy, and they were in each other's arms, a barrage of questions and answers going back and forth between them. Then the detective starting talking in Spanish, and Tanya entered the conversation, but Tara finally got Sam's attention so she could make sure he was all right.

"Meaning no disrespect, Miss Hill. I may be mature, but I'm not useless. Those scoundrels knocked us out unawares, and that was all there was to it."

She was glad that so far Sam seemed okay, just indignant that she had worried that he was too old to handle the situation. And he was indignant that they had been removed from the hotel in laundry baskets, along with a ton of dirty sheets.

"I'm so sorry," Tara murmured.

"Would you quit that!" Jimmy insisted, a protective arm around Tanya, as usual. "Tara, I started this whole thing. No, I didn't. Elliott started it all."

"Can't we just give him the stinking mask?" Ashley asked.

"That's the plan, I assume," Jimmy murmured, trying to sound cheerful. But his eyes met Tara's, and she knew that he was wondering, just as she was, how ruthless Tine was. Was he capable of killing them all?

She'd come to know too much about him to hope for much in their favor now.

"What do you think our chances are for escape?" she asked Sam.

"The man right outside the door is carrying a submachine gun. He could—" Sam cleared his throat. "It's a dangerous weapon."

"He could wipe us all out in thirty seconds," Ashley said bluntly.

"Then—"

The door reopened. The man from the lobby looked in. He pointed at Tara. "You, come on."

"She will not!" Ashley protested.

He ignored Ashley and grasped Tara's arm. Sam leaped to his feet; the submachine gun was whirled toward him.

"Sam, sit down. I'm sure I'll be right back. Don't forget, I knew Tine well once," Tara said, trying to sound assured. Yes, she knew Tine, and she was terrified! But she couldn't let it show; someone would wind up dead.

"Tara, don't—" Jimmy began.

"I'll be fine."

She wouldn't be, but she had to convince them. Oh, God. Now more than ever, thoughts of Rafe were crowding in on her, and her knees began to wobble as she was led back along the hallway. She thought of when she had looked up, that first time at the museum. Seeing the tiger, seeing Rafe. Feeling from that very first moment the sense of utter excitement. Wondering what it would be like...

And then knowing what it was like to be held by him. Loved by him. Touched...

She thought that if Tine were to touch her now, she would just as soon die. She'd known real tenderness, real care. Passion, beauty.

She swallowed sharply; surely Rafe figured somewhere in this. Tine would be coercing him as he had coerced her. He wanted both the Tylers, because he wanted the mask. He wanted them both stopped from hounding him. It had become an obsession. Tine was obsessive. He had never loved her, but had simply been obsessed.

She was scared that he would touch her. Scared that he would get Rafe. Rafe would do anything to prevent harm from befalling the rest of them. God, she wanted him. She wanted to be in his arms. She wanted . . .

Don't think! she warned herself. Don't think that Tine could trick him, could get him here—could shoot him. Kill him. In cold blood.

Deal with it moment by moment! she pleaded with herself. And she tried to convince herself that Rafe was no fool, that someone would miss them very soon, that maybe the police were combing the mountain at this very minute. Maybe she could even reason with Tine, convince him that he could never get away with it this time, that he would be found, that he would—

"Tara. I've waited a long, long time for today."

She stopped walking because he was standing there. At the end of the hallway, waiting for her. She didn't say anything; she was too wary of his next move.

"Let's go, Tara."

"Where?"

"A walk in the moonlight."

"I won't go."

"The hell you won't."

A second later she screamed, because he strode straight toward her, grim-faced, wrenched her arm behind her back and prodded her forward. Stay calm! she told herself desperately, and then she wondered, what good would it do?

He opened the door and pushed her out into the night. All she could see was darkness, though he seemed to know where he was going. The night had grown cool; she could see her breath in the dark. Under her feet, the ground grew rockier. Suddenly he yanked her back. She started to scream again, but he cut her off sharply.

"The ledge, you idiot. Another step and you'll be over it."

She saw it then, the point where the cliff ended. Below the city lights twinkled. So tiny, so far away.

"Sit down, Tara."

There was a tree with a clear space beneath it. Tara sat. He stood behind her and lit a cigarette.

"Tine," she murmured, when the silence became unendurable, "this is idiotic. You should have disappeared into the South American rain forest. You have to be crazy. If the authorities get hold of you this time—"

"I want that mask."

"Why?"

"Why?" He laughed shortly. "Simple. Money. I know the right channels. I could spend the rest of my life in outrageous prosperity with that thing."

"But you made good money!" Tara cried out.

"With Galliard, you mean?" he asked, amused. She felt the skin at her nape prickle. He had stooped down behind her. She could feel his breath touching her skin, and she tried not to shiver. The longer she could talk...

"I could have made a fortune with you, love. I would have known how to package you just right. But you didn't want me. And now you think you're going to marry Rafael Tyler. Hah! That's a laugh. I'm the one who dragged you out of the refuse, out of the gutter. And you betrayed me, you little bitch.''

''You didn't pull me out of the gutter, Tine—you tried to drag me down into it. I knew some poor, poor people, Tine, but not one of them would have stooped as low as you—for anything. They were all rich in something called pride.''

''I'm impressed, Tara. But it's a pity you feel that way. I might have taken you with me. 'Cause it'll all be over tonight, you know. I'll meet lover boy at midnight, he and boy wonder will get the mask—and take a tragic fall down the mountain.''

''You wouldn't!'' Tara almost choked on the words. ''Tine, don't be foolish! So far, no one can get you for murder—''

''Hey, it's easier to get away with murder than a few other crimes I could mention,'' he said lightly. ''I think that's about enough talk. It never was a high point with me. I missed you. That's the truth, you know. There's always been something special about you—''

''Don't be absurd. There's something special to you about anything in skirts,'' she said harshly, inching away.

She stopped when his fingers wound into her hair and jerked roughly.

''No, you aren't the only one, but you *are* special. I felt it when I watched you on that runway the other day. I had a hard time doing things slow and right, you know.''

He tightened his hold on her hair as tears stung her eyes. He was laughing at her helplessness. She felt sick, almost overwhelmed by the panic that was sweeping through her.

''Come here, Tara!''

She was so close to the cliff—but she didn't care. Blind instinct made her wild and furious. He wrenched her around by the shoulders; she brought her hands to his face and raked furiously, bringing a sharp cry of pain to his lips.

"You stupid little bitch—" he began.

And he released her for just one second.

The second had been enough. She was on her feet, still wild, unaware that she had nowhere to go. She tried to retrace her steps. Tried to race away from the dangerous cliffs so she could find a way down the mountain.

There was someone on the path before her. Coming toward her. She halted, then gasped and started racing forward again, relief singing through her. It was George Galliard.

Tara cast herself straight into his arms. "George! How did you get here? Oh, thank God! Are the police here? Tine is right behind me. George—"

He held her stiffly, looking over her shoulder. She turned, gasping and crowding closer to him. Tine was almost on her, wrath and cruelty on his features; along with the blood-red gashes she had torn across his face.

"George . . . ?" The name escaped her in a gasp. Tine kept coming closer. George's grip tightened—then he pushed her toward Tine. She stumbled; he caught her in a grip so venomous that she cried out.

"George?"

"Sorry, love," Tine said softly, with an edge of malice. "You hadn't guessed? How do you think dear George got his start? No one would buy his damn fashions. I never worked for him; he always worked for *me*. Gems, gold, artifacts, in and out so easily, because who would think to check up on a world-famous designer? He arranged this nice trip back very carefully, right after he talked to you and discovered that you were running a little low. He had a hell of a time squeaking by the authorities last time."

"Idiot!" George accused Tine suddenly. "Neither of us will get out of it this time! What the hell did you have to take half the town hostage for?"

"I only did what was necessary. Quit sniveling like an old woman. Go back to town. I hope you weren't foolish enough to be followed!"

Tara's knees suddenly gave out with shock. George! What had looked like salvation had been a merciless trick. She couldn't believe she had run to him for help and he had handed her right back to Tine.

"Get up!" Tine yelled at her. "George, get out of here! I've been waiting for the return of my love so patiently!"

He turned, dragging her with him. She screamed; she kicked; she fought.

And she knew he wouldn't loosen his hold for a minute. Not this time.

Rafe took five different cabs, stopping at five different places and coming out on five different streets before taking the final cab to Costello's office. He chafed at the time it took, but knew that he had to take the precaution. He burst in on the lieutenant so wildly that in retrospect, it was a wonder that the man had listened. But he did, and it was probably another miracle that he studied the ridiculous map with Rafe, stroked his chin and agreed that they could probably find the location.

"I'll call in one of my men—Juan Ortega. He's from the mountain, a farmer. But if it is not the place, Rafael, then—"

"It has to be the place," Rafe said hoarsely. "Jimmy is alive, and he wouldn't have done this without being certain."

They sat down and went through the particulars. The only way to get up there without being seen would be to take the back roads. That would take time. And they'd have to count on surprise. Neither knew if Tine Elliott was ruthless enough to start shooting or not. Since the woman had died last time, Costello didn't think that an effort at negotiation would be worthwhile.

Four of them would go: Ortega, who knew the mountain so well; a sharpshooter; Costello; and Rafe.

It was nearly ten o'clock when they set off.

They followed the city lights, then turned into the mountains. They could only go halfway by the main road. Soon they were climbing, and Rafe stared out the window at the mountain. Purple and haunted and shadowed, wild and primitive, and anything could be hidden there.

They reached a point where they could no longer take the car. They would have a long walk, he was warned, and they'd have to study the situation when they reached their objective—a hostage situation was always tricky.

Ortega did know the mountain. He walked easily; Rafe and Costello were panting.

"Here, this path," Ortega said. "If the map is accurate."

They walked until Rafe's muscles ached, though not as badly as his heart. Time was his enemy. And it was passing so swiftly. All he could see was the forest. Tree after tree, branch after branch. Eternal darkness.

Ortega stopped short. Rafe saw the lights seeping through the trees. Costello gestured, and the four of them scattered, circling the hut, which seemed to blend into a crevice of the rock and the forest.

It was the sharpshooter who found the right window. He beckoned silently to the lieutenant. Costello went around the front; Ortega went with him. Rafe and the sharpshooter stared at each other and counted off the seconds.

Then Rafe crashed through the window. The sharp-shooter followed, covering them both with a burst of fire directed at the door. Rafe found Ashley first and pulled her to the floor, shouting that the others should duck.

It was really ridiculously easy. The sharpshooter shouted to the armed man guarding the hostages that he would be a fool to die for the criminal *norteamericano*.

He gave up without firing a shot. By then, Ortega and Costello were coming in through the front, herding two more men ahead of them. To Rafe's amazement, one of them was George Galliard.

He couldn't dwell on that for the moment, though; he saw his brother and clasped him tightly in an embrace.

But then he even pushed Jimmy from him. "Where's Tara?"

"Out—out somewhere with Elliott."

"Wait!" Costello ordered Rafe. But it was too late— Rafe was already out the door, running into the night.

He paused a short distance from the hut, looking left, right and forward. The mountain was so dark. It seemed to have an evil pulse. No, the pulse was his heartbeat. It was the panic, the fear, the desperation bubbling up within him.

And then he heard it—a scream. Tara. Sick with dread, but galvanized, Rafe started running. He veered, he slid, he crashed into the trees. She screamed again; the sound was nearer.

He saw her, and his heart caught. She was so close to the edge. Struggling. And there was Elliott. A big man, his blond hair gleaming in the night. He was laughing as she screamed. Bending over her, saying something, taunting her, touching her...

Something burst inside Rafe's brain. He thought he could rip Elliott into a hundred thousand pieces, do it savagely, do it horribly. He didn't feel quite human. Power rippled through him and he didn't remember taking the last few steps; he was just there, driving his fingers into Elliott's hair, wrenching for all he was worth, tearing the man away from her.

Elliott came up swinging. Rafe ducked, something warning him that his adversary was tough. He pitched himself into the air, bringing his full weight down on Elliott. They wrestled, spinning in the dust, against the rock. Rafe felt it all. Elliott aimed a well-delivered blow at Rafe's jaw. For a moment, the night spun—stars bursting inside his head instead of against the sky. He saw the man's fist rise again; he saw the hate in the powder blue eyes, and he twisted just in time.

He saw Tara there, standing too close to the edge. "Move!" he shrieked to her. "Tara, damn you, move!"

He saw her indecision; he saw her anguish. She was trying to figure out a way to help him.

He catapulted, putting Elliott beneath him, slamming his fist against his jaw. He took a pause. "Get out of here so I don't have to worry about you, too!"

Elliott swung and caught Rafe's jaw again. "Go!" Rafe shouted.

Tara ran.

"Tyler!" Elliott raged. "If I go, you're going."

"Then let's do it, damn it!" Where the hell was Costello?

They started to twist again, and Rafe got in another blow. They broke and stood, coming closer and closer to the ledge. They used their feet; they used their hands. Rafe slammed a good right hook under Tine Elliott's jaw. Elliott let out a grunt and went down, but the impetus took Rafe with him—over the ledge.

So this is it, Rafe thought fleetingly.

But to his amazement he hit another shelf just a short way down. He looked over a few feet, dragging himself up, leaning against a rock.

He gasped for breath and dragged in the mountain air. Elliott was a foot away, out like a light.

"Rafael!"

Costello was above him at last. He saw Rafe and Tine, and he grinned. "You need some help?"

Rafe laughed. It felt good to laugh. "Yeah, yeah. I could use some help. Take the carcass away!"

Ortega and the lieutenant came down to collect Tine Elliott's unconscious form.

Rafe waved away Ortega's hand when he would have helped him. "I need to catch my breath. I'll be up in a minute."

Costello didn't really think when he passed Tara on the mountain path. There was terror in her eyes, fear, anxiety—she looked like a beautiful gazelle caught in bright lights, elegant, still, ready to bolt like lightning.

"My God, where's Rafe?"

"Down—down on the ledge."

She bolted.

Costello realized that he hadn't told her that the man was fine. He shrugged. She would see for herself.

Tara just ran, her heart racing. Only the moon and stars illuminated her way; nothing but raw emotion guided her. There was no time to think that he was a man who had betrayed her, too. She was terrified, more so than she had been through any of it. The fear for Ashley, the terror when Tine had dragged her out. None of that meant anything now, nothing in the past, nothing in the future. She only knew that if Rafe was injured or—oh, God! no, she couldn't even think the word—she would not be able to bear it. She had to hurry. If she could just touch him, she could stop his pain. It was madness, but it drove her relentlessly through the trees, over the bracken, branches ripping at her clothing, stones and roots tripping her. Nothing stopped her.

She found him just below the ledge. Scrambling precariously down to him, she clutched a decaying root and paused, her heart seeming to rise to her throat and catch there, no longer beating.

He was dead. Blood trickled from his mouth. His eyes were closed, and he was hunched back against the rock, as still and pale as the stone.

"Rafe!" Tara shouted in desperation. Frantically she scrambled the last few feet to reach him, kneeling at his side, touching his forehead, taking his hands.

"Rafe, Rafe, please, I love you so much. I've got to get help. Hang on. I'll be back. I've got to get them down here. Don't—don't—you have to be all right. You have to be. I love you. I love you—"

She started to rise. The hands she was holding moved; fingers curled around hers.

She didn't see his eyes opening to slits, still covered by the dark shadows of his lashes.

If she had, she would have realized that never before had he appeared so like a tiger.

Eyes glowing amber and gold, muscles corded, ready to pounce. He felt the greatest burst of triumph—and happiness—in his life.

"I love you." He was careful to keep his words a whisper.

"I love you. Please, I'll get help—"

"No!" he croaked, exerting more pressure against her hands when she would have risen.

"Rafe, you're hurt!"

Guilt touched him. He opened his eyes a little more and saw the terrible anguish on her beautiful features, in her moon-silver eyes. The guilt was painful, but there was the rest of their lives to consider, and he couldn't lose her now.

"Tara...you have to listen. Before God, I love you. I started falling in love with you the moment that I met you. The first night. And each time I saw you, I fell further under your spell. I thought at first that I was a fool, that you had bewitched Jimmy the same way, had led him into disaster. And then it didn't matter. I'd have died a fool if that had been the case, because I love you so much. Tara—"

"Oh, Rafe! It doesn't matter. Shh! You musn't talk. I'll get help. You need care—"

"No, no, Tara. Tell me you believe me. Tell me that—if I make it—you'll marry me."

"Rafe, you need—"

"I need your promise, Tara. Swear that you'll marry me...."

"Yes, yes, oh, yes! Now let me get help—"

He wasn't about to let her go. The tiger pounced.

He sprang up, sweeping her into his arms, kissing her lips quickly, pressing her against his chest and letting out a hoarse cry.

"Rafe..."

She accepted his hug at first, returned it with fervor and delight, but then, she realized that he was solid and warm and moving—and completely healthy.

"Rafe!"

Tara slammed her palm against his shoulder, pushing him away, her cheeks crimson. "You're not hurt at all!"

"I do beg your pardon. Elliott had a very nasty punch, and I've got a mile-long cut inside my mouth."

"Oh! You made me think—"

"Oh, yourself! Did you want me broken and bleeding?"

"No! No! Of course not! It's just..."

Her voice trailed away, because he was grinning, with relief, with a smug happiness that caught hold of her just as his energy could, just as the need to be with him had infected her from the very beginning. She was dizzy with relief, ready to throttle him—and then so incredibly happy that everything could have come out all right when it had begun so bleakly and horribly.

"You're terrible!" she accused him. "That was the most devious thing I've ever seen in my life!"

He brought her down to the ledge, kissing her swiftly again, staring into her eyes, hovering above her.

"Would you believe me if I swore never to be devious again?"

"No."

"Have a heart. You're supposed to trust your husband."

"Husband!"

"You just promised to marry me."

"You tricked me!"

He smiled down at her ruefully, his knuckles tenderly grazing her cheek.

"I had to have your promise. I might never have had the opportunity again, Tara. I had to make you forgive me." His smile left. He was suddenly, painfully serious. "Tara, when I knew that he had you, I almost went mad. And when I saw him with you, I think I did lose my mind. There were things I didn't say to you, but I swear, I never said I loved you when I didn't mean it with all my heart. I wanted to kill Tine. I felt like an animal. I wanted to kill him because he was endangering you."

She reached up and touched his hair, studying his eyes with tears forming in her eyes because she loved him so much and because she knew, with all her being, that he loved her just as deeply and that it was a good love, honest and real, and that it could and should last forever.

"Oh, Rafe." She smiled. "I do love you. And I'm glad you didn't kill him."

"In the end, I suppose, I'm not an animal. Just a man."

"Just a man," Tara repeated the words, a whimsical smile touching her lips. "Just *the* man who means everything in the world to me."

Slowly, he started to lower himself to her again. To touch her lips with the reverence that the night and the moon and the mountain demanded. He was just able to touch her mouth and taste the sweet salt of tears and the hunger and the warmth, when their moment alone on the ledge in the darkness came to an end.

"Tara! Rafe! Where are you?"

It was Ashley—anxious, concerned.

Rafe lifted a brow to Tara. "We're here, Ashley. Coming!"

"Are you all right?"

Tara answered her, curling her arms around Rafe's neck, meeting his eyes with a promise deeper than words, her eyes softening to a misted silver.

"We're fine, Ashley. We've never been better."

Rafe rose and helped Tara to her feet, and his arms were around her all the way up the cliff, as if he would never let her stumble again.

15

The mask was really unique. It was up high in a protective glass case, and there was a plaque beneath it, giving a few brief particulars: that it was Mayan; that it was ceremonial; that among its stones were forty-five diamonds, sixteen rubies, and nearly eighty small sapphires. It was on loan from a museum in Mexico City.

It was unique, probably beautiful in its way, but Tara shivered as she stared at the grinning golden face. It seemed to be an evil thing—and it had brought only evil. She didn't think she was superstitious, but she'd be glad when the mask was returned.

She left the Mayan display and hurried down the corridor, knowing exactly where she was going. And when she reached the room she wanted, she paused happily, staring.

This sculpture really was magnificent.

It was in the Roman section of the museum, with a plaque under it: Anonymous, A.D. 100, Black Marble.

Tara was still entranced by it.

Her life-size tiger, standing, watching. He was all power, all grace. There was nothing she wanted to study so much as the tiger.

Her back was to the doorway when she became aware that she was no longer alone. Someone had joined her in the tiger's room. Watching the tiger? Or watching her?

She looked up. In the glass case around a majestic granite centurion, she could see the reflection of a man. He seemed as tall as the centurion in the display case, seemed to tower in the dooorway, blocking her way. He stood there, as striking and haunting as the ancient works of art on display.

She grinned and reached out as he came around to her. There was a simple gold band on her hand now, one that nicely complemented the diamond she had still never managed to take off her finger.

"Hi," he said, slipping his arms around her to pull her against his chest so that they both stared at the sculpture. His chin nestled in her hair. "I thought you wanted to see the mask."

"I did. I hate it."

"It's only a mask," he murmured softly.

"Encased in glass," she agreed, adding, "just like Tine and George are caged behind bars. I still can't believe that George was involved."

"George kept Tine's business going once he couldn't flit back and forth between the States and South America himself. One of us should have figured it out before."

She didn't answer. He knew that she was thinking of the years she had spent with such ruthless people, never suspecting. She shivered beneath the silver fox fur of her coat, and he hugged her more tightly.

"It's all over now. And there were a few good things that came out of it. Jimmy would have never met Tanya, and they're certainly happy. Ashley would have never started her own business—and Mary might never have run off to Italy with my ship's captain."

She turned around, meeting his dark eyes, smiling at last.

"Myrna thought I was a sleazy felon!" Tara laughed.

"No. A felon, but never sleazy. And you made her day when you told her you'd be pleased to death to have her take care of things. Jimmy and I in the same year, keeping her busy with weddings. And Sam was so proud to give you away." He laughed happily. "And I've never seen such a beautiful wedding party—Ashley, Mary, Cassandra! And, of course, the bride. In silver that matched your eyes..."

She felt the golden warmth of his eyes, alive, tender and, as ever, hungry...like the tiger.

She lowered her eyes, staring back at the marble beast.

"The first time I saw you," she murmured, "I was astonished by the similarities."

"Yes?"

She laughed. "Between you and this tiger. I told you."

"Oh, yes, the tiger." Smiling, he moved around, surveying the sculpture. He gazed at her wryly.

"I'm not sure I find that terribly complimentary."

Tara grinned, walking around to him, slipping her arm through his. "Oh, I thought you were gorgeous. Full of intrigue and sleek power and grace and...well, you were on the prowl. And you were damned well ready to pounce!"

He grimaced. "You promised to forgive me."

"Oh, I have. And I meant to give you a compliment. The tiger may be dangerous, but he's also totally fascinating. I was drawn to him. And I was drawn to you."

He caught her hands, eyed the room, and saw that they were alone and pulled her close to him. "*Was* drawn?" he whispered in the tone that always sent her senses reeling.

She gave him a slow, enchanting smile. "Am drawn."

"What time did you promise to meet Ashley for lunch?"

"One."

"It's only noon. We've got plenty of time."

"Time?" Tara said, startled.

"The apartment is close. Come on!"

"Rafe!" she protested, but she was laughing. He took her hand and they started toward the door. He paused, looking back at the tiger.

"Thanks, pal," he murmured softly, winking.

Tara was almost convinced that the sculpture winked back.

They left the museum, ran down the steps, and hailed a taxi on the street. Sam was somewhere in the museum, but Tara would have been horrified if Sam had driven them. Rafe wondered what difference it would have made—Sam was surely old enough to know what went on in a marriage, but Tara would have blushed and objected strongly to being obvious.

That was one of the things he loved about her. She had the unique beauty and sensual appeal of a siren, but she had somehow maintained the innocence of an angel.

It was the siren who entered the apartment with him, though. She walked straight through to the bedroom, heedlessly shedding her coat.

He followed her, tearing off his jacket.

Then she was barefoot, curled up on the bed, smiling, as she awaited him. The sun fell through the glass overhead, catching her hair, making it a gold finer than any created by the earth.

He came over to her, and she rose to her knees, making a sensual act out of undoing his buttons, moving her fingers slowly, following each touch with a kiss, with the softest, hottest flick of her tongue. When she reached his belt buckle a sound rumbled in his throat, in his chest, and he caught her hair at the nape, raising her head to his, kissing her as sensation flamed higher and higher within him. She played her fingers against his chest and rubbed her hands down his torso, then caught the waistband of his pants. She broke the kiss and laid her cheek against the coarse hair on his stomach; with far less grace than she, he swore softly and tugged at her sweater, pushing her on the bed in his haste.

She laughed as he kicked away the remainder of his clothing and fell atop her, hands busy on the waistband of her slacks, eyes golden on hers.

"I'll never forget the first time I saw you," he murmured. "I'd heard that you were beautiful. I'd read that you were extraordinary... but none of it meant anything until I saw you."

"Lust at first sight?"

"Hmm. Something like that. I wanted to strip you right there in the museum."

He paused for a moment, gazing down at her naked breasts, touching them reverently with the palm of his hand, catching his breath as she moaned softly, her nipples rising to taut rosy peaks before his fascinated gaze.

"Right there," he murmured softly. "I could have swept you off, into the Egyptian area maybe, into a temple, because you looked just like a goddess, and I felt..."

"Like?" Tara breathed, her lashes falling over her silver eyes glazed now with her growing ache.

"Like thunder. Like lightning. Like Zeus!—ready to take on any form to seduce the enticing maiden."

His hands slipped lower, sliding away her clothing, teasing her flesh mercilessly with the vibrant power of his own.

"I never accused you of being a god," she told him, smiling as he tossed her jeans away and moved over her, his shoulders gleaming in the sunlight. "Just a tiger."

He lowered himself, carefully holding his own weight, until his lips were just a whisper away from hers. "Grr..."

She laughed until his mouth touched hers. Then laughter became a moan.

Whispers grew to a melody of passion, but the song that rose between them was more.

It was tenderness, and it was love. Fantastic and real and binding. And without thought, Tara knew in her heart that it had all been worth it. The past, and the treacherous road that they had taken to the present. Without the trauma, she would never have known that a dream could live. That her fabulous tiger-man could be real, could offer the love she had dared not believe in.

Tenderness and laughter, passion and fervor. She would marvel forever that she could be his wife.

And he her husband.

A tiger still, fascinating, intriguing, sleek and powerful, and delightfully...

Well, never quite, but sometimes, exquisitely tame...

And then sometimes, exquisitely wild.

Take 3 of "The Best of the Best™" Novels FREE

Plus get a FREE surprise gift!

Special Limited-time Offer

Mail to The Best of the Best™

3010 Walden Avenue
P.O. Box 1867
Buffalo, N.Y. 14269-1867

YES! Please send me 3 free novels and my free surprise gift. Then send me 3 of "The Best of the Best™" novels each month. I'll receive the best books by the world's hottest romance authors. Bill me at the low price of $3.99 each plus 25¢ delivery and applicable sales tax, if any.* That's the complete price and a savings of over 20% off the cover prices—quite a bargain! I understand that accepting the books and gift places me under no obligation ever to buy any books. I can always return a shipment and cancel at any time. Even if I never buy another book from Harlequin, the 3 free books and the surprise gift are mine to keep forever.

183 BPA A2P5

Name	(PLEASE PRINT)	
Address		Apt. No.
City	State	Zip

This offer is limited to one order per household and not valid to current subscribers.
*Terms and prices are subject to change without notice. Sales tax applicable in N.Y.
All orders subject to approval.

UBOB-296   ©1990 Harlequin Enterprises Limited

New York Times
Bestselling Author

LINDA LAEL MILLER

invites you to experience some

Daring Moves

Amanda Scott had been devastated by a broken love affair. But then Fate placed handsome widower Jordan Richards right in front of her...and chemistry took it from there. Was it possible that her life had just taken a turn for the better?

Just when things are looking up, this new relationship is challenged by the appearance of her ex-boyfriend. To avoid getting hurt once again Amanda decides to flee. But first she'll have to answer to Jordan—and he's not about to let her go without a fight.

In April, find out if true love can mend a broken heart.

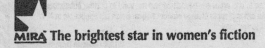

MIRA The brightest star in women's fiction

MLLM5

Now available for the first time in paperback!

SOMEBODY'S BABY

By *New York Times* bestselling author

CHARLOTTE VALE ALLEN

Snow Devane is devastated when her dying mother confesses that she stole Snow from a New York City supermarket thirty years ago. She is not Snow's mother. Snow is someone else's baby. With the help of friends and unexpected lovers, Snow begins to look for answers. Who was this woman who raised her? What happened to her "real" mother? And, most importantly, who is Snow Devane?

Find out this April at your favorite retail outlet.

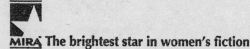

See what happens when two lovers are

Tempting Fate

By National Bestselling Author

JoAnn Ross

Donovan Kincaid—absentminded professor, rakishly
charming, last seen wearing one black shoe and
one brown....

Brooke Stirling—sophisticated college administrator,
determined not to let the relationship she'd once shared
with Donovan affect her new job. But sometimes fate
takes an unpredictable turn....

Look for TEMPTING FATE this May at your favorite
retail outlet.

Don't miss the thrilling stories of

HEATHER GRAHAM POZZESSERE

Order now for more romantic tales
by one of MIRA's most popular authors:

#66000	SLOW BURN	$5.99 U.S. ☐
		$6.50 CAN. ☐
#66005	A MATTER OF CIRCUMSTANCE	$4.99 U.S. ☐
		$5.50 CAN. ☐
#66019	KING OF THE CASTLE	$4.99 U.S. ☐
		$5.50 CAN. ☐
#66038	STRANGERS IN PARADISE	$4.99 U.S. ☐
		$5.50 CAN. ☐
#66089	EYES OF FIRE	$5.99 U.S. ☐
		$6.50 CAN. ☐
#66069	ANGEL OF MERCY	$4.99 U.S. ☐
		$5.50 CAN. ☐
#66079	DARK STRANGER	$4.99 U.S. ☐
		$5.50 CAN. ☐

(limited quantities available on certain titles)

TOTAL AMOUNT	$
POSTAGE & HANDLING	$
($1.00 for one book, 50¢ for each additional)	
APPLICABLE TAXES*	$ _____
TOTAL PAYABLE	$ _____
(check or money order—please do not send cash)	

To order, send the completed order form, along with a check or money order for the total above, payable to MIRA Books, to: In the U.S.: 3010 Walden Avenue, P.O. Box 9077, Buffalo, NY 14269-9077; In Canada: P.O. Box 636, Fort Erie, Ontario, L2A 5X3.

Name: _____

Address: _____ City: _____

State/Prov.: _____ Zip/Postal Code: _____

*New York residents remit applicable sales taxes.
 Canadian residents remit applicable GST and provincial taxes.

MHGPBL8

Look us up on-line at: http://www.romance.net